Dieses Buch gehört

Brigitte Fischer

A STRANGENESS

by

Jack R. McClellan

Bloomington, IN   authorHOUSE®   Milton Keynes, UK

AuthorHouse™
1663 Liberty Drive, Suite 200
Bloomington, IN 47403
www.authorhouse.com
Phone: 1-800-839-8640

AuthorHouse™ UK Ltd.
500 Avebury Boulevard
Central Milton Keynes, MK9 2BE
www.authorhouse.co.uk
Phone: 08001974150

© 2007 Jack R. McClellan. All rights reserved.

No part of this book may be reproduced, stored in a retrieval system, or transmitted by any means without the written permission of the author.

First published by AuthorHouse   2/27/2007

ISBN: 978-1-4259-8868-5 (sc)

Printed in the United States of America
Bloomington, Indiana

This book is printed on acid-free paper.

Chapter One

Reverently an aged man cradled in his arms a white frocked figure. His steps were slow and labored, cadenced to a funeral dirge, his shoulders humped forward to balance the weight of his burden. A bright Yorkshire sun caught tears that rolled down wrinkled cheeks, making them sparkle.

He entered the town square, buzzing noisily with people who had come to Tosten en Dale from all parts of North Riding for market day. As they mingled under red, blue, green and yellow canvasses waving gently in a soft breeze above tables spread with produce fresh from surrounding farms, they called greetings to friends, haggled over prices and discussed displays of farm machinery placed around the perimeter.

As the old man progressed along aisles of racked clothing the din of activity changed to quiet silence. Buyers and sellers turned to stare, transfixed by the pathetic scene.

"Mr. Minshell!" a voice cried out. "Let me help you!" A strapping young farmer rushed up, his arms extended to receive the girl he recognized as Minshell's granddaughter.

"Put her here, Tom. Reggie, get Dr. Poole." The commands were snapped with authority, the voice of Constable Ormand punctuating the silence. Tom carried the lifeless form to a table that had been cleared quickly. Carefully he placed the girl on it, stretching out her legs and arranging her arms at her side. Inquisitive onlookers formed a circle about the table to gaze in awe then commented in muffled murmers.

Dr. Poole broke through the ring of gawkers, paused to evaluate his task, then immediately checked for vital signs. He could find no pulse. "Carry her to my surgery," he ordered. It was there he completed his examination. Marks on the neck revealed the cause of death. He sat at his desk to make a report but got only as far as entering the date, 30 May 1770, when Constable Ormand opened his door. The two discussed the result of Dr. Poole's findings, death by strangulation. By the time Ormand left the surgery, the hubbub of marketing had been renewed.

Old man Minshall remained alone, silent and confused. Ormand placed a hand at his elbow, spoke comforting words, then guided him to the constable's office off the square. "Now, John, tell me what happened."

"I don't know what happened. I found my granddaughter in the abbey."

"How did you find her?"

"On the way to market. I took the path through Roche Meadow then into the abbey.

"In the south transept I saw this pile. It looked like a pile of clothes. I went to it. I saw legs. They were bare. The dress, everything, was bundled over her head. She was almost naked. I pulled the clothes from her face and saw Emma. My Emma! She's all I have!"

The old man shuddered, his face contorted in a massive effort to control emotions, but tears rolled down his cheeks. As sobs shook the frail body, gnarled hands covered his face to hide the embarrassment of emotional weakness.

Ormand gave him time to recover then asked quietly, "Did you see anyone?"

"Otley. As I carried Emma out of the abbey, I saw Otley. He was peering at me from behind a pillar. He hid when he knew I saw him."

"I'll get Mrs. Crewe to go home with you. She can stay a few days. You wont be alone, John."

Constable Ormand crossed the square. All eyes watched him enter the pub where he was greeted by a familiar pungent odor of ale. His appearance smothered the chatter of farmers now crowding their traditional market meeting place. They fully expected to hear a complete run down of Dr. Poole's examination, but instead the lawman went immediately to the publican.

"Manny, I want to speak to you. In private."

"Come inside." The barkeep at first look surprised, hesitated, then moved to oblige.

The two entered a room that served as both office and storage space. Ormand leaned against a keg, crossed one leg over another, then spoke abruptly. "Where is Otley?"

"I am not sure at the moment. He was in the backroom a short time ago. What is it?"

"You saw John carry in his granddaughter. You saw that she was dead. Dr. Poole determined that her death was due to strangulation. John tells me he saw Otley lurking in the abbey at the time where he found the girl's body."

"That doesn't mean a penny. Otley goes there all the time. He likes playing by himself among the old ruins. And, Constable, a lot of people walk through the abbey on the way to town."

"Dr. Poole says the girl was raped before being murdered. Otley is a suspect."

"A what! Otley! A suspect! Why that boy isn't old enough to know what it's for. You know he can't reason."

"Otley is growing, Manny. He's old enough to wonder what its for. Maybe he tried to find out. I want to see him. Now!"

"Ah, Edward, you know the boy can't talk. He can't tell you anything."

"Bring him here. Now!" The voice was stern.

The publican left the room. He returned shortly, the boy at his side. Otley was tall for fourteen and thin. He walked with a limp in each leg, the left one dragging a bit, and both arms, held outward at angles, shook slightly. He saw the constable and attempted a smile.

"Hello, Otley. Did you like being in the abbey this morning?"

The boy tried to reply. His face became distorted, straining to form words. The jaw moved awkwardly as he took in gulps of air, and his head thrust forward. His efforts produced no speech.

"Did you see Mr. Minshall in the abbey?"

Otley nodded, his head bobbing in jerks.

"Did you see anyone else?"

Otley struggled to reply. It was obvious he had information to give, but he had no way to communicate his thoughts.

The constable patted Otley's shoulder and thanked him for his help. Otley beamed in gratitude and his father told him to leave.

"There, constable, you can't say Otley did it."

Ormand pondered the thought. "I don't know. We may never know."

He noted the lingering crowd of people in the market square as he returned to his office. He knew his people. They wanted the latest developments before they left for home. He also knew there was a murderer in their midst and it wasn't Otley.

Mrs. Esterham watched the constable approach his office. She knew as did all the townspeople that Ormand had questioned Otley. "The idea." She spoke critically to a neighbor. "That poor boy. He knows who committed that dastardly crime. He'll find a way to tell."

A mumbling to herself continued as she walked the mile to Rochedale Manor, now in view beyond open fields beginning at the edge of town. The house was large by North Riding standards, its original portions having been constructed within the dormatory and refectory sections of St. Clement le Mer Abbey following dissolution of church lands in the sixteenth century. Succeeding generations of the Roche family made alterations and additions using some of the church stones in the new construction and leaving the abbey in partial ruins. Time and weather and lack of care contributed to the church's continued demise.

Mrs. Esterham followed the York road, crossing a wooden bridge over the River Dale, then took an abrupt turning to the right to enter a long lane leading to the house. On one side was Roche Meadow now populated with sheep. Rolling hills rose on the other side. Spring had flooded the countryside in shades of green while wild flowers splashed color profusely.

Inside the house Mrs. Esterham put her bulging shopping bag on the kitchen table and cook emptied it, saddened by the news that had already reached her. "Poor Mr. Minshall," she sympathized as she admired fresh vegetables coming out of the bag. "I'll fix a basket for him and Delly can take it over. I haven't asked Mrs. Roche if I can, but I am sure she will want him to have it. He'll need some help for a time."

"I'll tell you that murder caused a furor in the market place. Everyone is scared and angry. Poor child. And she an angel, a mere baby. She was all that was left to old man Minshall. How much more must he be asked to take? First his wife died. Then his son and family were taken in that awful accident. We said then it was lucky Emma stayed home that day, but maybe she should have gone with them. Now raped and murdered."

"You had better tell Mrs. Roche so she knows," cook advised. "I have tea ready to take to her."

Mrs. Esterham, housekeeper for the Roche family for many years, entered the sitting room and placed a tray on a table next to Mrs. Roche. Sun cascading through open shutters drenched her with a shaft of light to give her an aura of mystic stateliness. Approaching fifty, her hair already turning white, she was matron of Rochedale Manor, an extensive acreage supporting sheep and cattle which produced an equally extensive income.

The first Roche arrived with the Conqueror and was granted Yorkshire land by William for services rendered. Succeeding generations acquired additional acreage and their holdings developed. The greatest boon, however, occurred with the rise of the Tudors. Matlock Roche first fought for Henry Tudor during the Wars of the Roses then he cast his lot with the son, Henry Vlll, in his struggles with Rome. It was a gamble, for the Roches were Catholics, but the dice rolled favorably, and as a reward for support they were given the abbey with all its land. The family remained Catholic until the reign of William and Mary when they embraced tenets of the established church.

"Now, Mrs. Esterham, tell me the news from market square." The voice was warm and friendly, a Yorkshire brogue evident in soft tones. She sat erect in anticipation. Mrs. Roche was considered "of the people" since she was the daughter of a country squire who married into the upper class. Winsford Roche, heir to the estate, met her at a church function, courted her against family wishes, but his persistence prevailed. They married and she raised two boys and a girl. She buried her husband in 1760.

Ritually and in silence, Mrs. Esterham removed a cosy from the pot, poured tea into a cup, added hot water, a bit of sugar and a drop of milk then passed the steaming brew to her mistress.

She paused further to give a tidbit to Guy. Her entry had disturbed the dog's sleep but he rose in expectancy, stretched, wagged his tail then sat by the tray awaiting his treat which, through many years, had become established habit.

Kendall, the younger son, had found him as a homeless puppy, brought him home where he immediately became a family pet with full privileges of the house. At first he ran with Kendall and Radcliffe, the elder son, but later he preferred the company of Mrs. Roche. There were rugs for his private comfort, one in the study and one in her bedroom. Of nondescript origin, he appeared to be mainly a brown and white hound dog.

"I have dreadful news, Mrs. Roche." Mrs. Esterham's voice was dramatic. "Emma Minshall was found murdered in the abbey this morning. Mr. Minshall carried her into market square for all to see. Dr. Poole said she had been raped. Constable Ormand questioned Otley."

Mrs. Roche returned her cup to the tray and stared past the shutters. Recovering her composure, she spoke quietly. "Ask cook to prepare a basket for Mr. Minshall and see to it that he has food until we can provide permanently for him. Thank you, Mrs. Esterham. I need to rest before supper."

"Will you have a tray or will you eat with the boys?"

"I think it best I eat with them. You may take the tea tray with you. Thank you."

Mrs. Roche rose and walked to the window. Of more than medium height and trim of figure she carried herself with dignity. For ten years she had been master of Rochedale Manor, raising her children skillfully, directing a cattle and sheep business to make it profitable, leasing some of her property to provide added income, managing her home to make it a show place of the north country and taking a leading role in civic and social activities. She had earned the community's respect and she enjoyed her role.

A flower garden immediately in front of her was a profusion of color, benefiting from her constant attention as well as from a warm spring sun. Beyond was the abbey church. The sight of it tore her heart as Roche ancestors had torn the heart from the church when they stripped it of its granite stones. Remaining standing were a few partial pillars in the nave, portions of each transept and most of the choir with its reredos wall supported by four flying buttresses. The abbey had been founded by monks soon after the conquest who dedicated it to St. Clement le Mer, their local saint, protector of travelers.

To the casual viewer it was a romantic vista, a French gothic ediface with lacy patterns designed in grey stones, sitting gently in a sea of rolling grass being clipped at the moment by a scattering of sheep.

To a lonely viewer just informed of a tragedy, however, the abbey provoked unhappy memories of time in the past. Ten years ago two girls had been found within its confines, one of whom was Mrs. Roche's own daughter, both raped, both murdered. The culprit or culprits was or were never identified. At the same time as the murders, two girls were reported missing but they were never found. "She would have been twenty-two, a wife and mother, and I a grandmother," Mrs. Roche thought. "Is it starting all over again?" She concentrated on Ormand's men inspecting the area around the ruins.

Hands grabbed her shoulders and turned her about. Startled by the sudden intrusion, she looked up into the face of her son. "Hello, mother!" Radcliffe's voice was warm and filled with enthusiasm. "What magic are you planning for that garden of yours. You do have the touch of Merlin." He kissed her on the forehead then pulled her into a lingering embrace.

"Of course you heard the news." Hers was a quiet statement reflecting concern.

"Yes, mother." The young man's voice changed to a somber shade and the joy of greeting was gone.

"What do you know?" She backed away and looked at her son, searching for clues. She loved both her boys but Radcliffe took her interest since he concerned himself with estate business, spent time on the land with her foremen and, she recognized, he had acquired skills approaching expertise.

"The constable is searching for evidence. He is concerned about the reaction building among the people. They are talking about the missing girls and the two unsolved abbey murders and are fearful of a renewed wave of violence. I stopped in the pub on the way home. There was no other topic of conversation. All the men are incensed that Otley was questioned. They don't want him accused so the constable can say he solved the crime. It is likely the boy knows who did it, though."

"I saw Otley in the abbey earlier this morning," Mrs. Roche volunteered. "He is often there by himself. Poor child. With his problems he plays alone. I'm concerned about Mr. Minshall."

"I have just been to see him, mother. Mrs. Crewe is there. She will stay until we can get permanent help. I thought that would be your wish."

"Bless you, Radcliffe. You must never forget that we are always ready to be of service. Now tell me about your day. Would you like tea?"

"No, mother. I had ale at the pub. I rode about the herds most of the day and all goes well. We are having a fine lambing year and with the price of wool staying high and firm we should realize considerable profit, barring any catastrophe, of course."

"I am so proud of you. We do need your strong leadership. In fact I need a strong hand in matters of the estate, and you are such a strength to me." Her pleasure showed on her face which was alive with gratitude, a broad smile giving it accent.

Responding to his mothers pride, Radcliffe boasted a bit. "I have learned the estate management, mother. I could handle it by myself but I shall give you my faithful support as long as you are manager." It was the first time he had expressed himself so openly. It was his desire to replace his mother and assume the role of master of Rochedale Manor. After all, he was the first born and it was his right by primogeniture. "If she would give up I would be head right now," he wished tacitly.

Not only was Mrs. Roche grateful for her son's estate acumen, she was pleased with how he was developing as a man. At twenty-two Radcliffe was an excellent speciman. Six feet two, broad of shoulders and square of frame, he was solidly constructed. Brown wavy hair fell over a high forehead and his blue eyes were like her own. He had a ready smile that produced wrinkles on either side of his eyes and showed a fine set of teeth, giving him a handsome countenance. He seemed always to present a serious manner but quick to react warmly to others and steady at times of stress. This even temperament had given her a feeling of security, for managing a large estate meant dealing with people and problems, and Radcliffe seemed always able to face adversity without becoming unduly upset.

"It is the business end that needs more attention, mother. I do not understand all that goes on in the York or London offices."

"Then we need to get you to York and to London for some training. It would be well for both you and Kendall to spend some time in the offices of our representatives. After all that is where the price of wool is determined, and Kendall may take an interest in this part of our endeavor as well."

The mention of Kendall's name produced an immediate feeling of concern and she felt her body tremble. She had seen her second son in the meadow next to the abbey ruins prior to the discovery of Emma Minshall's body but not since. It was well past the hour when, by long established habit, he had tea with her. She did not want to associate these circumstances with the tragedy, but her anxiety to see and talk with her son was mounting.

Kendall was different from Radcliffe, she had long recognized, but the boy's light, gay attitude toward life appealed to her and she loved him the same as she loved Radcliffe. His interest ran to animals. He loved horses and spent undue amounts of time in the stables. He knew the herds and flocks well, always assisting with lambing and calving. At times of crisis he worked side by side with hired help to alleviate an animal's pain. She believed that because of Kendall's concerned interest a healthy stock was maintained. "I would like to be an animal doctor," he told her when but a lad, but his station as a Roche did not earn her encouragement. She wanted him to be more like Radcliffe, more oriented to management functions, directing not working with staff, preparing himself to administer family holdings.

"That is a good suggestion, mother. I'll speak to Kendall and we perhaps should plan a visit at least to York during August or September. What do you think?"

"Fine, son, but you will have to push Kendall. You know how he is when it comes to learning business procedure. Perhaps if you could include some social activities you might incite his interest."

"I'll arrange something and Kendall will go. Count on me"

"I always depend on you, son. Will we see you at supper?"

"Of course, mother."

Left alone, Mrs. Roche returned to the window and carefully surveyed the abbey ruins.

Her eyes could detect no movement and she concluded that the constable's men had terminated their search. A noise disturbed her concentration and she turned to discover Kendall entering the study. "Ah, my dear. You had me worried. I missed you for tea."

Kendall beamed his devotion as he strode forward to give Guy a pat on the head then to gather his mother in his arms. At six feet he was of slighter build than his brother, considerably thinner but more handsome. His hair was light brown with thick waves that rolled about his head. Long lashes blinked over hazel eyes that highlighted a sharply designed face with high cheek bones and aquiline nose. His smile formed dimples in his cheeks and revealed perfectly formed teeth. A slight clef was carved into his chin.

"I am sorry, mother. I should have sent word to you, but I didn't think I would be so long with the lambs. I was working with Henley Ludlow trying to save some sick ones. We are endeavoring to drop our mortality rate. But we shall have supper together."

She enjoyed the kiss he gently gave her then she felt him release her. "You do work so diligently with the animals. You and Henley have created fine herds, but I do wish you would give more time to the business end."

"Radcliffe is so good at that. Keeping books and counting profits are more to his liking."

"That is true but you must have a sound knowledge as well. I suggested to Radcliffe that you and he hie yourselves to York and London to talk to our agents. You can enjoy some social activities while you are there. He will be talking to you about it. Of course you heard about Emma Minshall."

Purposely she made her statement abrupt and stared to catch his reaction. She was surprised to note his casual reply. "No. Is she getting married?"

"She was found dead in the abbey." Her analytical stare continued to focus intently on his face searching for a clue.

"Emma! How! Why!"

The shock Kendall revealed appeared genuine. She started to relax, but she tried again. "She was murdered."

"Oh, mother! Emma! And after all John Minshall has been through. What is being done about it? Is John being cared for?"

"The concern is genuine," Mrs. Roche concluded to herself. "This one can never cover his true feelings. It was wrong of me to suppose even for a moment that he could have done such a thing, but . . . ." Aloud she answered his questions. "The constable has been in the abbey searching for clues. He has questioned Otley."

"What! That poor boy is suspect for everything that goes wrong."

She considered a final testing. "Did you see him in the abbey when you were there this morning.?"

Kendall stared with disbelief at his mother. "Why, I went directly to the stables this morning, met Ludlow, and we left immediately for Stillston Meadows. What makes you think I was in the abbey?"

"Ah, he has proof of his whereabouts." She spoke to herself, relieved. Aloud she answered. "As I puttered in the garden I saw you in the meadow near the abbey. You had on your favorite jacket, the brown one. I gave you no more thought for I know you enjoy browsing among the ruins."

"Mother, are you suggesting I am a suspect? I did not wear that jacket today. The morning was much too warm for that one." His tone was defensive and his face revealed shock.

"Of course not, Kendall." Her manner softened, relieved to hear the intensity of his challenge. "I only thought you may have been enjoying the building again. I didn't see the face of the man, only his back, and I did think of you because of the jacket."

"Most farmers wear that type of jacket. You know that. It could have been anyone passing through the abbey on the way to market."

"It probably was. Come, let us get ourselves ready for supper. Cook will be annoyed if we are late." She slipped her arm in his and squeezed tightly as she guided him out the door. Guy was right behind.

The dining room at Rochedale Manor was a Tudor masterpiece. Left intact from the original building was a sized, squared and polished inglenook fireplace but the refectory from which it was formed while shortened was sufficiently large enough to meet the needs of a family likely to entertain. The walls were covered with finely carved linen fold paneling while exposed unfinished beams supported the ceiling. From it hung two large burnished brass chandeliers that shed light onto the original refectory table which could seat thirty-six persons comfortably.

Mrs. Roche always presided at supper whether it was prepared for the immediate family of three or for a larger number of guests. Tonight was no exception. She and her sons were dressed formally as was their custom, and they were served under the glow of four candlesticks placed at the northern end of the table. As usual their conversation was centered on the events of the day and plans for the future.

"Schedule your trip to York around the racing meet in October," Mrs. Roche proposed. "Socials are always numerous during the meet. There is much enjoyable activity and you can combine business with pleasure. I shall alert our agent that you are coming. It should be a pleasing time for both of you."

"I for one shall look forward to going." Radcliffe spoke enthusiastically. "I intend to fathom the workings of the York office so

I can be assured we are getting a fair return for our product. It seems to me that we do all the work on the land and the city people get the money."

"You have a mind for business, Radcliffe." Kendall complimented his brother with pride. "You are earning the estate more profit all the time."

The brothers shared a deep mutual respect, one for the other. They enjoyed each other's company, were concerned for the other's welfare, and each sought opinions from the other. Each recognized that their interests varied and that these differences resulted in specializations that contributed to the total welfare of the estate.

"We would not be realizing profit if you did not promote healthy herds. We make a good pair, Kendall." Radcliffe was equally fervent in his praise.

"I'll go to York, mother," Kendall reassured her, "but the socials will be more to my liking. I wonder if Mr. Gunning will be attending the racing meet and if he is taking Carinna. Tomorrow I must talk to him."

"I claim some of her time, Kendall. She is not yours yet." Radcliffe smiled but he was in earnest.

Carinna was their only source of conflict.

Chapter Two

The following morning Kendall planned his first stop of the day at Compton Heath. He trotted his horse down a long approaching avenue bordered on either side by green meadows broken into sections by hedge rows. Most pastures were being grazed by flocks of sheep enlarged by spring lambs, but in one were mares supervising amusing frolics of their long legged colts soon to be judged for training as race horses.

Kendall passed through a gate at the top of the lane. Before him was a manor house, a stone structure built in the sixteenth century. Plain and sturdy in glistening sunshine, it boasted two stories with mullioned windows, their stone work appearing more like graceful lace succoring thick glass panes. Beyond was the River Dale and a rise of hills, green in spring grass.

Mr. Montague Gunning, squire of the manor, owned productive acreage but he was not in the same social class as the Roche family. He was widely respected, however, as a business man, master of a small but highly competent racing stable and a leader in the political affairs of Yorkshire. He was also the father of two attractive, eligible girls.

"Carinna, good morning," Kendall yelled. He had discovered the elder daughter kneeling to weed and work the soil in a rose garden. At seventeen she had captured the interest of all eligible bachelors in North Riding. Even dressed in work clothes, a broad brimmed hat

A Strangeness

shading her face, she was captivating. "It is impossible for me to tell you from your roses. Speak so I can."

"Oh, Kendall. You always make sport of me." Her laugh was musical and a smile gave her face a radiance that completely conquered him. "You come early today. Will you have some tea with me?"

"Thank you, no, but I would speak with your father after you share some time with me."

"Come to the bower." Her invitation was spoken with enthusiasm, the smile still on her face in anticipation of his company. She lay aside her hand tool and led the way to a rose arbor nearby. He admired her slim, shapely figure as she walked, the right amount of curves flowing below a trim waist. As she sat amid the covering of rose vines, his eyes darted about a well exposed cleavage, and he wondered what lay so amply covered beyond. "How is you mother, Kendall?" Her voice was lyrical.

"Mother is fine and she sends you her best wishes." His words were delivered mechanically for he was involved in wonder by the pixie face whose blue eyes literally danced before him.

Carinna removed her hat and shook her head to free her golden tresses so they would fall in waves about her shoulders. "What do you have planned for today?" She reached out to touch his hand.

He clasped her fingers, entwining his own among hers. Her hand felt minuscule in his. He stared at her disbelieving her beauty. Unable to control himself, he leaned down to brush a kiss across her forehead. Pleased by the sudden action she raised her face in invitation. His lips found hers. Without direction his arms enfolded her waist, drawing her close to him. She pressed her lips on his, her arms using his shoulders to draw closer. The kiss was ardent, lasting.

Gently he released her, but urgently he murmured, his lips just above hers, "Lets ride to Moncton Tor. The day is perfect for a ride." His passion was rising and he felt compelled to have more of her.

"I must ask father." She was breathing heavily. He could feel her bosom pressed against his chest rising and falling in rapid rhythm.

"We shall go together," he urged.

"Yes."

They released their embrace but he held her hand, warm and moist, as they walked through the garden and into the service area. Ahead was Mr. Gunning. Kendall released her hand as soon as he saw the back of Carinna's father. The man was of average height, trim of stature, and dressed in the customary habit of the Yorkshire gentry farmer, knee boots, corduroy jacket and brimmed hat. Hearing their approach, he turned. His grim countenance revealed his nature. As a widower he kept firm control over his daughters as he did on his land, his horses and his hired hands.

"Good morning, Squire." Kendall assumed a formal attitude instantly and used a title of respect demanded by Mr. Gunning. "The day is perfect for a ride. Sir, may I take Carinna to Moncton Tor?" There were no preliminary warm up statements or explanations. Kendall used Mr. Gunning's manner, short and direct.

The reply was in kind. "Carinna has too many chores."

Kendall knew better than to pursue his request. His fervent desire for the girl eased considerably after hearing the refusal. Her closeness, however, continued to excite him.

"Will you be going to York for the September racing meet?"

"It's likely."

"Will you be taking Carinna and Flora?"

"Perhaps."

Kendall felt a lift. The likelihood of being near Carinna for several days of socials stimulated his spirit. With more enthusiasm he inquired, "What horses will you enter?"

"I don't know yet."

Hesitating, then thinking it wiser to discontinue the questioning, Kendall took his leave. Carinna walked him to the gate showing her disappointment as well. "I am sorry, Kendall. I wanted to go with you."

He sensed a feeling of defeat as he rode away. "Damn!" he explicated with feeling. "I was ready. Carinna was ready. Somehow I must get around that man's protective barrier."

Despite the busy schedule he had planned for the day, he was too devastated for estate duties, not after a near miss with Carinna. He directed his horse toward Moncton Tor considering what could have been. "One day soon I'll manage that father of hers," he promised himself with conviction. Thoughts of the tor prompted a mental listing of his conquests and he smiled, feeling more confident in his prowess and allowing pride to build in his manliness.

Kendall was no stranger to women. The first one was not his conquest, however. It was he who was conquered. "By that wonton in York." His laugh echoed among the crags. "She did me in masterfully, taught me with skill and got me started as an independent lover. She told me that even as a beginner I had the skill of a veteran and I've proven she was right.

"Then there was that Masterson girl, glorious fun in the hay." The recollection prompted a satisfying smile. "I must get back to her." Kendall moved about in the saddle to accommodate the bulge forming at the crotch. "But Emma Minshall. She was far and away the best. She cried for more and I could not give her more. At fifteen! Poor little girl. I cannot go back to her. Pity."

Without his direction, Kendall's horse had taken him to Moncton Tor, a rugged peak with wild outcroppings of boulders rising majestically above the rolling panorama of North Riding.

From its summit he could see mile after mile of Yorkshire landscapes no matter the direction he looked, hills falling into valleys, some with rugged escarpments, wooded dales and glens washed by brooks and streams now glistening in the sun where they escaped protective tree cover. Sheep and cattle roamed freely in green meadows broken into sections by hedge rows and on barren moors where there was a scattering of copses.

The young buck dismounted, secured his horse, and let his thoughts go to what could have been with Carinna. Relief had to come. He allowed his hand to roam over the front of his pants, rubbing the bulge that was now massive. Unable to deter himself further he released his manliness from his trousers and held it extended, amazed at its length. A noise disturbed his reverie and in shock he looked up to see Otley staring wide eyed. Embarrassed, Kendall stood, feeling remorse for his wanton display.

Otley moved toward Kendall, managing somehow to maneuver his unsure steps among the rocks, his arms fluttering to maintain balance, eyes continuing to stare. Kendall stood as if hypnotized by the approaching boy. Aghast he saw Otley fall to his knees in front of him. He felt lips form around his extension. Kendall's hands went to Otley's shoulders to brace himself as he began push and pull motions. Feeling a climax coming, his hands went to Otley's neck.

He exploded. His hands remained on Otley's neck, tightening his grip as his feeling of disgust toward the boy heightened. The boy sank to the ground.

Kendall released his horse, mounted and left the scene, not looking back, loathing himself for participating in a demented act.

Radcliffe planned his day so that he could oversee some estate matters then make some purchases in Tosten en Dale. When his tasks were accomplished more quickly than expected, he entered the town pub which he found unusually well attended. Most tables were well occupied and there was a hubbub of active voices, a banging of mugs, and a movement of people. Recognized immediately, Radcliffe was invited to join a large table. He sat with a group of men and ordered ale. Instantly he was caught up in the dominant topic of conversation, for everyone had a comment to make about the murder of Emma Minshall. "It seems to me the murderer is no passerby," one farmer commented between gulps of beer. "He is someone she knew. Dr. Poole says there was no evidence of a struggle. A girl being attacked would put up a fight. I know Emma. She was a feisty one, quick to give battle."

"Now, Roger, you are angry over this whole affair like everyone else," came a response from a man across the table. "It could be she was surprised by an intruder in the abbey, someone who choked her first and then raped her. If so, that fellow is long gone. Now just who around here would do such a thing? We'll probably never know who did it."

"Well, we'll know before long." Another voice was more confident. "The constable says he has some ideas even though there isn't much to go on. He's not telling what his men found in the abbey as evidence."

"He'll have to do more sleuthing than he's done. First he thinks it's Otley. Then he doesn't. Then he does. Then he says Otley saw who did it. I'll tell you this, men," the speaker orated slamming his hand on the table to emphasize his feelings, "if he charges Otley, the whole town will be on him. There is not one person in Yorkshire who'll convict that poor boy."

A murmur of approval passed about the table.

"I for one think Otley knows. Problem is, how is he going to tell. You can't line up every man in North Riding then have Otley point to the man he saw." After his statement, the speaker lifted his mug and swigged a pint.

"He'll be able to tell." Another voice was assured and positive. "That boy is a lot brighter than he is given credit for. What do you think, Radcliffe?"

"I agree, Henry." Radcliffe's tone was serious. He knew the men were expecting wisdom from him. "If Otley did see something then the constable will learn of it. Ormand is a very capable lawman."

There was a nodding of heads and another voice was heard. " What worries me is what is worrying everyone. If the murderer isn't caught soon, we could have yet another murder on our hands. It could be that a maniac is in our midst. Remember ten years ago."

"Has it been ten years?" Radcliffe asked, surprised.

"You were a young one then, Radcliffe. Two girls found dead, two more missing, never found. Neither was the murderer."

"Yes, and the town has never forgotten. I for one want this one solved, and soon. I don't want my daughter to be another Emma." The speaker's hand slammed the table with severity.

"We need to get a committee organized to put some pressure on Constable Ormand."

The proposal received a drone of approval. "What do you think, Radcliffe?"

Radcliffe sat for a moment to create the impression of serious consideration. "That would be a drastic move, gentlemen. The constable knows your feelings. He is trying to make our land safe for all of us, and he was here ten years ago. He must have the opportunity to do his job without the pressure of a committee forcing him. He is as anxious as you are to make an arrest."

There was a stir in the room and quickly the normal undercurrent of chatter abated to silence. It was caused by the entry of a figure through the door. All eyes moved with the constable's approach to the bar. The normal voice he used to order ale sounded more like a shout.

A Strangeness

He took a sip, turned about, and glanced about the room. "Here's a chair, constable," an invitation rang out.

He took a step in the direction of the voice but was stopped by a question. "Any clues, constable?"

Instantly he identified the speaker. "We are making progress, Will. As soon as I have anything definite, I'll make a statement. Meantime we are hard at it."

"We just don't want a repeat of ten years ago, constable. Every father and mother in Yorkshire is alarmed."

"I am aware of that, Will. I don't want it either. A killer is loose and we'll get him."

"What about Otley?"

"Otley saw something. We are sure of that." Ormand proceeded to the empty chair and the undercurrent of chatter began again.

"Best we go along with him, at least for a time," the man next to Radcliffe said. He summarized the thinking of the pub's occupants.

Radcliffe finished his ale then bid the men good day. He crossed Market Square in the direction of his horse, a frown revealing the intenseness of his concentration. "People are fearful," he mused. "They have a right to be. So Otley knows who killed Emma." The silent comment was made as a warning to himself. "Maybe I can get it out of him."

Radcliffe guided his horse out of town and onto a path that paralleled the River Dale, past the abbey, then entered a wooded area. He had seen Otley earlier in the morning and supposed the boy would still be about. When his alertness availed him nothing, the horse, without guidance, went to the Esterbrook Farm, a site well know to him. Molly Esterbrook was a looker and enjoyed the attention of young Mr. Roche. She saw in his visits an opportunity for marriage, but so far she found his interests were only in her company. She would rather they were of the flesh.

Radcliffe was not a rounder, but life was no stranger to him. His first lesson in the basic facts of life occurred by accident. While his mother was aiding in an act of mercy at a nearby farm, he and a girl went to a barn and together they let curiosity run rampant. The escapade left him with a guilt complex which he had to fight whenever the male drive had to be satisfied.

He knew a few girls but he was reserved and proper in the pursuit of the act. He discovered that while he had the drive to participate with a girl he could not always perform. He was not sure this is what should happen, and he never built up enough courage to ask Dr. Poole or even Kendall about it. "That would be a loss of pride and it would show my ignorance," he justified himself, and he did not seek advice. He found enjoyment in petting and kissing, however, and promised himself he would have to be with more girls to get more experience.

A shout of "Hello, Radcliffe," startled his concentration and he was surprised to see Molly hurrying toward him. "How lovely to see you. Won't you come in. Dad is in town." The greeting was warm and inviting and carried an interesting inference.

He smiled in return but quickly explained he was on a task that begged completion and could not tarry. "Do come back when your chore is done, Radcliffe. You are sorely missed."

The urgency of the invitation did not go unheeded. It prompted the young man to hesitate. Immediately he saw this as a chance for more adventure with a woman, but he had made a commitment that even the anticipation of a frolic with a body as sweet as Molly could not deter.

He took his leave without a promise to return and continued on the lane until a path veered to the right. This he took for it was a haunt of Otley's. It led to Moncton Tor. "So the boy knows. The constable will get it out of him, but I shall get it out of him first." His declaration, spoken in a quiet inside voice was so adamant he startled himself. But the conviction was there. The higher he climbed the hill, the more determined he became in his quest.

"Suppose I don't find him today. Ah, then I have a problem. I shall intercept him near the pub. No one, especially the constable, can know the secret he carries. It must be done today!"

A disturbance in the copse interrupted his planning. He looked ahead to see a distinct movement. There was no question as to the source. The boy, try as he may, could not hide himself. His affliction did not allow for quietude.

"Otley?" Radcliffe's voice was raised, but it was friendly. "If that is you, stay a moment. Let me speak to you."

Otley did not show himself.

"Are you going to Moncton Tor or have you been there? I can take you home."

Radcliffe dismounted and went into the copse. Otley huddled behind a shrub, fear exacerbating the trembling. "Stand, Otley!" The command was spoken with fervor, delivered in a tone that required compliance.

Otley stayed as he was, shaking more from fear than from his affliction. He saw a hand coming toward him. He fell backward. The hands that grabbed him then jerked him up were strong. He felt two hands on his neck, squeezing, then he knew no more.

Virginia Roche rose earlier than was her habit. She had not slept well, if at all. Events of the previous day mounted in intensity during the night forcing her to toss and turn in the great, heavily carved, canopied fourposter bed she once shared with Winsford Roche. Visions of Kendall in the abbey linking him with the murder of Emma Minshall prompted memories of the past when her own daughter was found abused and strangled. Terror seized her for she was fearful of what could happen to her son if he had perpetrated Emma's demise. She strode the floor, back and forth, back and forth, until the dark of night faded into dawn. From her bedroom window she watched the first rays of sun strike the impressive ruins of the abbey. "How beautiful they must be in the eyes of a romanticist, but to me who has known only terror in its precincts, they are but formless rocks."

Terror for Mrs. Roche began ten years ago. Sun warmed the landscape as she watched the scene from her bedroom window. The ruins appeared majestic, sitting as they were in a sea of swaying grass bordered by the River Dale, its flow first smooth and quiet then breaking noisily into a stretch of white water. The remaining gothic walls of the abbey church resembled lace work and the arches soared in stateliness.

After breakfast that day she worked in her garden. She noticed with pleasure her daughter collecting wild flowers in the meadow then she saw Winsford coming out of the abbey, take their daughter by the hand and disappear into the south transept beyond her view. A game she thought, but when the child did not return for the noon meal, she herself went to get her. The gruesome discovery remained vivid in her mind. The deed was never solved since she did not report what she had seen to the constable or any one else.

Late morning took Virginia to her flower garden. She worked in a manner that placed the abbey in her vision. Her constant vigil was rewarded by a view of Otley as he crossed the meadow and entered the nave. She lost him when he turned into the south transept.

She debated an action she considered taking, hesitating to reassure herself, then she placed her tools together next the plot where she worked and headed for the abbey, her garden gloves still on her hands. Her determined intent frightened her. But she justified her purpose by convincing herself that Kendall's life could be more productive than poor Otley's who would remain forever a little boy.

Her strides through the grass swirled a sweet aroma to her nostrils, giving her a heady feeling, encouraging her on. For the first time in ten years she entered the abbey, passing down the nearly extinct nave then turning into the south transept, the very place where she found her daughter. Otley stood and watched her approach.

The boy greeted her in his way, appearing nervous because of his affliction, but smiling in recognition. "Good day, Otley. I see you often from my garden when you come here. No one comes here more often than you do, Otley. It is your abbey, isn't it. The abbey truly belongs to you."

He smiled and jerked, attempting to respond.

"You were here yesterday."

He seemed pleased that the great lady of Rochedale Manor would notice him. He tried to tell her that he was in the abbey yesterday.

"You saw Kendall here. You saw my son." Mrs. Roche's voice changed from pleasantness and warmth to a sneer. It gathered strength and rose to a higher pitch. She became challenging. He stepped backward in surprise. She pursued him, moving directly in front of him until she stared into his frightened eyes. Terror mounted as she began losing control of herself.

"Did Kendall do it?" she screeched.

Otley strained himself to reply. The struggling incensed her, stimulating the anger that was building. Her hands fell strongly on his shoulders and she shook him vigorously. "Tell me! Tell me!" she yelled.

Frustrated by a lack of verbal response and fearing his reactions indicated a charge of "yes," her gloved hands went to his neck and she squeezed, the leather of her gloves digging into his flesh. Maniacal now, she refused to let go.

Looking down at the prostrate figure, and realizing the immensity of her act, she was seized with horror. She stared at the gloves in disbelief then covered her face to hide the scene.

Mrs. Esterham rose at dawn tired and depressed. Events of the preceding day had unnerved her to the point that all during the night she fitfully reviewed her sorrows of the past.

First as a maid then as a housekeeper, she had been at Rochedale Manor for over forty years, becoming part of the family, enjoying each member's accomplishments and suffering pain for each one's defeats. She had helped raise each Roche child, no, more than raise, for because of Mrs. Roche's circumstances, particularly at the births of the children and then later when they grew, she was almost a birth mother to all three. Each child turned to her for affection, for satisfying wants and for guidance. She provided all as well as for covering childhood transgressions.

Ten years ago she anguished with Mrs. Roche at the loss of her "sweet little girl."

Later when Winsford Roche died so tragically, they wore the black of bereavement together.

During the years since, "the women of Rochedale Manor," as the community referred to them, supported each other in not only maintaining the estate but in increasing its wealth.

She knew Kendall had been in the abbey before the Minshal girl was found. She recognized the coat he always wore. She didn't tell Mrs. Roche, but she thought she had seen Radcliffe in the abbey as well, a place he rarely visited. She recognized immediately the fearful thoughts that must be going through Mrs. Roche's mind when she thought of Kendall and Emma and ten years ago. "I must speak to Otley. I shall have the truth from that young man before the constable gets it."

After attending to the needed morning chores, she put together a basket of biscuits, freshly made by cook, but adding a finishing touch of her own. She fiddled as she kept vigil, continuously reassuring herself that Kendall must be protected from any suspicion. Her patience was rewarded. In the distance Otley was about his usual rounds. She tarried further for she knew Otley liked to play for long periods in the abbey. At length, with basket in hand, she intercepted the boy, knowing full well that the way around any child was through his stomach. "Hello, Otley," she greeted him happily. "You chose a beautiful day to be about. How's for a biscuit to make it even brighter. Sit down here and uncover the basket."

Otley sat down next to Mrs. Esterham. He looked at the basket knowing full well what to expect, for many times he had been given treats from the Roche kitchen and they were always delicious. After some effort he pulled a colorful serviette from the basket to discover two kinds of biscuits, each separated from the other by a folded serviette. His eyes bulged in expected pleasure of discovery.

"Take one of these first, Otley." She pointed to the kind closer to him. "Good?" He nodded to her question after he took the first bite.

When the first biscuit was no more, she began to probe. "You saw somebody harm Emma, didn't you, Otley? Just nod your head if you did."

Otley's head gave a jerky affirmative nod.

"Have another biscuit." As he ate she praised him for being a fine boy, helpful to everyone and for always being truthful. Otley responded happily and laughed aloud. He rarely heard a compliment. "Now, Otley, since you never tell lies, tell me who hurt Emma. If you touch this first stick, you will tell me Kendall hurt her. If you touch this second stick you will tell me Radcliffe hurt her. If you touch this third stick you will tell me some one else hurt her. Now, Otley, touch the stick that tells me the truth."

Otley did not hesitate. With much effort he touched one of the sticks.

"Thank you, Otley. Take this biscuit" She handed him one from the second pile.

"Constable, Dr. Poole needs you." The request came from the door as Ormand worked at his desk. A late afternoon sun was just touching roofs of buildings on the eastern side of Market Square, and he was anxious to tie up the day's paper work and be on his way.

Anxiously he entered Dr. Poole's surgery, fearful of the worst. On the table was a body covered with sheeting. "The boy is dead, constable." Dr. Poole's voice was grim. "It is murder."

He uncovered Otley's head and shoulders. The face was somewhat distorted but the neck was badly bruised. "I was afraid of this." The constable spoke ruefully, incensed at what he saw. "I wanted to put him in protective custody but his father said no, and others warned me that protective custody would be interpreted by some of the townspeople to be an arrest and accusation of murder. You know what would have happened as well as I if I did provide protection. What was the cause of death?"

"I can't tell for sure and even with further examination I am not positive I can give an unequivical answer. It is either strangulation or poison. Blood analysis is not giving me much. These marks on the neck indicate some very drastic action, enough to cause death."

"Who brought him in?"

"Radcliffe Roche."

"Did he say where he found the boy?"

"I did not ask."

"Mmmmmmm." The constable pondered his next move. "I need to see Radcliffe about that. Can you tell me what kind of poison was used?"

"I can't be that definite. It could have been a concoction used with animals or it could have been from a homemade recipe. Animal poison is very common as you know, and people still use poisons they put together. Any number of country folk use recipes handed down by word of mouth."

"Could you get a better test? I'd like to follow up on the poison." Ormand returned to his office feeling depressed. He tried to prepare himself for the community reaction he knew would result from the latest murder.

Chapter Three

Emma and Otley were buried in Tosten en Dale church cemetery. Services were widely attended, people having come from all parts of North Riding, partly out of respect for the deceased's families, but mainly to express alarm over the murders of two children and the fear that there could be more. After the vicar committed their souls to heaven, the assemblage moved into Market Square where small groups of discontented citizens formed. Their action was compulsive since there was no effort on the part of anyone to organize a community meeting. There was a deep social need, however, for people to gather, to speak their minds, to take comfort in each other and to let somebody know of their concerns. A grimness was evident on faces and the mood was threatening. It was not the nature of Yorkshire men and women to take the law into their own hands, they had elected officials, but at times of crisis, they wanted to express themselves. A leader emerged.

Radcliffe Roche leaped onto the flatbed of a wagon standing at the northern perimeter of the square. He was recognized at once and his acceptance was demonstrated by the movement of people toward the wagon where they formed a large semicircle. Eyes lifted upward in rapt attention as if expecting a miracle to end their anxieties. "My North Riding friends," the young man began, his eyes moving about from individual to individual to give a personal touch to his oration. "We grieve over the tragic loss of two young people. You have come together, some of you from many miles away, to express your fears. You want to know what is to be done about our tragedies and what is to be done to provide safety for your defenseless loved ones."

Heads nodded in agreement and a murmur of assent rumbled through the crowd.

"Some of you have suggested we organize a committee to assist the constable. What do you think, constable."

Again the murmur rose, but it subsided as soon as Constable Ormand stood beside Radcliffe.

"As Yorkshire men you have the right to express yourselves in open meetings. At this time of crisis you are exercising that right. I hear what you are saying." Ormand paused to let his statement convey his concern for their welfare. "When Emma was brought to this square we considered the possibility that a transient may have done her in. But with Otley's death we have reason to believe the culprit is a neighbor, perhaps one who is standing among us right now. It is possible the same person committed both acts, or we may be seeking two murderers. There is no doubt, however, that the crimes are related, for Otley knew who killed Emma. Someone did not want Otley to tell." Heads nodded in agreement.

"My job is to find the murderer or murderers as quickly as possible. I am an experienced law man. I have an extensive background in the practice of keeping the law. I want the freedom to do my job without hinderance from a group of anxious committeemen who are emotional and who could point a finger at the wrong person. None of us want an innocent person accused. If I cannot get the murderer, I will resign."

"What clues do you have, constable?" someone called out.

"We have some clues but you will understand why I cannot discuss those here."

"When will you have the murderer?"

"I cannot give you a date, but our full time is already on these crimes."

"But our children are not safe, constable."

The comment hit the heart of all concerned.

The constable waited until the buzzing calmed then he spoke. "It is best not to leave children alone. Have them play in groups. Where possible parents can work out schedules so that children can be supervised by an adult, each taking turns. Have groups of children go to and from school together, the older ones watching younger ones. Tell children to be aware of strangers and to report anything suspicious. If you have doubts about anything, make an inspection and if you are still concerned, send word to my office." He had the full attention of everyone. "Be alert, but above all, be careful about shooting at anyone. You do not want to kill an innocent person. By working together we can rid ourselves of a menace that has struck our lives."

The constable turned to face Radcliffe, silently communicating he had completed his statements. He received a nod in reply.

Radcliffe faced the assemblage. "Constable Ormand has asked for our cooperation. We need to give him all the help he needs. Will you help?"

There was broad assent indicated by a nodding of heads and the turning of one person to another for expressions of agreement. No further questions came from the crowd and slowly it began to disburse, some men entering the pub, women going to their homes or to the homes of friends and others to their wagons for the trip home. The events of the day would have continued analysis wherever people met.

Left atop the wagon, the constable offered his hand to Radcliffe and thanked him for calming the crowd and for helping him give the people direction. "It would have been a difficult afternoon without your support. I appreciate your quick action."

When Radcliffe jumped down, Kendall immediately embraced his brother warmly and praised him for his leadership. "That was masterful, Radcliffe."

"Come on, constable," Radcliffe urged. "I'll treat all of us to an ale."

From her buggy Mrs. Roche watched the three men enter the pub. She felt proud that her son could rise to meet a difficult occasion, but inwardly she was fearful. She had cried for Kendall although he denied being in the abbey. "A lie to defend himself. He is only human."

She defended herself, too. "It is a mother's right to protect her son. I cannot let the constable suspect him. Otley would have involved Kendall."

The conclusion gave her some strength to face her own dreadful deed. A vision of Otley's face appeared again. She closed her eyes trying to erase the boy's bewildered expression. It had appeared frequently, especially during the night when sleep evaded her, as she dressed for the funerals, during the service, and now as she watched the square clearing of people. His eyes that shouted disbelief as her fingers closed about his neck stared at her again and again. She looked at her hands. "What was the source of strength to commit that awful act? I know. A mother's defense. I could not allow him to tell on Kendall.

"I left him coiling on the ground, the last convulsions moving him about, his eyes closed, the marks of my gloves appearing red on his neck. The horror of it!"

Her sob attracted Mrs. Estherham's attention. "Mrs. Roche, are you alright?"

"It is just all that has happened. We must take our basket to John and tomorrow we will call on Mrs. Willowby to pay our condolences for the loss of her son. Her loss is just as devastating as if Otley were a complete boy."

The two women entered their buggy. In all their years of association their salutations never relaxed to intimacy. It was always Mrs. Esterham and Mrs. Roche. Yet there was deep understanding and respect one for the other, a caring that had grown out of living and working together under one roof for many years.

Tillie Hetly married Arthur Esterham while she was a maid at Rochedale Manor. He was a sickly man, a fatal respiratory problem racking his body until he could fight no more. He left her with a child, a girl, who inherited her father's poor health. Tillie made Rochedale Manor her home, nursed her daughter through illness after illness until she married. Mrs. Esterham was already the housekeeper when Virginia Barkeley arrived as the bride of Winsford Roche.

The housekeeper trained the young Mrs. Roche for her role as future matron of Rochedale Manor and she was eminently successful in guiding her apt pupil. Virginia became in time like her own daughter filling the void left by the loss of her only child.

The buggy stopped before Minshall's cottage, a small stone building fronted by a garden filled with color. Mrs. Crewe admitted the women and all shared their grief once more. Included in the basket was sufficient cash to provide adequately for John's care. There would be more, payments to relieve the tragedy of guilt.

The drive home continued in silence. Mrs. Esterham was first stunned then she felt some relief when she heard the cause of Otley's death was by strangulation, but is was only for the moment. No matter what Dr. Poole had said, she knew how Otley died. "It was an ancient concoction given to my mum by old Mother Thatchley, the crone in the village who learned wizardry from gypsies."

She, like Mrs. Roche, justified her performance on the grounds of parenthood. "No, he is not my son, only one step removed. I could not let Otley tell on him. I could not loose that boy. What he did to Emma was a crime, but he must have had a reason. One day I shall know."

Remorse haunted her. Every waking moment gave her a memory of the dead boy accepting her kindness, "a trust that was his doom." There were tears not only for Otley and herself but more for what would have been had she not taken her action.

The pub filled rapidly, and although it was his only son who had been buried that day, Manfred Willowby manned the kegs. Ale flowed in quantity, for his patrons wanted to drown their fears and find relief in the company of friends.

Radcliffe bought a round for everyone and he toasted the constable with wishes for success. He mingled among the tables speaking to the men, and after a number of mugs he sat down heavily in a chair and dropped his head on his arms spread atop the table. Tears began to flow amid some heavy sobbing.

Kendall immediately came to his brother's protection, warding off sympathizers and reminding them that it was he who brought the boy in. "He has kept it all inside. It has to come out. Let him be."

But Radcliffe's own thoughts could not let him rest. He reproached himself for what he had done, not understanding what had occurred, but feeling penitent for his transgressions. "Why? Why?" he charged himself. "Why does it happen?"

Kendall stood above his brother waiting for a sign of recovery and thinking of his own last meeting with Otley. "How could I have allowed such an act. It was Carinna, my need for Carinna or any girl. I had to let go. He surprised me. He looked fascinated. It happened so quickly. I could not stop. How can I tell anyone? I am so ashamed. And after, I left. I did not even look back." He peered down at his hands as they turned for him to see his palms. "They were on his neck." He shuddered at his thoughts. "I could not have done it!" He screamed silently at himself. The feeling of guilt would not go away.

Radcliffe moved after a time and raised his head. Kendall motioned to those nearby to pay no attention. "Shall we go home?" he suggested. The young man rose and together they left the pub. The horses knew the way, first the road to York, over the Dale bridge, onto the first road leading to the right. No words were spoken until they dismounted in the stables.

"Will you sit with me, Kendall?"

"Of course."

They climbed the stairs to Radcliffe's room. "Brandy?" he proposed as they entered. The room was large, remodeled from the second level of the abbey dormitory. During the Tudor period it was the priest's room, for its windows provided a broad view across the meadow to the Dale as well as along the extended lane leading to the house. It was believed that those approaching could be identified and suspicious strangers thus seen could give a resident priest in a Protestant countryside ample time to hide.

Kendall sat down and took a sip of brandy as Radcliffe went to one window to gaze at the abbey. "I am so distraught over what happened." His voice reflected fatigue. "First Emma and then Otley. Everyone, the whole of North Riding, wants results, but Ormand has no clues, not even one. You saw their mood. If we have another murder there will be trouble and things will get out of hand. Innocent people will be hurt. What do you think?"

The question surprised him. "I agree."

"No. I mean what do you think about the deaths?"

"I have no idea. I don't know one person who would kill, particularly a child like Otley."

Radcliffe turned to look at his brother. "That is the whole thing. No one knows anyone who would kill. But some one did. The constable isn't sure the two deaths are related. At first glance one would think Otley was killed because he saw who killed Emma. But that is not necessarily true. We could have two killers, two people we know and don't suspect. What do you know about Emma?"

"Emma? What do you mean?"

"You were seen in the abbey before Emma was found. Mother saw you."

"Mother told me she had seen me, but it was not I she saw. I did not go to the abbey. She saw someone in a coat similar to mine and assumed she saw me. She did not see the face of the person wearing the coat. Do I have to prove I was not there?" Kendall hesitated, his scowl indicating deep concern. "If I have to show proof I don't think I can. I was with Tenley for a time that morning working with sick lambs, but I left to take care of some other chores. I don't believe anyone saw me doing that work. It could be difficult if charges are brought against me. I did stop by Compton Heath to see Carinna during the morning but I wasn't there long."

"You do like Carinna, don't you?" Radcliffe kept his eyes on his brother. "Keep in mind I have an interest there." He smiled then quickly grew serious. "She could be a witness to verify some of your time, but you should be prepared with an alibi or attempt to find someone to substantiate your locations. It may come to the point where the constable will start questioning anyone and everyone who could remotely suggest a clue. He could start here since we are so close to the abbey."

"Are you suggesting I am guilty of Emma's death?"

"Oh, Kendall. Now. It is only that I am concerned. Mother saw you. If you were not there, you must be able to prove you were elsewhere. We don't know who else might say you were there. After all, the meadow is like a public park. Many people use it, and on market day people pass through to save time walking to town. Anyone could point a finger at you just to name a suspect to clear up the crimes. You saw the people's mood. Fright does change things."

Alarm for his own safety grew as he considered his brother's statements. "So that is it. I am to be charged."

"Nonsense. I just want to make sure you are protected."

"If they say I killed Emma then they will say I killed Otley to prevent him from talking. I don't even know where Otley was found. Come to think of it, where did you find Otley?"

Radcliffe turned to stare once more out the window. His eyes caught a glitter of sun on water where the Dale curves around an edge of the meadow. "I am not sure." His speech slowed and there was wonder in it. "I can't even recall where I was part of that day. I do remember walking my horse by the river, there, near the abbey. I had been at Moncton Tor and was going to Tosten. Otley was lying in front of me across my horse. The sight of him shocked me. I took him to Dr. Poole."

Kendall studied his brother. Shock grew across his countenance as the impact of the confession hit him. "Moncton Tor! That's where I left Otley! Among the crags!" he reminded himself, fear grabbing his very being as he recalled choking Otley.

"Did you say that to the constable," he asked in disbelief. To himself he added, "The guilt could be mine. Did I kill him and leave him in the crags?"

"No. When he asked me where I found Otley, I said in the meadow next to the abbey."

"My God! He killed Otley thinking he was protecting me!" Kendall shouted to himself.

He walked to the window, put his arms around his brother's shoulders and squeezed. "You have been working too hard, carrying the weight of the whole estate business. Let's go to London. It is time to get away for a while anyway. We can stop in at the office handling our business, get acquainted with procedures, but mostly we'll have a good time. We are both ripe for change. Let's talk to mother."

Radcliffe let his head fall on Kendall's shoulder. The protection from fear gave him confidence and he mumbled a "yes."

Mrs. Roche was in her sitting room, Guy next to her, awaiting tea and trying to relax from the highly emotional activities of the day. "Ah, my boys," she greeted their entry. "Come sit with me. Mrs. Esterham will have tea shortly. I am so proud of what you did today, Radcliffe. You saved a potentially dangerous situation and protected the constable."

"He showed all his leadership qualities, mother. Racliffe must have inherited all of father's skills." Kendall wrapped some complimentary swats on his brother's back before the two sat down.

Mrs. Roche heard Kendall praise his father. She knew the truth, however, but never had she belittled her husband in front of the boys. If they ever were to learn the true facts, they would have to get them from someone else. "That is unlikely for only one other knows. The secret is safe there."

Mrs. Esterham entered with tea service for three, quantities of scones, bread, butter and and jam and a larger than usual teapot. "I heard the boys coming, Mrs. Roche. I know they enjoy cook's efforts." She removed the cosy, poured tea and distributed hot water, sugar and milk to each one's liking. "Will you dine at seven, Mrs. Roche?"

"Thank you, Mrs. Esterham. That will be fine." The housekeeper withdrew.

"Mother, Radcliffe and I had a talk about your suggestion to visit the London office. With your permission we are thinking we should go very soon, perhaps next week. That will give us time to put everything in good order before leaving."

"Oh, I'm pleased, Kendall, particularly that you are going, too. How long to you plan to be gone?"

"We didn't discuss that, mother, but we want enough time to make the long trip worth while. What would you say to a month?"

"That is a long time, but I think we can manage here. Let's say no more than a month, and if you have your fill of office work before then, come home."

"It won't be all work. London has a social side." Kendall's enthusiasm for the plan oozed out of his statement.

"I shall call all foremen for a meeting, and we can anticipate needs, assign duties and assure ourselves all will be cared for to our satisfaction." Radcliffe had now warmed to Kendall's proposal, and encouraged by his mother, he was already organizing for the leave.

"I must get word to our London agent that you will be dropping in and requesting that he do a bit of instructing." After the first moments of surprise had passed, Mrs. Roche felt pleasure in her sons' acceptance of her suggestion, particularly the apparent ardent willingness of Kendall to go. "Of course I know it is the lure of London's gayety that attracts him," she acknowledged to herself, "but at least some learning may cling to him."

June rains were heavier than normal and served to delay the boy's departure. Radcliffe used the time to work with foremen and care for anticipated problems. He also organized a wardrobe he would be wearing in London.

Kendall called on Squire Gunning to advise him of his and Radcliffe's forthcoming absence. "May I request, sir, that as you have time, please call on my mother. It may be that in an emergency or if unexpected problems should arise, you could provide assistance and may I add, sir, expert assistance."

"I can do that, Kendall." He was pleased that the request was made since he knew that Rochedale Manor was served by the finest cattle and sheep men in Yorkshire, men capable of handling any emergency. He was further flattered by the compliment paid for his skills.

Squire Gunning saw in the request an opportunity to visit Mrs. Roche. In his younger days he had known Virginia Barkeley as a neighbor's daughter, had called on her then as a potential suitor, but instead chose Lille Rogers as his bride. As a widower he had considered Virginia Roche as a second bride when Winford was killed, but he saw problems in the match. Of course resulting from the marriage would be his control over the Roche estate, but she could claim his own extensive acreage were he to predecease her. "And I am more than a few years older than Virginia. There is need to provide for my own Carinna and Flora, at least until they take husbands." Economic reasons, therefore, took precedent over matrimonial interests which, he admitted, were not too strong. "At my age it is the convenience that matters and I am getting by." The wink he gave himself had reference to his housekeeper.

"May I speak to Carinna?" Kendall tried to cover his enthusiasm for the affect he was having on Squire. His primary purpose for riding to Compton Heath was his need to see her. The request spoken so eloquently to Squire Gunning was only a ruse to get on her father's side and gain some time alone with Carinna.

"Why, I believe she said she would walk to Ilkson Crags and even to Mockton Tor." The information was given only because the young man had paid him unusual respect and placed him off guard. Immediately after speaking he had second thoughts. Recollections of Mollie Peeks erupted, the only girl he ever got around, and he knew what a hot blood like Kendall could do.

Recognizing his error too late, however, he quickly added, "If you see her tell her I need her at once."

Careful to take his leave in a gentlemanly manner, Kendall promised he would. He directed his horse toward Ilkston Crags. An anticipated meeting with Carinna away from her observant, protective father excited him and quickly he felt the results growing. He touched his manliness as if to reassure the instrument that there was reasonable hope for pleasant use.

Ilkston Crags was a geological phenomenon to north country people. During a mighty eruption eons ago tremendous forces within the earth shoved huge quantities of molten rock to the surface. They cooled to form massive needle like structures of various heights clustered together as if tied. Because of an escarpment that fell away at their base, they created an awesome scene from a distance.

Kendall searched the environs of the crags, walking among boulders that had broken loose from the main clusters and rolled to rest at a variety of distances beyond. There was no Carinna. He continued on toward Moncton Tor where he discovered her walking on a path.

"Carinna, wait!" He yelled loudly so that she would know of his approach. She turned.

Before him was a picture of winsome beauty, the wind catching her auburn hair to toss it off her shoulders, the smile lustrous, an immediate reaction to his unexpected presence. "You are so exquisite," he complimented her. Leaping from his horse he rushed to her, wrapped his arms about her and kissed her forehead. Her arms went about his waist and the two stood like the crags, molded together. Releasing her gently, she raised her face to his, eyes closed, expectant. His lips found hers, and she closed her hand on the nape of his neck to press his mouth more tightly on hers. She felt a probe with his tongue and she released her lips to permit entry. He felt the quickening rise and fall of her breasts on his chest and she could detect his mounting hardness. He pushed his head upward so he could mumble ardently on her lips his urgency. "I must love you completely."

Simultaneously they broke their embrace and she led him, holding onto his hand as if in fear he would get away. They entered a cavern, the opening so small they both had to crawl on their hands and knees to pass through. The cave was shallow but the roof was high enough to permit him to stand. In the muted darkness he grabbed her wildly. He lifted her and gently placed her on the floor of the chamber. Quickly they disrobed, he helping her, she helping him.

He kneelt above her, hesitating in his purpose to admire the wonder of her beauty.

Tenderly he touched her nakedness, marveling at the softness of her skin, then letting his finger tips roam freely about her. She lay enthralled, her eyes closed, pleasure expressed in a smile that crossed her lips.

He lowered his head over hers, praise abounding in his anxious eyes. Lovingly he kissed her lips, her eyes. She felt a moistness at one ear then the other as his tongue explored. A nip was taken of the lobe causing her to squirm. He disappeared from physical touch for a fleeting moment then she felt him at her neck, a tongue roaming. Hands began stroking her legs and she became aware of his moving position. Her legs began moving outward as she accommodated his movements, his fingers roaming along her thighs, even higher. She felt him on her, at first lightly, his head between her breasts, kissing, then the roaming of a tongue again, a pinching with his teeth. His weight came more heavily on her and slowly, gently his hardness mastered her.

After, they lay side by side, her head resting on his arm that folded around her. Neither spoke. There was no need. For her this was fulfillment of a longing. For him it was ecstacy, a reward for the preparation with other women that had preceded this supreme experience, the consumation of love.

Chapter Four

Wagging her tail in full abandon, Bonnie greeted Radcliffe lovingly. Her delight was summarized in a loud bark which she let linger in a hum, and a grin showed on her face. He returned her affection with some gentle words and a vigorous rubbing of her hind quarters. Bonnie was an outside dog, having shown no interest at all in entering the house. Instead she preferred the stables where there was always more interesting activity and the daily anticipation of a run. While she liked Kendall and occasionally joined him, she preferred Radcliffe. The sheep dog alertly watched as a groom saddled a horse then led him from the stable. Barking was vociferous when Radcliffe mounted. She waited until a direction was taken then she bounded ahead in unreined happiness.

Radcliffe was on his way to Compton Heath. He had written previously asking to see Squire Gunning as well as for an opportunity to visit with Carinna. A reply was received specifying the date and time. He rode now with thoughts centered on the meeting. He was dressed in a manner suited to his station, a requirement that would be expected by the father and he hoped impressive on the daughter. This was a strategic encounter, as Radcliffe viewed it, for Kendall was his adversary, a formidable suitor.

"Of course Kendall is not serious in pursuing her for marriage." he reasoned. "He likes the ladies and is playing the field. She is undoubtedly a much fairer prize than a lot he has seen but to him she is only one among many. I must be more careful in my quest, however. The girl I choose will become mistress of Rochedale Manor. Carinna has that potential." He was pleased with the practical, business like manner in which he approached the requirement in selecting a wife. At this point he gave no consideration to the lusty dimension.

Radcliffe was also aware that a union with Carinna could add Compton Heath property to Rochedale Manor. "That would depend on what provision Gunning has made for Flora, of course, but it would be an excellent acquisition nevertheless." Visually he conjured money resulting from the new lands and a possible inheritance of a small but excellent racing stable. "That could be a new hobby for me."

Bonnie stopped her run, listened, then began barking. Radcliffe stared in the direction the dog pointed. He saw a figure on foot, a girl approaching on a walking path. He directed his horse forward at a walk until he identified her.

"Good day, Flora. What a pleasant surprise on this sunny day." He dismounted and offered his hand. Gently she accepted it. What he saw surprised him.

At sixteen Corinna's sister had suddenly developed into a beauty, no longer the little awkward girl he once thought her to be. The dress she wore complimented a slim figure that curved at the hips and showed an enticing protrusion at the breasts, her bodice falling low enough to excite the male view of an inviting cleavage. Sun glistened on teeth exposed by a captivating smile and her blue eyes danced at his warm greeting. Blond hair was pulled back and tied with a red ribbon, the tail falling almost to her waist. Here was a dimension he had not considered in his marriage planning.

Flora eyed him with the power of a conqueror, for that is what she was attempting to be. She had read her father's correspondence with the principal heir of Rochedale Manor and she knew of his coming visit. She planned her timing perfectly to intercept him on his approach. It was her further plan to beguile him if she could, and if not, at least to impose herself on his thinking. "After all he has not spoken for Carinna and I could be the young Mrs. Roche, heiress apparent to lofty Rochedale Manor. Carrina can have Kendall."

"You are on an errand and I am delaying you," Radcliffe apologized, but he hoped she would stay. He felt an interest growing.

"Why not at all. I was taking a walk when Bonnie's barking startled me. I was at first fearful after what has happened to Emma and Otley, then I saw you. Father has warned us about wandering too far. But you have removed that fear." She tossed him a coyish look and let her lashes fall.

"Of course your father is right. We don't know whom you might meet, and one so fair as you could be in danger."

She took his hands in both of hers and spoke demurely. "If I had a protector such as you, I should not have to fear anyone."

At his age he should have seen through her wiles, but even her inexperienced cleverness was having an affect. He was beginning to succumb, acting as clay in her hands. "Then I shall walk you home. What a pity that you must be in fear."

"How good of you, Radcliffe, if I may call you so."

"Of course, Flora. Please use my given name. You are no longer a child. You are a lovely young lady. Why, I am only a few years older."

They started walking, he holding the reins of his horse in his right hand and she, pressing her advantage, slipped her right arm through his left. He could feel the movement of her body as she pressed against him.

"Father tells me that you and Kendall will be going to London for a time. How fortunate you are. You will be part of the gay life, all the parties, all the dances. I should so much like to go with you. We would have such a marvelous time together. You could show me the city."

"That would be fine, indeed, Flora, but your father would not permit that, and Kendall and I are committed to conducting business in London."

She pulled his arm to stop him. As he turned to face her she looked longingly into his eyes. "Oh, Radcliffe, you wont be gone long. I shall miss you."

He stood above her gazing down at her pleading eyes. He detected a feeling growing within himself. He dropped the reins and both hands went to her shoulders. He felt her arms go about his waist. Slowly his head dropped onto hers, her eyes closing in anticipation. Their lips met. She pushed hers against his and tightened her hold at his waist. He felt her body curve into his. A strange feeling emerged. He felt compelled to act. His head began to ache. His hands left her shoulders and glided to her neck.

She felt his body tense over hers. His kiss became ardent and she could feel his hands cross her shoulders, touch her neck and begin to tighten. Fearfully she loosened her embrace, forced her arms between the two of his and pushed vigorously to free herself from his clutch. She looked into eyes that appeared glassy. He seemed in a trance.

"Radcliffe!" she called in alarm. "Are you ill?" The blank stare continued. She grabbed his arms and shook him. He appeared to tremble. He bobbed his head and his eyes cleared. He seemed to be in a daze for a moment He found her staring at him, startled, and he watched her for a moment.

"Forgive me, Flora. I have been getting these strange headaches. Kendall says I have been working too hard. Getting away to London will help. Come. We must get to Compton Heath."

"I am so sorry, Radcliffe. Let me steady you." Once again she placed her arm through his, thrusting her body next to his so they rubbed. As they walked she guided her hand into his and clasped it tightly. "Promise me you wont spend all of your time working while in London. I shall want to know all about the socials, what the ladies wear, and the plays. I have never seen a play. It must be glorious being an actress."

Her attack began afresh and by the time they approached the gate to Compton Heath, both were talking and laughing gaily, his illness on the path quite forgotten. Flora left him at the entry with a caressing handshake, holding his free hand in both of hers, and pleading coyly, "I would like to see you before you go to London. Say you will come to see me."

"My dear, I shall try. It would be very pleasant for me to see you once more. I am so glad we met today." He watched her departure, she deliberately rotating her derrier expressively, he staring in wonder at the awesome gyrations. A feeling of ambivalence struck him, upsetting his plans. He had come to Compton Heath to establish a definite liaison with Carinna. Now here was Flora presenting herself for his examination. "She is a young filly, but that kind matures in a hurry," he considered. "I shall have to give her consideration."

Radcliffe directed his strides to the service area where he fully expected to see Squire Gunning. He was told his host would meet him in the house. Leaving his horse, he returned to the front portal, used the heavy ringed knocker, and was shown to the study. It was an academic room with a large desk, shelves holding some books, and two chairs. Before long Guinning entered.

"Good day to you, Radcliffe. Tea will be served shortly. Kendall tells me you are planning a trip to London."

Squire Gunning's personality characteristics were well known to Radcliffe. He wondered how such a person could have fathered two daughters so different from him. Flora, he believed, had shown during their short talk more life than her father could muster in a life time.

"Yes, sir. We hope to learn more of the business functions of our London agents, and that is the purpose of my visit with you. I would like to ask if you would talk with me about the inner workings of a London office so that when I arrive I shall not be completely ignorant and will be able to ask intelligent questions."

Squire looked at the young man. Immediately he felt his ego rise, and a positive reaction toward Radcliffe began building. "This one has the business interest," he considered to himself.

"Kendall arrives and merely tells me they are going to London. He wants me to be a watchman.

"Radcliffe arrives and asks me for help. He is the one alright. He is the boy who will carry on the Roche tradition. Carinna needs to become better acquainted with Radcliffe."

A smile broke the crusted face drawing a frown of amazement from Radcliffe. "I am honored you would ask." The comment was unusually friendly. "Of course you need some background. Like your own father who would have prepared you, I shall inform you."

Radcliffe gave an inward sigh of relief. "The plan is working. 'Through the father get the girl.' Who told me that? He will support me in my quest for Carinna. Kendall will have no chance."

The discussion went on for almost two hours. Radcliffe was surprised at the store of information Squire was sharing with him. His own interest grew, he asked questions, pursued topics, evaluated procedures and Squire developed each subject. It was the housekeeper who ended the meeting. "Your noon meal is ready, sir."

Both girls were in the drawing room when the men entered. Greetings were exchanged then Squire led the group to the dining room where Radcliffe seated each of the sisters. He was directed to take a chair opposite, a position he appreciated for the advantage was his to observe and compare. He paid just enough attention to participate in the light banter but mentally he designed a check list to guide him in an evaluation. Quickly he came to a conclusion. "Both are lovely to look at, each has a beautiful face, and they have comparable conversation skills. There is one major difference, however. It is maturity. Flora at times acts the child while Carinna acts the young lady, poised and assured. It is she who meets my needs for the future Mrs. Roche. Flora in time could be trained, but the question is how much time. I don't have the patience. It is to Carinna I must direct my interests."

The decision bothered him, however, for he did not feel entirely secure with it. Each time he looked at Flora he recalled the feel of her supple body and the sweetness of her kiss. "Her kiss? I did kiss her, didn't I. I must have."

There was a red ribbon about Flora's neck, tied attractively to compliment the bow in her hair. It was not there when he embraced her. She placed it appropriately to hide noticeable blemishes she did not wish her father to see. She did not have faith she could account for them adequately should he inquire.

Surprisingly Squire did not dominate the conversation. It was Carinna who played the hostess, seeing to it that he had enough to eat and involving each person in discussing a variety of topics. It was Flora who brought up the subject of the murders, but it was Squire who brought it to a close with an admonition. "I do not want either of you two girls leaving this house unless you tell me. We do not know who is out there looking for the likes of you."

The meal over, Squire spoke in his usual authoritative voice. "Flora, I need some help. Carinna, see to it that Radcliffe is made comfortable. Come, Flora."

Disappointment showed immediately. Of course Flora knew Radcliffe had asked to see Carinna. She had read his note but she was hoping against hope that her father would permit her to stay with her sister.

Squire caught her reaction. He knew his younger daughter well. "She is like her mother, boy struck," he reminisced. "I recall how Lillie Rogers chased me. I would perhaps have been married to Virginia Roche if it had not been for Lillie's skillful wiles. She heated me beyond control, got me in the hay, and then said I had to marry her or she would cause a scandal. Flora would take Radcliffe the same way. No. Carinna is better for him. She is better for my purposes, too"

His stare was enough. Flora followed him out the door while Carinna gestured Radcliffe to the drawing room and toward the sofa. She sat beside him, leaving a respectable distance between them. "You will be leaving soon for London. I do wish you a very happy holiday,"

"Thank you, Carinna. We are looking forward to a pleasant time although business is our first purpose for going."

"But, Radcliffe, you must see some plays. When you return I want to hear all about them. The actresses particularly. I want to know what fashions the ladies are wearing."

Radcliffe was becoming nervous. She was making conversation, he recognized, while waiting for him to state his purpose in seeing her. It was her voice, the lilting quality, that got in his way. "How long will you be gone?" He heard her say.

"We are not sure. The length of our stay will depend on how well our business goes."

Carinna looked at the man opposite. He was attractive, handsome certainly, and his big frame added to his appeal. His dress was irreproachable and refinement glowed in his polished manner. "But he lacks his brother's charm. What the French say, 'bon vivant.'"

"Carinna," he opened. "I asked your father's permission to see you."

She almost snickered, but she recovered quickly. "Kendall did not ask, he just took," she thought to herself. The remembrance of the taking pleased her. This Radcliffe is not the same man who stood on the wagon after the funerals and spoke so eloquently. Now he has a problem. I sit untouched by him because he is unsure of women. Perhaps it is shyness."

"Now may I ask permission to visit you? I would like to know you better and for you to know me. I have admired you for some time."

His statements were anticipated. She had no question about what he would say. It was only the manner in which he would express himself that caused her to wonder. "So this is the way of telling me he has selected me as the next mistress of Rochedale Manor. No doubt he wants to court me for a time then present his petition to father." She smiled openly, for his interest pleased her, but to herself she commented, "Be not over anxious, Carinna. Follow your strategy. Make him earn his conquest." The pause had given her the time she needed to maneuver him into her scheme.

"Radcliffe," she beamed, "you are sweet to say so. You for some time have earned my esteem. I was so proud of you for handling that unruly crowd after the funerals. Because of you we have had no community problems. That is a great tribute to your skills." She permitted her hand to glide in his direction until it rested in the space between them.

'Why, thank you, Carinna." He noted her hand and took it in his. "I shall endeavor always to earn your respect." His hand closed tighter on hers and she returned the gesture with a gentle pressure of her own. "Then you will permit me to call on you?"

She directed some power into her reply. "I shall be honored indeed, Radcliffe. In fact I shall look forward to our meetings and dread the wait between them."

"Oh, Carinna. You do please me. May I ask for your time as soon as I return from London. I shall make every effort to perform our duties in the city very quickly and return post haste." He raised her hand to his lips and kissed her palm.

"I shall await your return with great expectation." She arose leaving her hand in his. Immediately he stood placing himself in front of her so he could feel her body touching his. She slowly lifted her face and gently aimed her eyes at his.

He read the message and lowered his lips onto hers, resting them lovingly as his arms went about her waist and drew her to him. She returned his kiss strongly enough for him to feel pressure and he sighed. Breaking his hold he stepped back and gazed into her eyes. "Why must I go to London? I would rather stay here with you. I shall think of no one but you, Carinna, while I am gone. You are all I knew you would be."

"Sweet Radcliffe. I, too, shall think of you and long for your safe return. Bon voyage."

He turned quickly and left the room.

She stood staring at the door, thoughts evaluating the effectiveness of her plan. "He will come courting," she assured herself with a nod. "To have two Roches seeking me is indeed a conquest." She turned and strolled to the window. He was just passing through the main gate, Bonnie jumping and barking in advance.

"Radcliffe is so different from Kendall, reserved, proper. Very much the gentleman. But how would he be as a husband?" She tapped her finger on the sill. A smile broke the serious concentration. "Ah, Kendall. I know how you would be as a husband. You have demonstrated those skills. Perfection." Pleasure mounted in reflection. "But would you be faithful? I would feel safe with your brother about that question. But you, Kendall. I have a feeling you know your way around. I was not your first. Would I be the last if I married you? I wonder if a wife's bed would be enough for you.

"I have a feeling Radcliffe has not learned all about life as you obviously have. It is his unsureness that leads me to believe so. He would not be a rounder. Marriage for him would be the beginning and the end."

She moved from the window and began pacing slowly up and down the drawing room. "What is it I want? Take Radcliffe and I get the role of mistress and all it encompasses.

"Take Kendall and I get the second son's portion but all the pleasures of the bed." She stopped by the table and tapped her finger on it.

"You don't have to make a decision now, Carinna. Follow your plan. Let time be on your side. You have both men, one in each hand."

Her musing was broken by the opening of a door. Squire Gunning entered. "Did Radcliffe speak to you?" His query was abrupt. "He wasn't here long."

"Yes, father."

"What did he want?"

"He asked my permission to call on me."

"What did you say:"

"I gave him my permission."

"Ah. I gave him no permission to see you again. It was only for today."

"You don't object, do you father?"

Gunning stared at his first born. "She is my love child. I was in love with Lillie Rogers that night in the hay. Now my baby is to be mistress of Rochedale Manor." A feeling of satisfaction engulfed him. "I must see to it that nothing interferes with her opportunity." Aloud he asked, "Has Flora returned?"

"I have not seen her."

"That errand should not have taken this long." He turned and went to the door. "That Flora. She is so different from Carinna. Like her mother. I sometimes wonder if she is mine."

Flora had not known her mother. Lillie Gunning died shortly after her birth. An epidemic that swept the north of England took many lives. Squire Gunning was left to raise his daughters alone aided by legions of housekeepers who came and left. Mostly they could not abide the squire either because of his autocratic attitudes or his amorous attacks. Carinna was easy to direct, but Flora rebelled at her father's constant haranguing. She did not dare defy him but she took advantage of every opportunity to get away from the house. She soon learned that by volunteering to run errands she could escape him and then by using various ruses prolong the periods of freedom.

At such times she played games, sometimes with the sons of hired hands and sometimes with the fathers. She was always skillful enough to know when to stop her amusements, however, not because she wanted to but because she feared her father. Although she thought she knew the facts of life, she had yet to know a consumation.

It was the desire to get out from under her father's heavy thumb that led her to make plans. These included Radcliffe and Kendall. So far Kendall had not reached for her baited snare.

He always played up to Carinna when he came to Compton Heath. But she was not giving up on him. "After all if Emma made it, so can I."

Thoughts went to her friend, murdered by a person still unknown. It was Emma's stories that gave encouragement to Flora. Emma liked to taunt Flora with her own freedom. The stories she reported about her escapades were often based on fact but always embroidered with fantasy. Flora was wily enough to question the veracity of some her tales.

"Kendall is different, Flora."

Emma told her friend not long ago, "He knows what to do to make me love him. I've made up my mind I am going to live in Rochedale Manor. I am going to be the future mistress of that fine hall. I am going to marry Kendall. He has already told me he likes me. Do you know why I wasn't killed with my family in that accident? I had a date with Kendall. That was the day he told me he liked me. I figure I wasn't killed because I was meant to marry Kendall. I was meant to meet him and not go with my family. It is all a divine plan, but I have a plan of my own. I have a plan that will move me higher. I have a date next market day. I can leave the house to go to market then on the way to Tosten I will stop in the abbey. He will meet me there. I have a date with the handsome beast and I am going to marry him. After he loves me I will tell him he has to marry me. I have his child. I heard my mother tell a story like this. It will work."

Flora shuddered. She had given much thought to what Emma had told her, even considering going to the constable. "But that would not help me. If Emma planned on Rochedale Manor, why not Flora!"

Since the murders Flora gave time to planning what she would do with the information.

"If worst came to worst, I can tell Kendall to marry me or I will tell the constable Emma's story. I will be in Rochedale Manor one way or the other, Kendall or Radcliffe. Which ever opportunity presents itself, I shall be ready."

The errand completed, Flora hurried to the lane leading from Compton Heath in the direction of Rochedale Manor. She chose a site where she could hide yet observe the lane for several hundred feet. The wait was not long. Radcliffe appeared riding his horse at an easy gait. She stepped into the lane and heard Bonnie bark. She walked toward Radcliffe, a noticeable limp showing in her left leg.

"Flora, what is it?" Radcliffe evidenced concern as he called out. She stopped, assumed a grimace of pain and rubbed her thigh. He dismounted quickly.

"I fell crossing Loxley Stream. I stepped on a rock that turned under my foot and I fell," she explained as he came up to her. Quickly she caught her mistake. He started to ask why she was not wet, but she anticipated his inquiry. "I managed to keep my balance until I got beyond the water."

"There can't be any broken bones. Perhaps some badly bruised muscles."

"Would you look." She sat down immediately and pulled up her skirt. He knelt beside her and saw bare flesh. She looked up to see his face, a blushing red. "Forgive me. I should not have asked you to look. It is only that you are so wise. You could help me." She put a winsome pleading in her voice.

He placed a hand on her thigh. The skin was soft, white and so pleasing to the touch. He struggled to gain control of his emotions, looked away from the loveliness she offered and caught her eyes, pleading for him. He explored her visually then let his hand move upward. She moved slightly to lift her skirts higher. He heard Bonnie bark interrupting his intent. Checking quickly he saw nothing but Bonnie kept up constant barking. "Come, Flora. I'll get you on my horse and take you home."

She cooperated without a protest, the limp suddenly gone. He mounted his horse, pulled her up to sit in back of him and off they trotted. She fastened a tight grip around his waist and leaned against his back. "How strong he is," she marveled. Aloud she revealed her impression. "Radcliffe, I can feel all your muscles as you ride. You are a strong man."

Ahead was her father riding rapidly. He reined his horse and stopped. Radcliffe quickly explained the circumstances and continued to the stables. Squire helped Flora dismount. She thanked Radcliffe profusely as she was led away.

"I must see Carinna after London," he reminded himself on the way home, "but that Flora. She has a way." The ride gave him time to think. His conclusion as he entered his stables was that two women can be more interesting than one.

Chapter Five

A buzz of final activity was evident in the manor house. The boys had packed travel trunks and these were being moved from their rooms to be tied in position atop a coach. Cook had been baking and these treats were being wrapped lovingly to be placed in baskets. Mrs. Esterham was making sure the interior of the coach was comfortably appointed with cushions and foot rests, and Mrs. Roche was checking the contents of hand bags each boy was to carry, the personal needs required for overnight stops along the way.

Attired in proper dress for travel, the young men appeared at the main entry, their three quarter length coats tailored impeccably, boots polished and trousers pressed. Both dogs bounced around them barking, old Guy trying at first to match Bonnie's exuberance then giving up with only his tail wagging.

Radcliffe responded to another admonition. "Yes, mother, we shall return as healthy as we are at this moment." She received embraces and kisses from each of her boys and quickly applied a handkerchief to her eyes as soon as they climbed inside the coach. Sadly she watched the coachman guide his team of two around the circular drive, through the massive wrought iron gates and down the lane toward Tosten en Dale, her hand fluttering in a final goodbye. It was the first time since they returned from Oxford that they would be away from her for more than a few days. Loneliness was already setting in.

Mrs. Esterham stood beside her and noticed the forlorn look. "Now, Mrs. Roche, they are adult men and need to get away. Independence is good for them. They will be just fine."

"It is not for them I am distressed. I have concern for myself. Already I feel like a desolate old lady."

Mrs. Esterham was startled by the pronouncement. It was the first time in years she had heard anything so negative from her employer. "Then we need to get ourselves busy. It is time we make plans for our annual party. July is next month and we have tarried too long. You rest for a time then I'll come by with my pad and we shall make preparations"

Mrs. Roche did not object. Of course it was time to plan. "Very well. I shall be in the study." She went to her favorite chair and sat, gave Guy, who was already next to her, a pat on the head, closed her eyes and let her thoughts drift. Otley. An image of the boy would not leave her. His haunting face was ever present showing his astonished eyes as her gloved hands clasped his neck, the coloring of his face changing to blue when his struggle for breath failed. She looked at her hands. "How could you use them on a defenseless child? Oh, yes, to save a son, but in the process he will lose a mother. Well, I did what impulse made me do. I was wrong. I will pay."

She continued to stare at her palms now revealing the process of aging. "Before Otley you were used to kill a man. You are the cause of my desolation. You remind me. You give me no rest." She slammed her palms together in a frustrating effort to silence their affect on her, but they only created a loud pop which disturbed Guy enough so that he raised his head to question her.

"Well now, Mrs. Roche, I trust that was a sign of pleasure in thinking of a new idea for the party. I recall you always enjoy our annual party." Mrs. Esterham's interruption saved her from further memories. "You had such a good time last year with all our guests."

"Yes, it was delightful. But give the sun his due. Please schedule another day such as you did last year, one full of sunshine. Rain always plays such havoc with an outdoor party, and summer is so unpredictable. This horrid Yorkshire climate. One never knows what to expect."

"I shall have to speak to the gypsies about that." The off remark caused Mrs. Esterham to pause and permit a thought to carom around her mind. "I think I have an idea. Would you consider a fortune booth this year? We could hire a gypsy to tell fortunes. In fact we might have a carnival theme and use a variety of booths."

"What a delightful idea. We have not done that before. Now then, what kind of booths shall we have? " It was the first show of enthusiasm from Mrs. Roche since the murders.

The two women continued to discuss the summer party, a tradition of long standing, unbroken by any master of Rochedale Manor as long as anyone could remember. The social provided an annual opportunity for everyone in the community to visit the house and to enjoy for one day a gala event. It was a way for the family to establish a bond with neighbors and for the people of North Riding to identify with the Roches as friends.

The women concluded the theme would be "Carnival Time." "I have an idea, too, Mrs. Esterham. It would be splendid to hire a traveling carnival troupe for the day. They could arrange all their activities in the meadow near the house and we wont have to plan each one separately. We would have less work and we could enjoy more of the day ourselves."

"Why, that is an excellent idea." The housekeeper warmed immediately to the suggestion and added, "I shall start making arrangements at once and depending on a date when a troupe is available, that will be the day for the party."

"Now what about other booths of our own? We need to continue the traditional ones."

"Of course. I'll take care of those except for the church booth. Will you meet with the ladies to plan?"

"You know the ladies, Mrs. Esterham. They prepare all year. We merely have to think of a theme for their booth to attract buyers."

"That is almost what cook said to me. She just said, 'You have only to name the day. I have all my helpers alerted.'"

"Bless her. Our party day requires a lot of work, but we know from all of our past experiences what to do to get ready. Cook is always prepared."

Pleased with their promising beginning, the two talked on, discussing decorations for the great hall, music for dancing, the need to speak to Manny Willowby for ale and the other myriad of details attendant on party giving.

"You made a proposal I have been considering in a cranny of my mind." Mrs. Roche's face took on a serious demeanor. "It's your idea of a gypsy booth. I like the thought, but you know how some people are about gypsies, all the superstitions and the fears. Many do not take to fortune telling. They think it is silly and against the teachings of the church."

"That is true, but this is a day for fun. People don't have to believe what a gypsy tells them. They can listen, enjoy the prattle and forget it. Anyone who doesn't like the idea doesn't have to go to her booth. I doubt the vicar would complain after all you do for the church." Her voice was becoming adamant.

"You convinced me. Let's make a call this afternoon."

Their carriage crossed the Dale, turned right onto a road immediately beyond the bridge, and continued paralleling the river for a time. Heavy rains of late spring followed by a warming trend had turned the landscape to a verdant green. English elms were producing light green leaves while oaks, scattered intermittently along the river allowed their gnarled branches to spread protective custody over shady areas. Splashes of color appeared where red poppies clustered in profusion.

A gypsy encampment was close to the river, their richly painted mobile home carts arranged in a semicircle under a giant oak. At the center was a stone fireplace from which a thin spiral of smoke emerged gauzelike permeating the area with a homey aroma of burnt wood. Horses grazed in the meadow beyond. A dog lay stretched out in front of one wagon. No person was in evidence.

The Roche groom stopped the carriage, stepped down and approached the encampment. The dog, disturbed by the intrusion, stood up and barked angrily. A figure emerged from a wagon, a portly, dark skinned woman dressed in a bright red skirt and green blouse. A patterned cloth was tied about her head and a quantity of bangles and beads was spread about her person, their jangle creating musical sounds as she came forward.

"Mrs. Roche wishes to see you," the groom addressed her. He turned to retrace his steps and the gypsy followed, the dog trailing alertly.

At the carriage she was greeted from within. "Good day. Do you give readings?"

"I do, madame. It is two shillings. I read either cards or palms. Come to my wagon."

Mrs. Roche considered the invitation. She had not intended to have a reading but suddenly the idea sounded intriguing. She turned to her companion and whispered, "I think I shall, then we'll talk business. Come with me and wait outside." The two women followed the gypsy to her wagon. Mrs. Roche entered. Mrs. Esterham remained outside. "On guard," she laughed.

A Strangeness

The wagon's interior was as brightly decorated as its exterior. It contained bunk beds, a sink with cupboards and cabinets, all in wood, and a crude table with chairs. A gesture invited Mrs. Roche to sit down. The women sat opposite to one another.

"I am Madame Zorkina. I receive payment first." Seeing the schillings on the table she added, "What would it be, cards or palms?"

"I don't know. What would you suggest?"

"Let me see your palms."

Mrs. Roche presented her palms. The gypsy examined them then recommended with finality, "Shuffle the cards." Heavily designed over sized cards were spread on the table face down. "Like this." Madame Zorkina mixed the cards. Mrs. Roche repeated the example, spreading them in sweeps of the hands, intermingling the cards to effect a mix. "Make no noise. Do not ask questions. Now put the cards in three equal piles." Directions were followed. "Answer only the questions I ask." Mrs. Roche nodded in understanding. "These piles represent the past, present and the future." The gypsy sat quietly, closed her eyes, relaxed her body and sank into deep concentration. Mrs. Roche smiled inwardly, not believing the power of gypsies to tell fortunes, but marveling at this one's showmanship. Slowly the lady opened her eyes, shook herself and reached for the pile of cards she had designated as the past. She picked up the pile, placed each card from the pile in a precise location on the table, then studied them intently. "I see a large home. There is much land. There is money in the home. But you are not happy. I see blood."

Mrs. Roche's eyes opened in amazement. She started to ask a question but remembered the gypsy's admonition.

"I see a gun. It was fired. I see blood on the floor. I cannot tell who is holding the gun. Now there are tears, many tears. They are tears for a man. A girl, too? Yes, I see a girl. Such sadness you have

67

had." The gypsy gave Mrs. Roche a sympathetic glance. A stare of disbelief was returned.

"Now to look at the present." The second pile was picked up and the cards spread out.

They were studied earnestly. "More sorrow. You are worried about a man. Your son? Ah, he is in difficulty. There has been a death. Oh? One? Are there two deaths? The cards are not clear. I see a journey. People in your family are on a trip, a long one. I see difficulty." Her hand trembled and her face flushed noticeably as she picked up a card and slowly took it to her breast where she pressed it tightly against herself. "Right now there is trouble. The card doesn't tell me what kind of trouble."

Mrs. Roche gasped. "Oh, please. My boys! Tell me! Are they in danger?"

The gypsy relaxed her body and her hand came down to rest on the table, the card in it. Her face cleared as she lost her concentration. "Please, madame. The spell is broken. I asked you not to interrupt me with questions. Now I have lost the power to tell you."

Mrs. Roche squirmed under the disciplinary scrutiny, but worry for her sons' safety mounted. "Please! Are they alright? I must know!"

Madame Zorkina glowered at her. "Let me be," she hammered out emphatically . "No more questions!" She again settled back in her chair and made an obvious effort to concentrate. After what appeared to be an eon of waiting for Mrs. Roche, the gypsy said, "I see no blood but I cannot bring the card to tell me the facts it knows." She passed to the next card. "More happiness is showing. There is a party. You are preparing for it. There will be much pleasure. Ah. A man. I see a man who is interested in you. The card does not tell me who it is, but it is a man you know well. Before long he will come to see you. He has thoughts of marriage."

Mrs. Roche tilted her head in wonder. "Who could that be? Marriage at my age?" The thought revolted her.

The cards were cleared and the third pile was picked up. "Now, madame, shuffle the cards. Your future will be revealed in them. When I close my eyes shuffle them then make a row of them before me, placing each one on the table very carefully, side by side."

Mrs. Roche followed the directions precisely. In time Madame Zorkina opened her eyes and examined the cards. "There is love in your heart for your sons. This love will direct you to take action, an action that will end with blood. Yes, there is blood on that card. Oh, here are girls. Girls will enter your life. This card asks me to tell you to be careful, very careful. Your sons are involved. I see a wedding. It is not clear if the wedding is just planned or if the wedding actually takes place. A trip of some kind is concerned. The wedding is somehow associated with the trip. I see someone trying to get your property. A man? A woman? I cannot tell but the card says to me you must be on guard if you want to hold your property." The gypsy looked up at Mrs. Roche. "Now for your question."

"My sons. Tell me my sons are safe." Worry was profoundly evident in her plea. Much of what she had just been told was smothered by anxiety for the safety of Radcliffe and Kendall.

"Madame, the cards do not tell everything. If you had not interrupted me, perhaps I could have learned more, but since your sons are in your future, I must guess they survive whatever trouble is now befalling them."

Mrs. Roche sat for a moment, thoughts scrambling about her mind, questions forming, but only one was uppermost, the welfare of her sons. Quickly she rose and went outside, took Mrs. Esterham by the elbow and guided her away from the gypsy's home. "That woman told me that even now Radcliffe and Kendall are in trouble. She cannot tell me what trouble.

You go in. Maybe your fortune can tell us. The boys are yours, too." She took some shillings from her bag and gave them to her housekeeper.

Mrs. Roche's agitation was obvious and while the request to enter the wagon was a surprise, it was the last statement that startled Mrs. Esterham. "Does she know? Of course not. Never in twenty-two years has she questioned. She has never given me one clue that she even suspects. 'The boys are yours, too.' She just means I took so much care in raising them that they are like mine." She stepped into the trailer and said, "I would like my fortune told."

"That will be two shillings. Sit there." Receiving her payment, she added, "Let me see your palms."

Mrs. Esterham turned her hands to rest their backs on the table, palms up, fingers outstretched. Wrinkles were plentiful. "They are to be expected at my age," she acknowledged to herself. There was also evidence of arthritis in knobs about the knuckles and joints.

The gypsy studied her lines a moment and announced, "You have good palms to read. The creases are deep and there are many. Palms hold your fortune. I can see past, present and future. Look here." A forefinger traced a major groove. "This is your life line. It is the main one. All other lines relate to this one. It tells me, mmmmmmm, let me study." The finger traced lines under deep concentration. It was evident the examination would be thorough.

"You have had an interesting life. Always helping. Oh, but you had tragedy, too. Those in your immediate family died. I see a boy you love. No, there are two boys. One boy appears to me to be more strongly attached to you than the other. He is not your boy. You provided for him and now you protect him. There was a tragic death, a shooting? Yes, I see a gun. And blood.

"Did you pull the trigger?" Madame Zorkina looked up at Mrs. Esterham's stare. "Do not be afraid. A gypsy will not tell. A gypsy tells to you what she sees in your palms, only to you. What you tell about yourself is your business. A gypsy tells no other."

"What are the lines telling you?" The question was delivered in firmness, Mrs. Esterham staring directly at the eyes of the gypsy.

"The lines are not always completely revealing." After a pause the reading continued. "I see much activity, a party perhaps, and you are planning it. But you are worried. You are worried all the time. It is about a boy. Two boys? You are protecting them. Or is it one boy. Oh! You know some secrets the gypsies know about poisons. You know how to make one that kills. Do you use the poison?"

Mrs. Esterham stared the gypsy down.

"The boys are in trouble. Are they in a coach? A gun is on them. They are on a trip.

"Ah, I see girls in their lives. There could be trouble for them. The girls are anxious."

The gypsy said no more as she analyzed other lines. "Your lifeline is solid. You will continue to live for a time, but there is tragedy in it for you. There is a gun. Your hand is near the gun. A man will be shot. One of the boys? I cannot tell. Is it a question of property? Or are you still trying to protect him?"

Mrs. Esterham pulled her hand away. "The future is not for us to know." she snapped. She rose instantly and left the cart, going immediately to Mrs. Roche and speaking sympathetically. "If it is a problem with the boys they handle it fine, for they arrive in London. She says they are to meet some girls. Shall we return home?"

"What about asking her for the party?"

"Well, I for one don't believe a word of her hokus pokus, but I am sure she is entertaining. Why not. Those who want to hear her prattle can go to her booth.."

"Very well, ask her to come out."

The three discussed a fee then came to an agreement. The date was open depending on the availability of a carnival troupe. No. She could not charge each person. Yes. She could place a dish on her table for gratuities.

On the return ride, Mrs. Roche announced that her first task would be to write her London agent to inquire about today's trouble with the boys, "And to have either reply at once. I must know what happened. It seems to me that if Madame Zorkina as she calls herself could say there was trouble she could also say what it was."

Both fell to silence, each thinking about the gypsy's readings and each bothered by her revelation. "After all," Mrs. Roche summarized to herself, "if she could tell me so much about the past that was right, why can't she tell me about the future and be definite." Her thinking was heavily concentrated on the gypsy's comments when to her resentment she heard Mrs. Esterham.

"We really should do a bit of planning for the party. While waiting for you back there, I wondered what we could do for the children. Of course there is the river for wading and the carnival rides, but for an all day party, we need more variety. What about a marionette show?"

"Even I would like that. Do you suppose we could get a monkey, a live monkey, one that would not bite? That would be a child's delight. Marionettes and a monkey."

"A wonderful idea. Keep thinking."

There was silence then Mrs. Esterham spoke again. "Don't think me too ambitious in planning, but I am wondering about a traveling theater group. The boys spoke of one the last time they were in York. Maybe we could entice a group to come here to put on a play."

"I like your idea but we don't have a theater. Pray tell where could they show their play?"

"I do believe we could arrange the great hall. It is large enough. Of course if the day is nice we could use the chancel of the abbey. That would be something, wouldn't it. The old monks would turn over in their graves if they knew we were thinking of such a thing."

"Why, that is a jolly good idea. I like it. Of course use the abbey. It should be used for something. I do believe, however, we should do something practical about all our dreaming. Let us get ourselves to York with a list of our ideas and see if they are worth putting to work. What do you say to Thursday. We could come back on Saturday."

"That should be delightful. Shall we say yes?"

"Agreed."

When they passed through the main entry of the house, Mrs. Esterham suggested that Mrs. Roche rest in the study and that tea would be brought in. Guy greeted her approach with a show of warm greeting, his long thin tail gyrating happily. "Did you miss me, dear one. I missed you. Come sit next to me so I can pat you." She was no more seated when Mrs. Esterham came up to her.

"Squire Gunning is here. He asked to see you."

"Oh? Show him in and tell cook he is here. Serve tea at once and warn her that he may join us for our meal."

Gunning greeted Mrs. Roche in a manner that for him could be called friendly. "Hello, Virginia. It is always a pleasure to see you."

"Why Montague, and pleasant for me, too. How are Carinna and Flora? Please sit down, here, near me. We shall have tea presently."

When he was comfortable he addressed her. "I do want you to know that during the boys' absence I am at your service. Should there be any need at all, please call on me. Kendall alerted me of their absence in London and asked me to provide assistance to you should you have need."

"Well, that young man." The tone to herself was harsh. "He did not tell me he had spoken to Montague. The idea!" Aloud she was more gentle. "It is very kind of you to offer. Should there be a need, I shall indeed call on you. I do hope you do not mind Kendall's intrusion."

"Not at all, my dear. Had he not spoken to me I would have called on you to determine your welfare."

The approach of a tea cart brought an end to the stilted tete-a-tete that was developing.

Mrs. Esterham served and then retired. Before the need of more conversation, Squire evaluated to himself the lady who could have been his. "Those awful days when she lost her daughter and husband have not aged her. She is still a lovely creature, so handsome, grown more attractive with the passing of years. And she was almost mine. Drat my poor luck. But the second time around could bring better results. Shall I try again? Why not. Rochedale Manor would be a second prize. Go ahead, Montague. She can only say no."

"Are you having a good year, Montague?" The entry of the tea cart had given her as well an opportunity to consider her former suitor. "He has not changed. He is still stilted, self centered and so direct. He has yet to relax, to be pleasant. He could never develop a warm, friendly personality. It is just not his nature. I am sure he is here to see what chance he has to court me again. Kendall gave him the entry he needed."

"It has been a good year for me and all sheep raisers," he replied matter of factly. "Yours has been good, too. That is the problem. With so much wool on hand, we can expect the price to drop. It is the old story of supply and demand. We have too much supply to keep up the present price. I asked Radcliffe to inquire about this possibility while in London."

"Radcliffe?

"Yes. He came to Compton Heath to see me about his trip. He asked me to explain the work of agents. He is a very knowledgeable young man and will make in time an excellent master of Rochedale Manor."

"It appears my sons are turning to you, Montague. Neither one told me of his visit with you." The idea of her boys seeking advice elsewhere was a matter of concern that alarmed her.

"Now, Virginia. I would believe they know I am an expert and they have need of information. They do me an honor coming to me. After all they have no father to turn to, and in a way I satisfy that need."

The impact of that statement was not lost on her. It prompted her to assure herself silently. "For ten years they have been without a father. I have been and still am both father and mother. I am not a failure. Look at them." Aloud she stated, "You do have two daughters, Montague."

The inference was not lost on him. "Ah. I do indeed. Marvelous girls. Radcliffe asked for permission to see Carinna."

The declaration stunned her. This son who always discusses his thoughts with her going to Compton Heath without her knowledge! Speaking to Carinna! Is he promoting an interest of the heart? Why didn't he tell me? Why is it I must learn of his actions from this man? To cover her surprise she reached over her chair and patted Guy. The action gave her pause to reply. "Carinna is a lovely girl."

Kendall thinks so, too. He stops to see her."

"This is too much," she commented to herself. "Kendall I can understand. He often is impulsive. It would be just like him to call on her without Montague's leave, but in time he tells me what he is doing." The thought was revealed on her face.

"You do not know of their visits?"

"It may be they either thought the visits insignificant or their preparation for London became more important."

"I am sure it was the latter."

"Will you have your meal with us, Montague?"

"No thank you, Virginia. You are kind to ask. But I do remind you I am at your service and I do ask for your permission to call on you."

"If we do need assistance I shall. All our friends know they may call at any time. Our door is always open."

Mrs. Roche did not readily calm her anger after Squire took his departure. "Imagine my boys allowing me to face that man without telling me what they had been up to. Of course he wants me to know about their interests in Carinna. He sees in her an opportunity to marry into the Roche family. And the gall to ask permission to see me. I would not have him in my youth and certainly not now. He probably thinks if Carinna can't become a Roche he will marry me."

The thought recalled a statement made by the fortune teller. "What was it she said? 'There is a man interested in you. He has thoughts of marriage.' The idea! Montague interested in me. Why, I would not give him the time of day."

She made an emphatic decision. Each night as they meet for supper, she would require reports from her sons that would include a daily accounting of activities including visits with girls, especially with those whom they were considering for the Roche name. "I am mistress of Rochedale Manor and I intend to be such. I will not be embarrassed again by Montague or anyone else." She had to admit, however, that such a policy for grown men would be difficult to put into effect. "But I shall try!"

On Wednesday the Rochedale women drove to York. They left at sun up for the distance required more than half a day barring any unforeseen misadventure and a rest was necessary for the horses. Fortunately there was no rain to hinder their progress. "Are you aware of the boys' interest in Carinna, Mrs. Esterham?" It was inevitable the subject would surface. Mrs Roche could not keep family affairs from the housekeeper and the long ride together made time available to talk.

"Why no, Mrs. Roche. Did they tell you such?"

"No. I learned from Squire Gunning."

Quick to defend them she suggested gently, "It is possible they just stopped at Compton Heath as they rode by and Squire made it appear more than it is."

"It could be that for Kendall but for Radcliffe, no. He asked Squire for permission to see Carinna."

"Well good for him. It is about time he started looking for a wife."

"That is just the point. The woman he chooses becomes mistress of Rochedale Manor the moment he marries her. Then I become a dowager shunted to the back room." It was the first time she felt her position threatened. "Furthermore I must have the right to approve or disapprove the girl either boy begins to see seriously."

"It could be that neither Kendall nor Radcliffe is serious and because that is so, they did not think it necessary to tell you. I for one am pleased they are visiting girls. Kendall has been getting around, not seriously, but Radcliffe has not until now shown any interest in girls."

"You are right, Mrs. Esterham. But I must make sure that the next Mrs. Roche for either boy has my approval."

"But it is Radcliffe who inherits."

"True, but should anything happen to Radcliffe . . . . . ., well, I must be sure of Kendall, too."

The coach slowed noticeably and Mrs. Roche gave Mrs. Esterham a quizical stare. "It does look like difficulty, probably a highwayman, unless it is a wheel or some other mechanical problem."

When the coach came to a complete stop, Mrs. Esterham peered out the window. "Just as I thought, highwaymen, two of them. Now don't say a word. I'll do the talking."

Their driver came to the door and angrily said, "They want you to get out. I couldn't talk them out of it." He opened the door then helped each lady to alight.

"Good day to you, Mrs. Roche."

The greeting from one of the masked men startled her, and she responded quickly, "I realize I am well known but not by bandits."

"Come now, good lady. I even know your sons. In fact I met up with them just the other day, on their trip to London. We had a chat but they beat me out of some horses. Now I need to ask you to cover their debt. Give my friend here your cash."

The second highwayman approached the travelers. "See here," Mrs. Esterham boomed out, "You taught us long ago to leave our cash home. We have very little."

"It may be enough. Give him all your money." He snapped the order.

Cash was placed in a bag and taken to the leader. "It is not enough. Look inside the coach." The cohort entered the coach and presently came out with a pillow. "Look what they used for a hiding place. The pillow was slit and out fell a quantity of pound notes.

"Ah, ha. Good searching. Tell your sons, Mrs. Roche, that the horses are now paid for. They will understand. We should have slashed up their coach but you see how we learned by that error." The two rode off leaving the women angry.

"The idea. How much did we lose? And to pay for what horses? Mrs. Roche was incensed.

"We must have given up fifty pounds between us. I deliberately sewed the money in the pillow so as not to lose it. I had an idea we might meet up with highwaymen. What do you suppose they meant by paying for the horses? We'll find out when the boys come home."

By late afternoon the Minster of York appeared on the skyline. It grew larger as they approached, dominating the city. They passed through Roman walls and drove in traffic to the York offices of Steiner and Ross, agents to the Rochedale Manor estates.

"What a pleasant surprise, Mrs. Roche." Mr. Ross was genuinely pleased to see her. "I hope we can be of service to you. Do sit down."

The firm of Steiner and Ross, a branch of the main office in London, had held the Roche account for generations. "First off, we need cash. Highwaymen took every penny we had. But our main purpose in visiting you is to seek your assistance. We are planning our annual party and I want to do something different. We shall have a carnival theme, and we need a traveling company, preferably one with animals. Whatever date is open with them in late July is fine for us. Do you know someone with a monkey, a small monkey, one for children to pet without being bitten?"

"Such things are out of my line, Mrs. Roche, but I shall put a staff person on it immediately. How much cash do you need?" How long will you be in York?"

"Until Saturday. Fifty pounds."

"We shall try to line up something for you by then. Please come in Saturday morning." He called a boy.

"I have another request. We need a troupe of players. We want to offer a play."

"That should not afford a great problem. It will be a matter of coordinating dates."

"Now, Mr. Ross, we can feed all those who entertain for us but we cannot house that great number."

"I believe a traveling company will have their own means for sleeping, and a theater group can be bedded in your barn or stable for one night. Where will the play be presented?"

"In the chancel of the abbey if we have no rain. Otherwise we shall have to use the great hall."

"What play shall I ask for?"

"I don't know. Shakespeare? What is current? Shall we let the troupe decide?"

"Have you thought of fees?"

"I shall leave that to you, Mr. Ross. There should be enough money in estate coffers to pay reasonable expenses. I shall want to see all the bills, however."

Mr. Ross smiled broadly. "A Rochedale Manor estate books are in excellent condition. No bills are ever paid without an accounting by Mrs. Roche."

"Oh! I almost forgot. For the children we need a marionette show."

"That is easiest of all."

"Very well, I shall return on Saturday. Mrs. Esterham and I will be at our usual inn if you should need us."

The boy returned with fifty pounds and Mrs. Roche signed for the cash.

Chapter Six

Having assured herself that all planning for the summer party had been completed and all participants notified of the date, Mrs. Roche sat quietly in her study, her hand resting on Guy's head, the old dog sitting at her side looking lovingly into her face. "Would that all living things could love so devotedly as you, Guy." She clasped his head between her hands and leaned down to caress his face to hers. "But that can never be. You are the only one that has remained loyal."

She raised her head and looked at him, returning the love he gave her. His paw came up and tapped her leg, begging more attention. At fourteen he was showing his age by a growth of grey hair at the muzzle and by murky eyes that, she thought, could very well be going blind.

"No, Guy, that is not true. The boys are loyal. It is just that they are men seeking their own lives, becoming more independent, telling me less and doing more on their own." She thought of the gypsy's words, 'You are not happy. I see blood.' Those words caused her to reflect. "Those cards told the gypsy what I cannot tell anyone for I shall carry to the grave the source of my sadness." She leaned back in her chair, closed her eyes and thought again of her past, wondering what went wrong, where she made a mistake, what she should have done but did not. The thinking made her young again.

"Virginia, Montague is here. Are you ready?" It was her mother's voice. Montague Gunning was calling to take her to the Roche's annual summer party. He had asked Mr. Barkeley for his permission and received approval. She had hoped someone else would ask, but Montague was first. She dressed for a warm day, a light summer frock, white with purple ribbons about the waist and bodice and one tied about her light brown hair to create a tail which she had pulled over her left shoulder and arranged down her bosom. At eighteen she was attractive, not beautiful in the sense of having features that stopped boys and earned their stares, but lovely enough that she was considered fetching. Mothers said she was the wholesome type. At five feet seven she was tall and rather thin with few curves. She recognized that other girls appealed to most boys, but she had her share of callers. She had been told by some boys that her blue eyes were alluring and skin white like milk, but they were only flattering her, she recognized. "After all, all Yorkshire girls have milk white skin."

"Good morning, Montague."

"Good morning, Virginia."

He took her hand in greeting. He was a stern looking young man of twenty-three who should have been married at this age, but he told others he was not because he was looking for just the right girl. She noticed he did not smile with his greeting. "Do you mind walking to the manor. My parents needed the wagon."

Most boys by his age would have been on their own, but as an only child, he would inherit the family property and already Montague knew how he would enlarge his holdings, increase the flocks and make money. He would not always be the poor Gunning boy.

A long row of wagons, carts, buggies and other kinds of transportation was approaching the mansion. On the way Montague haled a ride from a friend and Virginia was pleased for she wanted to save her energy to enjoy all the activities. Montague got her some punch while he took ale. Together they toured the house, roamed about the meadow and walked through the abbey ruins meeting friends, stopping to talk and taking part in all the offerings.

In the afternoon they met Winsford Roche. At twenty he was the sole heir to Rochedale Manor. Six feet tall, burly in stature, he made a handsome appearance. Virginia was taken by his warmth. He had spoken to her at church on occasion but he never tarried. He was always with his parents who left services immediately after shaking hands with the vicar. "Montague, you and Virginia come into the house for dinner. I shall have a place for us at a table." It was an unexpected invitation but offered sincerely. Long tables had been arranged in the great hall with a buffet placed along one wall. The three chatted amiably as they ate, Montague questioning about Rochedale flocks and Winsford giving information. Virginia had little opportunity to take part until Winsford included her in a discussion centered on recent church social events. Both laughed at her recollections and Winsford became animated at times, much to Montague's chagrin. It was obvious to him that Winsford was making a play for the girl he brought to the party.

The following Wednesday Mr. Barkeley received a note from Winsford Roche requesting permission to call on Virginia. On Saturday afternoon he arrived. She and Winsford sat in the drawing room of the modest cottage and chatted. She was nervous from just the idea of being alone with a man of his station but she desperately tried not to show it.

Mrs. Barkeley had sat with Virginia the day before to discuss a protocol for the meeting. "This is not a good association, my dear. It is not wise for a girl of your social status to meet with a man who is of the highest social level. No good can come of it. Be friendly but do not encourage him. I do not want you to be hurt."

Virginia was friendly to Winsford, she let him hold her hand, but she in no way encouraged him. She did not know exactly what her mother meant by not being hurt, but if her mother believed that then she would be obedient. She was to learn later the meaning of her mother's warning.

Winsford returned for a second meeting and very quickly he became a frequent caller. She allowed him to kiss her hand and then her lips but she did not return his advances.

One day a carriage appeared at the Berkeley cottage. A groom knocked at the door and announced that Mrs. Roche wished to see Mr. and Mrs. Berkeley. Mrs. Berkeley received her. Almost at once Mrs. Roche came to the purpose of the visit. "I have just learned that my son is calling on your daughter. I have spoken to Winsford about his error and have asked him to stop. He does not wish to stop. Mr. Roche and I believe he should find a girl within his station. Now I must ask that you not let your daughter see my son."

"Mrs. Roche," came her reply, "I cannot close my door to anyone. I have told Virginia not to encourage your son and she has not. I do believe that since he is the one who comes here, he is the one who needs to be disciplined. We shall understand if does not call again."

During the next meeting, Winsford held Virginia's hand and confessed that his parents were adamantly opposed to his visits. "I told them that I loved you, social station be damned, and that I intended to marry you." He embraced and kissed her passionately.

She pulled away. "Winsford, no good can come of our marriage. I am too far below you in station. Your parents will never accept me. It is best we do not meet again."

"My darling! I shall not hear of it! I shall speak to your father now. Please ask him so see me." Virginia brought her father into the room then excused herself. "Mr. Barkeley, I want to marry your daughter."

Mr. Barkeley started to protest, but Winsford quickly interrupted. "Please, sir. I know your position. I love Virginia. I hope she loves me. Your daughter is an intelligent girl with an excellent upbringing. She is very capable of bridging the distance between our stations. I assure you there will be no problems in that regard. May I ask your permission to marry Virginia."

A note with the Roche crest arrived at the Berkeley cottage. It conveyed the message that Miss Virginia Barkeley was invited for tea on Sunday afternoon at four o'clock.

Virginia appeared at the appointed time, fearful. She was ushered into the study where Mrs. Roche received her. Tea was served. "Miss Barkeley, neither Mr. Roche, your parents nor I approve of your marriage to Winsford, but my son is insistent. He will listen to none of us. Therefore, I have asked him to wait one year. I do believe that during this period he will see the error of his ways. I must ask you, too, to discourage him."

Virginia sat with her cup of tea balanced in her hand trying desperately to control herself. Of course she understood class levels and that the Roches were at the top. Of course she understood Mrs. Roche's objection. But she knew, too, taking away all the money and property from the Roches, she was as good as they. The facts remained, however, that they had the money, the property and the station. She took a breath and stated calmly, "Mrs. Roche, it is your son who has confessed his love for me. I can in no way control his emotions. If he stops seeing me I shall understand."

In six months a second note invited Virginia to Rochedale Manor. "Miss Berkeley, my wishes have not been considered." Mrs. Roche was haughty in her demeanor showing almost contempt for the girl in front of her. "You and Winsford have continued to see each other. He now informs me there can be no other girl for him. He is determined to marry you. That being the case, I must prepare you for your responsibilities. We shall meet frequently so that I can give you instruction."

Virginia met with Mrs. Roche. Lessons were taught with disdain, the teacher blaming the pupil for a marriage that should never be. There were constant digs at the girl, belittling statements and an arrogant attitude ruled the meetings.

Virginia armored herself for the ordeals. In the beginning she found the confrontations challenging, then when a feeling of hatred began to develop on the part of her tormentor, she became determined that she would prevail despite his mother's efforts. Love for Winston was not the question. It was her victory that became all compelling.

"Love for Winsford?" Virginia wondered what love was. Not having been in love before she questioned if she was in love. She enjoyed the attention Winsford paid her, but he was not sorely missed during his absences. Other girls told her they dreamed of their young men, longed for them and could not wait for them to return. She admitted to herself it was not like that. His kisses did not inflame her as their lovers' kisses inflamed them, whatever inflamed meant. It made no difference. She would prevail over Mrs. Roche.

A wedding announcement party was given at Rochedale Manor only because social protocol demanded it. The great hall was decorated adequately and the guest list included required names. Word was conveyed that the marriage was not to the Roche's liking. It would not be an affair to remember.

Banns were read on three successive Sundays before the congregation followed by a wedding in Tosten en Dale parish church. Virginia's gown was provided by Mrs. Roche, a gown she had worn some years ago in this same church. This gesture was made mainly out of a feeling of duty, however. The nave and chancel were decorated appropriately and a subdued reception followed. After a honeymoon at Harrogate Spa, the couple returned to Rochedale Manor where for eight years Virginia paid the penalty for her conquest.

Mrs. Roche at no time forgot that Virginia had not acceded to her wishes. She was not wanted as a daughter-in-law. She was not accepted as a member of the family except when social etiquette required such acknowledgment.

Virginia was rarely invited to have supper with her husband and the senior Roches, and Winsford never challenged his mother's refusal to include her. At Sunday services in Tosten church, she sat with her parents, never in the Roche pew. She was not invited to participate in family socials, either small gatherings or large events.

Winsford was not strong enough to break the determination of his mother. She allowed him from time to time to share a bedroom with his wife, but she directed him to interests far from the mansion, activities that took him away for days. She encouraged acquaintances with other women, inviting some to the house for a period of time, and sending him to other families of his rank.

At first Virginia was mortified, crushed by the demeaning actions of her mother-in-law. She had not expected that retribution would take this form. She almost broke under the treatment, but from somewhere she found strength, mostly from her own grit. She adjusted in time and constructed a crust that proved to be a safeguard. She had the friendship of only one person, a maid.

Her marriage bed was a disappointment. She had received no instruction at home and not having experienced a relationship herself, she was not sure what to expect. Since she was fully acquainted with barnyard activities, she suspected humans performed in the same manner. Winsford, she discovered, either did not know what to do or was fearful of performing since it was the end of the first week while they were at Harrogate Spa when he made his first attempt.

She blamed herself and her own ignorance for his failure. He slept in bed with her occasionally but rarely coupled, and when he tried it was a failure. She attempted to help but did not know what to do or where to get help.

Six years later a girl was born. It was an easy delivery, the child was healthy, and Virginia recovered quickly. Although disappointed that the first birth was not the male gender, the senior Mrs. Roche assumed management of the nursery. That was too much for Virginia to accept. She rose to her full height, openly challenged her mother-in-law for the first time, and set terms for Mrs. Roche's participation in the nursery. She won in surprisingly easy form, for Mrs. Roche wanted access to the baby, albeit a girl, and had she not acquiesced to the terms, she feared total exclusion.

Feeling her first success in establishing authority, Virginia attempted a second confrontation. The Roches were entertaining, a supper party for twelve persons of status in North Riding. Virginia appeared as the call to be seated was given. There was no place for her, and should she be seated, there would be thirteen at table, a number that would be unbearable for a hostess. Not willing to cause a scene by challenging her daughter-in-law, and rather than risk being censored by her guests, she begged a sudden headache and departed. As the now ranking lady of the Roche family, Virginia was seated in the chair of the hostess. She conducted herself admirably.

The following day Mrs. Roche summoned Virginia to her study. "See here, young woman," she addressed her daughter-in-law in bitter tones, "you are not to intrude where you are not wanted. Never. Never! Repeat what you did last night!"

The response was simple. "I, madame, will make that decision." She turned and departed.

A Strangeness

The two strategic victories gave Virginia confidence. She kept her armored crust honed and stepped into her mother-in-law's domain. She began to appear at teas, uninvited, baby in arms, gaining attention and feeling more assured with each entry. Completely on her own she invited young people to an evening soiree. Although no other Roche was present, not even her husband who pleaded illness, those present enjoyed her party.

Gaining strength with each flurry into enemy territory, she found a second summons. "Discontinue these blatant excesses or you shall be locked in your room," she heard her Mrs. Roche orate.

"Attempt that, madame, and I shall take my baby and depart Rochedale Manor. The gossips will soon know how you preside at this mansion."

The summonses stopped.

During all the years since her marriage, Virginia's father-in-law rarely spoke to her. He obviously was dominated by Mrs. Roche although he appeared to his associates to be complete master of his estates. "Perhaps he runs the business side and leaves all else to his wife," Virginia thought. He came to the nursery to see the baby and showed great affection for her. It was during one of these occasions that he spoke to her.

"This lovely child is proof of what fine children you can bare. We need an heir to continue the Roche line. We must do something about it." Reluctantly she knew she had to.

In 1748 boys were born, twins, although they were not identical. It was a memorable day for Virginia, for the twin births were completely unexpected, there having been no multiple births on either side of the family. Winsford was absent from the house and Mrs. Roche was away as well, having accepted an invitation to spend a few days with friends. Mr. Roche was off on a hunting trip. The delivery was not expected for another two weeks and no difficulty was expected.

Such was not the case. Pains began on Thursday. Only the maid was available to provide assistance. The doctor in Tosten was sent for but he was on an emergency. No midwife could be found.

After a day of labor, Mrs. Esterham, the maid, was worried. Young Mrs. Roche should have delivered. Although never involved in assisting at a birth she decided to take action. She gave a potion to the mother, something she remembered midwives talking about. When sleep came, Mrs. Esterham began exploring and found a breach. She maneuvered the child and brought it forward. She worked with the boy until it yelled vociferously. Virginia rested until the potion wore off. When she opened her eyes and demonstrated enough strength, she received in her arms two babies, healthy boys. Delight showed in her eyes and she beamed at Mrs. Esterham. The first born was named Radcliffe after Winsford's father. The second boy was named Kendall for Mrs. Roche's father. Virginia had no part in the name selection.

Birth of the boys changed behaviors at Rochedale Manor. Mrs. Roche must have believed that Virginia had paid her dues for disobedience, for she relaxed her demeanor, praised Virginia's efforts, included her in all in-house activities, made sure she was invited to other homes, and she no longer referred to Virginia's humble origins.

The elder Mr. Roche spoke to her affectionately and took pride in claiming her as his daughter-in-law. The boys became his pride.

Winsford played the role of an interested father. He doted on the boys and showed increasing adoration for his wife. He left home less and planned his day to be with her some part of it.

Joy in the house was short lived, however. Within a year Mrs. Roche died unexpectedly. Winsford was devastated. He seemed to lose perspective immediately. He found excuses to be away from home, taking long trips and accepting invitations to go hunting and fishing.

Most of Virginia's nights were spent alone. He lost interest in the boys. He had long forgotten he had a daughter.

Mr. Roche appeared one day and asked to speak to Virginia. "My dear," he began, "Winsford is behaving peculiarly since my wife died. I know this is not unknown to you, but I need to talk to you about him. I no longer have any influence on my son. His mother doted on him, demanding he spend time with her, did his thinking for him and smothered him with love.

"She permitted me very little time with him. I was surprised when he stood up to her and demanded he be permitted to marry you. It was a dreadful scene. He raved. She raved. When he said he would leave home for good, she gave in.

"I know it was difficult for you during your first years. But that is past. I need your help with the business of Rochedale Manor. Winsford has never taken an interest in how we make money on the estate. I must assure myself that when I die there will be someone in charge who can take over with authority. I need to teach you so you can protect my heritage for your children. We cannot let Rochedale Manor go under."

Mr. Roche taught Virginia all he knew about the estate, its lands, holdings, rentals, herds, flocks and its economy. She was an apt learner. His instruction took her away from the house and required that the housekeeper assume more responsibility for the children although they had a nursemaid, tutor, riding instructor and for the boys, a male companion to take the place of the absent father. Before long the foremen took direction from Virginia and gradually Mr. Roche retired to his room. When he died Virginia was for all practical purposes completely in charge of Rochedale Manor.

Winsford came home more frequently after his father's death, but when he spent a night with Virginia, he rarely attempted to make love. One night he awakened and fondled her. He began to love her then suddenly his hands went to her throat. Frightened by the unusual action, she broke free from his hold and leaped out of bed. She lit a candle and looked at him. Tears fell from his eyes. He asked forgiveness saying he had a painful headache.

Over a year passed during which time he came and went in broken intervals. One evening she, by chance, heard a loud voice. Recognizing it as his, she passed through an open door and was surprised to see him talking to a portrait of his mother. "I hate you. You made me what I am. You made me dislike. . . ." He must have heard her for he turned quickly and discovered Virginia. She made it appear she was just entering the room, but she could not be sure he did not see through her action. That night he again, during an attempt at love making, tried to choke her.

Again he blamed a severe headache.

It was the last time they shared a bed. The next day Virginia moved to a separate bedroom. She believed she had to for her own safety. He retained their room. Not once did he challenge her action.

The following year two North Riding girls were declared missing, first one then a week later a second. A massive search was conducted by law men and hundreds of volunteers. Even Winsford volunteered his time and was assigned as a leader for one group. The girls were never found.

Winsford took to staying home. He at times rode about the estate and beyond but he was always home by evening. Later he began walking. One September day she noticed him as she worked in her garden. He entered the abbey. She was pleased for she thought he had gone there to be with their daughter whom she had seen go to the ruins earlier. By evening when the daughter did not appear, Virginia went immediately to the abbey and found two girls dead.

She came screaming to the house. Winston rode immediately to Tosten for the doctor and the constable. Later Virginia thought it strange he did not go to the abbey to see for himself what she had discovered.

The community was alarmed. First two girls missing. Now two murders. Were all related? None was solved. The doctor determined that both deaths were due to strangulation.

Following the funeral of their first born, Winsford made an attempt to show more interest in the boys, spending time with them, riding and hiking and discussing lessons. He spoke to Virginia about returning to bed. She considered his request but delayed responding. The last choking had alarmed her and she wanted more time to make sure he had no more headaches.

One night Virginia awakened to see her bedroom door opening. Enough moonlight came through open shutters to identify easily the familiar objects in her room, and her eye caught the figure of a man fully clothed coming toward her. It was Winsford. "Virginia, come back to me. I need you. You are my wife. You need to be in our bed."

"No, Winsford. Your headaches make you do strange things." He looked at her. "You know about my headaches? They come more frequently." His eyes appeared strange as if they had a far away look in them, dreamy, wondering. "Strange those headaches. I try to remember what I do when I get the pains. I saw two girls in the abbey. I tried to love them. Come, Virginia. I need to love you."

"Oh, Winsford! Those babies. You killed those babies. Our baby!"

"No, Virginia. I merely loved them. How could love be murder?" He put his hands to his head. "The pain, Virginia. The pain. Come, I need to love you."

He grabbed her and with one effort pulled her out of bed. She screamed knowing that no one would hear her. They were isolated in this part of the house. Down the hall he dragged her, clasping tightly one arm while she resisted, her free arm trying to grab anything, her body sliding on the floor, her screaming increasing. He forced her into his room and slammed the door. He stood over her and lifted her up with a jerk. "Now get in bed!" His words were ground out in a sneer.

At that moment the door opened. Mrs. Esterham entered, gun in hand. She walked toward the two, the weapon aimed at him. He hesitated, his eyes fixed on the gun. Suddenly he lunged, grabbing for the weapon. He pulled Virginia with him. All three struggled for control.

A shot was fired. Winsford took the bullet in the neck.

The women stood, startled. Reacting quickly Mrs. Esterham spoke softly. "Now, Mrs. Roche. It is almost daylight. I shall send for the doctor. Come to bed. You must rest. When the doctor comes and later the constable, let me talk. You repeat what I say."

The doctor came. Mrs Esterham explained that Mr. Roche had taken to hunting. "Yes, that is true," Virginia agreed.

"The gun must have gone off as he handled it," Mrs. Esterham added. "That is a true statement, too," Virginia mumbled.

"Yes, that is what happened. A very sad accident, indeed," Mrs. Esterham said with finality.

Guy gave her another tap with his paw. She had not petted him in the last few moments and his loving from her was not yet satisfied. She rubbed and patted his head again and named him as the best dog that ever lived. One pet was more precise than the preceding ones. It put an exclamation mark to her demonstration of adoration and he seemed to know he would receive no more. He moved away to take his place next to her on his rug.

"Yes, the gypsy was right. I was not happy during those early years of marriage. It was the birth of my daughter that gave me my first taste of happiness. Such a sweet child. And then the boys. After that Winsford did not matter.

"Strange man, that. I never knew him. He never loved me. He used me. He must have known he could not perform as a man and was afraid to choose a girl in his own class for fear the word would get around in his own circle. He knew I would find out, but who was I to tell. I never became friendly with anyone after I married, even with the girls in my station who quickly drifted away.

"There must have been a serious health problem to cause his painful headaches. I still wonder if they were related in some way with his inability to make love. They came when he wanted to perform. His hands ended on my neck. He wanted to choke me." She shuddered then shook her head trying to rid herself of the memory.

"The choking. Those two girls in the abbey died from choking. At his hands? I shall never know. Could it be he did try to love them, had his terrible headache, then choked them. He said he did love them. One his own daughter!" Tears came to her eyes. "I don't want to believe what happened. No other person knows of his affliction. It cannot be proved now, anyhow. Only I can wonder about those deaths and think his hands did the ghastly work."

Mrs. Esterham entered the study. "Constable Ormand is here. Will you see him?"

For a moment she hesitated, still thinking of the past. "Show him in."

Ormand entered, shook Mrs. Roche's offered hand and sat down at her request. "Will you have a brandy, ale?"

"Thank you kindly, but nothing." From his seat he could look out the window, past the garden, and see the abbey ruins. "I would like to ask some questions if you don't mind, Mrs. Roche. I could come back another time if the present is not convenient."

"The present is just fine, constable." She forced a friendly smile but inside she was fearful.

"I have been pursuing every possible clue to Emma and Otley's deaths. I am questioning anyone and everyone who might have seen something that would give us a lead, however insignificant it may seem." He looked directly at her. "Did you see anyone in the abbey the morning of Emma's death?"

"Yes, I did. As I worked in my garden I saw people pass through the abbey. Market day increases the traffic. My eyes being as they are and from this distance I cannot name any of them."

"I had a report that Kendall was seen. Did you see him near the abbey?"

Hesitating a moment to maintain her composure she replied calmly, "Why, yes I did. At least I thought it was Kendall. The man wore a coat identical to Kendall's. He was in the meadow, however, not in the abbey. Kendall is often in the meadow, being next to the house as it is, and especially when sheep graze." She hesitated then offered, "I asked Kendall if it was he I had seen, and he told me he had gone directly to Stiliston Meadows that morning."

"Did you see Radcliffe in the abbey?"

"Why no, constable. It is strange you ask about Radcliffe. Why?"

"I have a statement that Radcliffe was seen in the abbey that morning. Do you know where he was at that time?"

"Why, I can't recall at this moment. Both boys are very busy with business of the estate and business takes them many places. Radcliffe rarely goes to the abbey, but Kendall enjoys the ruins. As a boy he played there frequently." She gasped inwardly. "What have I said? He will be accused!"

The constable recognized the disturbed reaction to her own volunteered statement and made a mental note of it. "We are thinking more and more that Emma and Otley's deaths are related, mainly because of the strangulations and because Otley gave indication he knew who killed Emma. Would you think about the next day, the day Otley was found. You recall that Radcliffe brought the boy in. He said he found the boy in the meadow near the abbey. Do you recall seeing anyone in the abbey that morning?"

"I can't recall seeing any one other than Otley. I don't think so, constable. I went to the abbey that day. I saw Otley there and I spoke to him."

"What time was this?"

"I would say sometime before noon, perhaps middle forenoon. I made no special note of the time. It was not unusual for Otley to be in the abbey. He played about the ruins frequently."

"That is true." The constable hesitated, thought, and then went on. "Are you aware of any special poisons used in the work of the estate? I ask because Dr. Poole thinks there could have been poison in Otley's blood. He can't say for sure, however, that death was from poison."

"My sons would know the answer to that question. I confine my work with the business end these days, not the work with animals."

"Do you recall from your past any tales about poisons, stories about making poisons, anything about the folklore of Yorkshire related poisons?"

"I do recall hearing such stories, mainly as a girl when gypsies appeared, but nothing about the making of poisons, such as a recipe."

"Well, I am in hopes of getting some lead as I ask questions. I am questioning everyone and you have been helpful. Thank you, Mrs.

Roche. When the boys return from London, I will want to question them, too. Goodbye."

She kept her composure until he left then she felt her heart palpitate. "I did not tell all the truth. How could I? How could I tell about Otley?" She became distraught. "It was Kendall I saw. I know that coat. I know his shape, his walk. He was in the meadow. He could have gone to the abbey. What can I do to protect him? Someone else saw him in the abbey. He will be questioned when he comes home. Oh, Kendall!"

For the first time she admitted to herself that he could very well be the murderer. The thought ravaged her. She gasped for breath, fearing she might faint. "Is it like father, like son.

"The abbey is my undoing."

Chapter Seven

Having seen to Mrs. Roche's comfort after their return home from York, Mrs. Esterham retired to her own room. Try as she may she could not shake thoughts of the gypsy fortune teller. They continued to haunt her. "She said she would not tell anybody anything. At least she could say enough to raise suspicions and then there would be questions. That gypsy knows I pulled the trigger that killed Winsford." She sat in her rocker moving back and forth. "Who would have thought when I came to this house that I would be involved in a shooting. I was a girl when I arrived at Rochedale Manor. Winsford's mother hired me as an upstairs maid. Let's see. How old was I? Thirteen. My father said he could not afford to keep me home any longer and I had to help the family by making some money."

One memory kindled another until Mrs. Esterham was reliving her past. "Winsford was a problem boy. I think his mother made him a problem, always babying him, fearful he would be injured if he played with other boys, keeping him home with her when he should have been off to school, rarely letting him be with girls when he should have been seeing them. That tutor was with him when she was not supervising him. He met every morning with her before lessons began and after the noon meal they went somewhere together.

"Mr. Roche wasn't much of a father to Winsford. I don't ever remember that he took the time to teach the boy anything, even horseback riding. It was a stable groom who taught him to ride properly and that was over the protests of his mother.

"She's the one to be blamed. My the scenes when he wanted to do something she didn't want him doing. The temper tantrums. But she always had her way. The boy was never allowed to think for himself. She told him what to do and how to do it. Until he was almost grown he never had boys to play with.

"Mrs. Roche had her room and Mr. Roche had his. I don't think he ever entered hers after Winsford was born. They were always civil to one another but never loving. I don't recall ever seeing him show her affection, even an arm around her. He let her rule the house, Winsford and him. She did what she wanted and he went along.

"As Winsford became taller and began to fill out, she still managed him. There was that day when he wanted something. Maybe he was sixteen at the time, and she said no. His temper rose and he shook her. She placed a hard smack across his face that made him cry.

'There were other scenes like the time she walked into his room. He was standing in front of the big mirror playing with himself, watching his manliness grow. She walked up to him, put her arm around his waist and kissed him on his bare chest. She took him by the hand, naked as he was, to her room and closed the door. This was not the only time. There was evidence when I cleaned up that he stayed nights with her, many nights.

"When this started she extended his association with friends, inviting a few boys to stay at the house from time to time, and if he went out it was always in groups. Never did he call on a girl by himself.

"A meeting between Mr. and Mrs. Roche brought a change, however. They were at breakfast. He said that at nineteen Winsford should be thinking about getting married. She said in good time that step would be cared for. He reminded her there had to be an heir.

"One day I heard them in her bedroom. Winsford was saying, 'But I don't want to. I am afraid. I don't know how. I don't know what to do.'

'Now, dear boy. I shall guide you. Just follow mother's directions as I show you what to do. You must marry. Your father wants an heir. The Roche line must go on. I have a girl in mind, just the girl for you.'

'Not that one. I would die if I had to do to her what you have me do to you. I hate doing that.'

'Mind me, Winsford.' Her voice had a snap to it.

'Very well, but I must choose the girl.'

'She must be someone in your station, not just anybody.'

'I shall marry the girl I please.'

'We shall see.'

"She coached him as to what to do about petting and then kissing a girl. She had him practice on her. The day he came home and told her he was going to marry Virginia Barkeley there was another scene. 'Why that strumpet, from her lowly station. She the mother of the Roche heir! I wont have it! The idea! No!'

"The conflict continued, but Winsford would not give in. She changed her tactics. Instead of fighting him she gave her consent with the understanding that he continue to look for another girl before a final decision was made. She criticized Virginia Barkeley at every opportunity and had him meet other girls, all equal to his station.

"Finally he said to his mother, 'If I can't make love to Virginia she can't tell anyone in our station who knows us. I wont be so embarrassed.'

"I became head housekeeper at that time. Instead of just being the upstairs maid, I now had the responsibility of supervising the entire household staff including affairs in the kitchen. I was given rooms for my husband, my daughter and me and we moved to Rochedale Manor. It was to be my permanent home for the rest of my life. Mrs. Roche trained me thoroughly. I learned the requirements of social entertaining, proper use of table settings, and etiquette in every form. I enjoyed my association with her for she treated me with respect and never showed anything but courtesy in our relationship. She was exacting in all requests and I learned precisely what she wanted and how everything was to be done. During my husband's illnesses she was concerned and caring, providing a doctor and giving me time to nurse him. She took care of all details when he died. She paid attention to my daughter during her growing years, giving her gifts and clothes. While she maintained an employer relationship between us, she was always kind to me.

"When Virginia Barkeley came to live in Rochedale Manor as Mrs. Winsford Roche, everyone changed. Mrs. Roche became curt in addressing me. She snapped orders and became critical. Maids were let go for no reason and new ones did not last long. Mrs. Roche was in the house very seldom. Winsford kept his usual association with his mother. She continued to dominate him in every way, even to having him spend nights with her and not allowing him to be with his wife. But he tried to be kind to Virginia.

"I felt sorry for the young Mrs. Roche. She was alone in what for her must have been a sea of horror. I made it a point to see her, to speak gently to her and to ask what she needed, trying then to provide it. Mostly she needed companionship. During Mrs. Roche's absences I worked out excuses to visit the girl's room. I would start a conversation. Soon we both looked forward to the meetings. I brought her needle and threads and she started making baby things, 'for the baby one day I shall have.'

"She asked me about family activities and I made reports on each member as I knew them, omitting some of course.

"She wanted to know the proper way to do things, entertaining, for example, and what clothes to wear for various occasions. I soon became her teacher, preparing her for the time when she would be mistress.

"At times my daughter would visit me after her marriage and I would take her to Virginia Roche's room if Mrs. Roche was absent. She needed young people and my daughter helped fill the void.

"As time passed Virginia Roche and I became close friends, and because I was older I rather suspected she looked to me as a second mother.

"The inevitable had to happen. I heard Mr. Roche saying over supper, 'Winsford, you have been married long enough to produce an heir. Get busy. Six years is a long time for me to wait.' Mrs. Roche replied for him. 'You will have an heir. Winsford is very capable. It must be Virginia's fault. I am going to speak to her.'

"When the girl was born, Winsford was keenly disappointed. He said to his mother, 'I have to go through all that again to get father his heir.'

"It was about this time when young Mrs. Roche began exerting herself. As she came out, we discussed her duties and responsibilities before each event. With experience she became more confident. She blossomed physically, too, a happy countenance replacing the drab face she formerly presented. Her spirits lifted and she fairly bounced. Then she became pregnant again.

"My personal life changed at that time. My daughter came to live with me in trouble. She was pregnant without a husband, he having died several months before. Her general health was not good and I feared for her safety. She had attacks when she could not catch her breath. She would lie in bed perspiring and complain of being cold. Mrs. Roche gave me time to be with her. As time for her delivery approached she worsened.

"I shall never forget that day. Because Mr. and Mrs. Roche and Winsford were away, I had given the maids a day off. Suddenly my daughter began screaming. Her baby was born as she expired. I had only enough time to prepare the child when the nursemaid called for me. 'Mrs. Roche is in labor,' she informed me. This news was completely unexpected since her baby was not due for two to three weeks. I sent the maid for our doctor and I went upstairs. Mrs. Roche was in dreadful pain. I tried to comfort her until the doctor arrived. The maid returned after endless hours to report that not only was the doctor on call in the country but that the midwife was on call as well. 'Go for Mrs. Gillingsworth. Quick!'

"I had to check on my daughter's baby and after one quick trip, I brought him upstairs with me. The pain was obviously excruciating for the expectant mother so I prepared a potion hoping to relieve her. I discovered the baby had breeched. With some effort I delivered a boy. An idea crossed my mind. No one knew my daughter had delivered. No other person was present when Mrs. Roche delivered. When Mrs. Gillingsworth arrived she saw twin boys in the mother's arms and so reported it.

"The furor over twin births was so great that no one had interest in my problems. My daughter was buried but I had her baby. I always knew which boy was mine.

"Winsford acted the proud father. He told his mother without restraint that he created these boys and that he had done his duty to his father and all the Roches from the Conqueror on!

"I was in the room next to the mistress when I overheard a conversation. 'I went to bed with you, mother, for the last time.' It was Winsford. He spoke with finality. 'I hate what you made me do for so long.' She replied, 'You cannot stay away from me, dear boy. Those headaches will drive you to me. Those hands of yours must be tethered when you get those headaches. Who else will take care of you as I have done. I know what to do to help you when you want some love. You will be back.'

"He paid less attention to his mother and more to his wife. Then Mrs. Roche died. Winsford was affected instantly. It was as if he had nothing left in life. When he stopped paying attention to the boys, I assumed responsibility for some of their care, and when Mr. Roche began teaching his daughter-in-law the estate business, I took full responsibility for managing all three children. It was a pleasure, for one was mine. All three came to me for love, advice, protection and to solve their problems.

"All three needed a father. The girl particularly was at that age when a man's direction was necessary. I spoke to her father. He thanked me but nothing came of it. She did not exist for him. I asked men in the stables to teach the boys about horses and riding and they were splendid.

"I came upon Winsford one night by accident. I had checked on the children before retiring when I heard him talking. I stopped by his door which was ajar. 'These headaches. These headaches,' he moaned. 'They are killing me.'

"Shortly after, our little girl came to me. 'Mrs. Esterham, father looked at me with the strangest eyes. His hands came up. They reminded me of claws. I thought he was going to grab me.' It was not long after that she was found in the abbey with the other child.

"Do I think he was the murderer? Yes. I know he was the murderer. I was in the study reviewing the cleaning job just performed by a new maid. Winsford entered. He did not see me. He saw his wife. She was in the garden. He stood watching her. Anger was evident in his eyes.

"His hands went to his head. It appeared he was having another headache. He stretched his arms out and his fingers looked like claws.

'You women. You women ruined my life,' he spat. 'My mother died before I could get her.' His hands shuttered. 'My daughter died so easily. Now you, Virginia.' There was horror on his face. I feared for my life if he should see me. I did not move.

"Then that awful night. I should have been in bed but I could not sleep. I took to walking. As soon as I heard Virginia Roche scream I knew. I grabbed a gun and ran upstairs to his room. There he was. Claws on her neck. He grappled with me and her for the gun. It exploded.

"Yes, the gypsy was right. However she learned of it, I killed Winsford Roche. That man was insane, a manical killer. I could not allow him to kill his wife."

Mrs. Esterham continued to rock in her chair. At sixty she was Mrs. Roche's senior by twelve years, a bit portly, hair grayed, but the spirit that guided her through difficult years had not lessened. "My one great disappointment was that I was not able to save my daughter."

Thoughts of the latest abbey murders surfaced as they had done frequently. "Ten years later we have another killer. Like father, like son? Perhaps. Is it an inherited mental problem? Otley told me who did it. The constable could have found out, but he could not think of a way for Otley to talk. He did not raise children."

She gave consideration to her responsibility. "I cannot tell the constable. Otley could have felt his importance and pointed to any stick. What he told me could be wrong." The decision justified her silence.

Events of the morning of Emma's death were fresh in her mind. She saw Kendall in the meadow, but at that time there was no significance to has action. Later she saw Radcliffe in the abbey. That had more significance since he rarely went there. "Now I must look for the clues that will help me know more for sure. His father had pains in his head. They came before he strangled. I wonder if he has the same affliction."

Horses hooves disturbed the quiet of her room and she rose to look out her window. "The constable. I knew sooner or later he would come here." She opened the main entry door after he used the knocker. "Good day, constable." Her greeting did not belie her anxiety.

"Good day to you, Mrs. Esterham. You must be preparing for the summer party."

"Yes, we are and if plans work out well, it will be the best ever."

"I hope so. May I see Mrs. Roche?"

After she left him in the study with Mrs. Roche, Mrs. Esterham managed to hear all their discussion. She made mental notes of the questions and answers. "Strange. I didn't know she talked to Otley in the abbey. Oh, ho, the poison. So Dr. Poole has an idea about the poison."

As the constable left the study, she met him.

"I am questioning everyone. May I ask you some questions?"

"Of course. We can sit in the drawing room."

Once seated he began. "Recall the morning of Emma's death. Did you see anyone in or near the abbey?"

"Of course, constable. On market day the path through the meadow is busy with people. I would guess about a fourth of the people attending market use the meadow to get there, men and women both."

"Are you exaggerating?"

"I can't guarantee a number, but it is a goodly one,"

"What time is the most use made of the path?"

"Why, I would say early, at least by seven-thirty. No later."

"Mmmmm. Of course. Could you name any of the people."

"I guess so. The ones I saw going through the meadow that day are the ones who go through it each market day."

"Did you see Kendall in the meadow that morning?"

"I certainly did but that is no different from almost every morning. He does a lot of checking before he leaves the house area."

"Did you see him go into the abbey?"

"You know I just don't stand and watch every move that boy makes."

"Of course not, Mrs. Esterham. Did you see Radcliffe in the meadow?"

"I saw Radcliffe. But don't ask me if he went into the abbey."

"Very well." The constable paused and contemplated. "You have been around here many years, Mrs. Esterham."

"Now don't ask my age, constable."

He ignored her remark. "Do you recall hearing stories about home made recipes for poisons?"

"Of course. There used to be lots of stories. Old wives tales. As children we were frightened when they were told. A cauldron was necessary. Some berries of this and leaves of that and a dead rat. But don't ask me for a recipe." She hesitated and turned very serious. "I wonder if a gypsy could help you with that. They aren't far out of town."

"If you think of anything specific you have not told me, keep it in mind. When the boys return from London, I'll be back." She watched him leave.

Ormand trotted his horse down the long lane toward Tosten. He had not learned much from his visit, he considered. "Neither of those women is telling all they know. They only affirmed what facts I do have about Kendall and Radcliffe. Both men were seen in the abbey or in the meadow the morning of Emma's death, but the time was early, when shoppers were headed for market. I figure Emma had not been dead long at all when John found her, not more than one hour at most, and he picked her up just before noon."

Mentally Ormand reviewed what he knew and placed all the facts in order:

. Shoppers walked through the abbey, most by seven-thirty.

. Kendall and Radcliffe were seen about that time.

. John Minshall reported that Emma took great care in bathing and dressing before leaving the house that morning. He thought she left about nine, but certainly before nine-thirty.

"It would take more than fifteen minutes to reach the abbey if that is where she went directly from her house. John said she was not going to market but was not sure of her plans."

. Emma was not reported as having been seen in the abbey.

He mulled over the flimsy facts. "I doubt if Emma was killed and brought to the abbey, although that is a possibility. Someone would surely have seen her being carried across the meadow to the abbey on such a busy day. She certainly had plans to meet someone or she would not have taken such pains to clean herself and put on a new dress. Too bad old John didn't ask her where she was going or the name of the person she intended to meet. With all the careful preparation she made, I must guess she was meeting a young man and one she wanted to impress. There were no signs of a struggle where she was found in the abbey. If she had been accosted she would have put up a fight. She was a husky girl. She may have given herself freely to whomever she met."

He crossed the bridge and turned onto the road leading away from town and in the direction of the gypsy camp. "It may be that a discussion with Kendall and Radcliffe will clear up their actions. I can't get too excited about reports of their presence in the meadow and abbey. After all they live right there and could be moving about their own property without a specific purpose or intent.

"There is a possibility that a transient could be involved but Emma's preparation knocks that out. No. It has to be someone she knew and thought a great deal of. She was at the age when boys were important, even Kendall and Radcliffe despite the difference in station. Damn. If only I could have got it out of Otley."

Ormand guided his horse into the gypsy camp. A dog instantly began barking. The alert brought a man from a house wagon. He approached the constable who dismounted and identified himself. The two spoke casually for a moment then the constable explained the purpose of his visit. "I am searching for home recipes for poisons."

"My wife might help you." The gypsy returned to his home and shortly reappeared with his wife. "Constable," she informed him, "gypsies may never tell how anything is made except to another gypsy. We are sworn to secrecy when we learn to make any potion. If you return tomorrow I will have for you a couple of the strongest concoctions."

'Thank you. I shall return tomorrow."

The next day he called for the potions and received them without questioning their ingredients. The woman did warn him to handle them with care because of their potency.

Dr. Poole, cautioned by the constable that he would be bringing in some poisons, began analyzing them. By evening he was prepared to say that one of the poisons appeared to be similar to the chemicals in Otley's blood but he could not be absolutely definite.

"Now to find the person who knows the gypsy's secret." The constable looked grim.

Chapter Eight

The York road left Tosten, paralleled the River Dale for a time, then swung up a crease in the hills to cross a stretch of moors, a broad expense of land, wild and lonely, marked by patches of copses, an occasional outcropping of rock, and flocks of sheep. Infrequently their coach passed a stone croft, barren in its isolation and seeming inhospitable without landscaping. Often, when the road dipped into a valley, it became entangled in a village, a collection of cottages surrounding a church, a spire or square tower rising above the settlement.

Shortly before noon the coachman stopped his team at the Fleece and Bar to give his horses a rest and to water them. The inn also provided Radcliffe and Kendall a meal and some very welcomed ale. "It wont be too bad a run, Kendall. We are in no hurry and there is no need running the horses. It is rather nice for a change being on the road and away from the demands of Rochedale.

"It is indeed." Kendall smiled at Radcliffe. "No more chores for a while and who knows whom we'll be meeting. Some choice bits, I'm hoping. Now have a look at that barmaid for a beginning." Preparing trays was a comely girl, a bit buxom but pretty of face, who enjoyed taunting her admirers by throwing very ample bosoms at them.

"Calm, Kendall. We aren't even close to London. Save some of our energy for our big city belles."

When she took the brothers' orders the maid swung her posterior toward Kendall, and as she expected, received a pinch. She protested his freshness with a saucy wink, an action she knew would bring a generous gratuity.

The public room was not crowed, a few men standing at the bar, some eating at tables.

Two caught Radcliffe's eye for they appeared to be glancing his way then whispering to each other. When the girl finished serving Kendall with a flourish of flippant comments bracketed in smiles, Radcliffe made an aside to his brother. "Heed me, Kendall. Look at me and don't move your eyes elsewhere. Across the room at the corner table are two young men. Perhaps twenty. They seem to be noticing us. As you get an opportunity, have a look and tell me what you think."

Kendall lifted his mug and as he tipped it to his lips he glanced at the corner table. Both men were looking at him. Quickly he made a judgment. "We must be thinking alike. Good for you and your analytical eye. Let's just finish eating slowly as if we hadn't noticed them, then we'll leave."

Before they finished, however, the men left the room. They were dressed for riding, high boots and leather coats dusty from the road.

"We need to warn Tom," Radcliffe advised, "and please, Kendall, don't be a hero if we should meet them on the road."

At the coach, Tom, Radcliffe and Kendall held a discussion until they reached an understanding. "Instead of taking the York road to the city," Tom suggested, "I can turn off for Doncaster. That might interfere with their plans." Agreed, the coach was directed onto the road. To the point of the turn off there was nothing untoward and Tom held some hope that his change of plans might have thwarted the two men. Such was not to be his good fortune. Where the team slowed to mount an incline he became alert. At the crest were two mounted men, each with half face masks covering their eyes and each wielding guns. Tom brought the coach to a halt where the road leveled and he alighted. There was no doubt that these two were the men at the inn.

"Gentlemen, step out," came a curt order from the spokesman.

With the command, both brothers left the coach. Kendall had wanted to shoot it out but Radcliffe reasoned him out of his scheme. It angered him to think that these men were about to make a heist without so much as a challenge, but Tom was in danger of being shot and he was convinced a life was worth more than the loss of some money.

"I need your cash. Just toss your folders over here." The direction was given in an easy manner by the leader.

Both brothers reached into their coats, pulled out their money folds, and tossed them at the feet of the highwaymen. They were opened. "Well, you don't travel with much cash. Come, now, gentlemen, you surely can do better than this."

As agreed beforehand, Radcliffe was the spokesman. "You would understand that on roads made dangerous by highwaymen we would not carry much cash, just enough for inns."

"That may be true for some travelers but certainly not for the Roche heirs. You waddle in money, and we want some." It was the voice of the leader. His tone was demanding as he completed his last statement. It was obvious that the holdup was not only planned but that the highwaymen knew their victims and anticipated an ample take.

"You are welcome to search." Radcliffe was firm. "You will find we speak the truth."

"We accept your challenge. Any move on your part will be interpreted as an invitation to an unnecessary shooting. Our guns are loaded and aimed. Radcliffe, take five paces from your brother and stop. Prepare to be searched."

The silent highwayman approached Radcliffe, searched every part of his person, then backed away. No cash was found. He moved to Kendall, repeated his actions, and with no better success.

"Look inside the coach."

A thorough search was made of the coach interior, all to no avail. "You do travel at a minimum. Pity. The cash in your folds hardly pays us for our efforts. I know your horses, however. Excellent beasts. I can make good use of them. Driver, unhitch the team."

Tom stared at Radcliffe.

"Hesitation tells me you refuse. It would be senseless to shoot good beasts. I can even shoot good men."

Radcliffe nodded and Tom unhitched the team, a steady stream of swear words blasting the air as he worked.

"Interesting," the leader observed, "you now have no money to purchase new horses. If you pay cash for new ones, I shall see you presently, for I shall know you duped me. I could slash your pillows to find your hidden money but I do not wish to cause you more inconvenience on your run to London. The horses will do me well. Do you wish to change your minds? Your horses for your money."

Radcliffe remained silent. He glanced at Kendall who was fuming but fortunately controlling his temper. Returning to the highwayman he requested calmly, "Before you depart, perhaps you would be good enough to direct us to someone who would grant us two horses on faith."

"I shall sell your horses at the farm you just passed. You might inquire there." With that the two men rode off, the team running behind at the end of reins.

Kendall spoke angrily. "A couple of shots when they first confronted us would have knocked them out. We knew what they were up to. Now we are out the horses and our cash."

Radcliffe stayed calm. "Supposed we missed and they hit us. A highwayman is always ready and most are good shots. No. We were right to do just as we did. We lost little money. None of us is injured and we can get the horses. The cash we hid was not found, they did not want our valuables, and the coach was not ravaged. They could have ripped us apart."

"Of course you are right but it riles me no end to have to give in to these bloody . . . .."

"Well, I'll bargain with the farmer for the horses." Tom joined Radcliffe in a walk to the farm. The distance was not far and they soon had the farmhouse in sight.

"They made a deal alright," observed Tom. "The farmer is still in the yard and near the front gate are the horses."

"That is interesting. It seems to me he left the team there purposely to get our attention. I'll bet you, Tom, that farmer is in league with our thieving friends. Let me do the talking. Do you have your gun ready? When I whistle, draw it."

As soon as the two passed through the gate, the farmer appeared to act surprised. "Good day, gentlemen. What be your wish?"

"Good day to you. We are in need of a team. What is your price on these horses?"

"You are in luck. Have a look at them. Just decided to sell the pair. Fine team. Been working together for some time."

Radcilffe began checking the team with Tom following his example. Their nods communicated instant agreement that both were the Rochedale steeds. "What are you asking?"

"I'll take thirty pounds the two"

"That is a bit much, isn't it?"

"Not for these two. They have many years of work ahead of them. You will find them a bargain." As he evaluated the horses, Radcliffe looked about for evidence of the highwaymen. He convinced himself they were gone with the outside chance they could be lurking on the premises and observing his actions. He decided to take the risk. Leaving Tom, he moved to the rear of the team to place the farmer between them. Radcliffe turned to face the man. "Sir, you have stolen property. Those horses are mine." He whistled his signal. Instantly guns were drawn. "You know the penalty for receiving stolen property. We'll just relieve you of any guilt. Tom, prepare the horses for mounting. And, sir, you keep your silence."

Tom worked quickly and mounted as Radcliffe covered the farmer with his weapon.

When he mounted they ran the horses to the coach, harnessed them quickly, and moved onto the road, rapidly increasing their pace under Tom's direction.

Kendall howled loudly as he listened to his brother relate the story and soundly slapped Radcliffe on the back. "You are the shrewd one. Those highwaymen will be rousing mad, mad enough to give that farmer's bottom a thorough lashing."

"Well, we didn't do too badly. It pays to hide money. The hollow heels on our boots was a good idea."

"Leave it to Mrs. Esterham to prepare us"

Both men used large, soft throw cushions to absorb bumps, rested their legs on comfortable foot rests, and they munched on cook's treats as the trip continued. Stops were made at wayside inns for daytime rests and nighttime sleep. A storm broke south of Peterborough, however, and by afternoon the downpour was so heavy it was necessary to make an early stop. Tom drove the team into the yard of the Crown and Rose where he saw to the horses while Radcliffe took care of lodging. A room was booked for the brothers and Tom was placed in the general room.

After bathing the three men entered the public room for supper. A familiar aroma of ale, common to all pubs, made them welcome and they went to the bar. Radcliffe ordered a round. The room was large with a huge stone inglenook fireplace constructed into the west wall. Within it flamed a lusty fire cooking a large joint of beef turning on a spit. Kendall discovered a comely lass joking with a merry table as she served. He eyed her, indicating a need for more ale. As she took his order he directed his hand along her leg and noticed she did not object. He got the impression that she either liked the attention or expected it.

By supper time Kendall was feeling affable, too amiable thought Radcliffe, and a table was taken. From the kitchen the maid brought three plates, each with a slab of rare meet cut from the joint swimming in juice, a portion of peas and a serving of roasted potatoes. She gave Kendall a wink as she placed a dish before him and received a pat on the rump. He accepted her gesture as a sign of encouragement and he winked in reply, indicating acceptance of her message. The exchange left him in anticipation.

Supper over the three enjoyed a brandy together then mingled with other guests until the innkeeper announced closing. Kendall had eyed the maid continuously during the evening, letting gestures and eyes silently communicate his invitations. The brothers retired to their room and got into bed, side by side. Radcliffe very shortly started to snooze, but Kendall, wide awake, waited and wondered if she would come. He was not disappointed. Within the hour the door opened. The bar maid slipped in, slide the bolt in place, and undressed. She placed her naked body next to his. Instantly he began his conquest.

His sleep disturbed, Radcliffe awakened. At first startled by the interruption, he soon realized what was taking place. He raised his head to watch, assumed a more comfortable position, his head resting on a palm above his elbow, fascinated by his brother's performance.

He was quickly stimulated to a point of feeling his own manliness.

Kendall received the girl in silence letting her curve her body to accommodate his own. He caressed her gently kissing her where his lips fell and allowing his hands to roam about her form. He cupped her breasts, tonguing each one, and picked at her nipples. Without pressing his weight on her, he maneuvered his body over hers to place her next to his brother. Now between them he continued his preparation, his hands roaming to her thighs. Casually, but with intent, he took his brother's hand and guided it over her body. He felt Radcliffe's attempt to withdraw, but Kendall tightened his grip. Slowly her legs parted. He lowered his face again to her breasts and then down the cleavage, down, down. Without lifting his head, he let go of Radcliffe's hand, reached across the girl's body and placed his own hand on his brother's back. Gently he pressed, encouraging Radcliffe to take part. He was aware of Radcliffe's hand being withdrawn from the girl. It was placed on Kendall's forearm, a push indicating that the answer was negative. Kendall looked up at his brother, first questioning, and then inviting him to join in with more emphatic facial gestures. Equally emphatically Radcliffe refused.

The girl by this time was aroused by Kendall's expert tactics. She pulled him to her and climbed on top of him, kissing where she could find him, roaming her hands about his body, grasping his extended manliness and moaning. Her legs went to the sides of his waist squeezing him mightily as he forced entry.

Her scream of pleasure startled Radcliffe. He looked at the pair and marveled at their wild gyrations, each one expressing joys in wondrous unrestraint. He felt his head begin to ache and he stared at the girl, his eyes focusing on her neck. It became a magnet to his hands. They began crawling toward her.

Kendall gasped and relaxed, puffing loudly then quieting until he rested in silence under her form. Their quietude broke the spell that engulfed Radcliffe and he shook his hands as if ridding himself of a demon. The headache persisted.

The coach continued its run to London the following morning. The heavens were bright again after the rain and the landscape presented a sparkling green, the sun making fields of dew glisten. It was Radcliffe who introduced the subject. "You are indeed a master, Kendall. It was obvious she enjoyed the escapade and you certainly did. Wherever did you become so expert?"

"Experience is the best teacher, I think is the old saying. One learns something from every effort, but this one was ready. Very satisfying."

"Thank you for offering her to me. I must admit I am not always comfortable with women. There is something that happens. I am not sure what it is. I want to master them but . . ., I don't know."

Kendall considered his brother's confession but did not pursue it. There would be an opportunity later. He changed the subject with, "Shouldn't we be thinking of a place to stay in London?"

"I have the address of an inn in Chelsea recommended by some chaps in York. I did think of staying in the City near the agent's office, but the inns in that locale are old and may not be the best. This one is new, has the latest conveniences, and we can have our own rooms. Since we are staying for a while we might as well be comfortable."

"Good idea. I must say I am tiring of these roadside inns. The food is the same and the beds are not clean. I awake to scratching bites from the vermin."

On the fifth day the boys entered London. Tom had some difficulty but the Chelsea inn was located, the coach stored, the horses stabled, and Tom was given a folder of money with the admonition to report every few days until it was determined when the return trip would be scheduled. The inn indeed was modern, roomy, boasted the latest accouterments and proved to be comfortable. Kendall found the food very acceptable and Radcliffe was pleased to room alone.

The next day the boys reported to the agent's office.

The firm of Ross, Byers and Millersly was located south of St. Paul's Cathedral in the heart of the financial district of the City, a brick edifice constructed after the great fire of London.

A convivial greeting was extended by Mssrs. Ross and Byers who obviously anticipated the boys' arrival and planned well for their visit. Coffee was served in an impressive conference room lighted by brass chandeliers, made comfortable by leather chairs placed about a finely carved oak table and enhanced by hand tooled paneling on which hung excellent oil paintings. Conversation was light and friendly with the hosts full of admiration for energetic sons helping their widowed mother. "I shall be your tutor while you are with us," announced Mr. Ross, "but before we turn to the operations of business, you boys need to see London and enjoy some of our social life. I have taken the liberty of engaging two charming young ladies to be your guides, if that arrangement is convenient to you. I am sure you will receive some interesting invitations as a result. Have your lodgings been cared for?"

Radcliffe gave him the name and location of the Chelsea Inn.

"I had spoken at a private club for you but no matter, that can wait. Perhaps some evening, or if your Chelsea inn does not prove to be satisfactory, let me know and we shall get you in the club. It is an exclusive men's hostel and excellent. Many interesting activities. May I say when you will be calling on the young ladies?"

"That is very kind of you, sir. Would day after tomorrow be satisfactory, perhaps in the afternoon?" Kendall warmed to the idea.

"Fine. What do you say to tea and you can get acquainted. Mind you, the ladies are not to take all your time. You are to let them know when you are available. Now, about business. Perhaps next week we can chat."

Having agreed to Mr. Ross' proposals, the brothers departed. "I would say the company of Ross, Byers and Millersly is doing very well." Radcliffe was serious in his evaluation. "Did you note the fine furnishings. That is a successful operation."

"Successful at our expense? Well, we'll just have to find out. Anyhow I like the idea of meeting the girls. This stay in London could be an adventure." Kendall had a gleam in his voice.

"Perhaps. It depends on the girls. I am glad I spoke to Squire Gunning. He gave me good background and suggested several questions to ask. We wont be talking to Mr. Ross without some sense of his ways."

"You spoke to Gunning? About what?" Kendall thought immediately about Carinna.

"I wanted some preparation for this trip so Squire gave me two hours of his time. He was very helpful."

"Did you see Carinna?"

"Indeed I did. I asked Squire for permission to speak to her."

"And?"

"She is a charming girl, Kendall. I could be very serious about making her Mrs. Roche."

Kendall thought about the cave and wondered how far Radcliffe got with her.

"She promised to see me again when we returned home."

"It is likely she will have to choose between the two of us, Radcliffe. I have a deep feeling for her and she has promised to see me, too.

It appears that no matter which of us she selects, she will be Mrs. Roche."

The two walked along Fleet Street in silence, passed Temple Bar, each considering how he was going to court Carinna.

Sharply at four in the afternoon on the appointed day, Radlciffe and Kendall appeared at the entrance to a portentous town house in the Westminster district of London. Extensive landscaping surrounding a fashionable two story brick building, designed in the William and Mary style, gave evidence as to the social status of the inhabitants. Radcliffe used the polished brass lion head door knocker which brought a maid dressed in formal livery to the door. She greeted the brothers and guided them to a large drawing room richly decorated in shades of yellow, carpeted with orientals, and furnished with deeply upholstered sofas and chairs. Overhead was a finely carved plastered ceiling from which hung three chandeliers cascading prisms while on one wall hung brocaded drapes opened to permit sunlight to brighten the room. Gold framed portraits and oil landscapes adorned one of the walls while a floor to ceiling mirror covered most of another. Opposite the windows was a fireplace of carved wood painted white.

Diana and Cecilia Isham appeared after a polite delay, swishing exuberantly into the room, both dressed in tea frocks. Greetings were exhanged after appropriate introductions then personal assessments began, each man appraising each girl, each girl making judgments of each man.

Light repartee was the vehicle with subjects caroming about the men's journey, the frightening actions of highwaymen, socials in London, entertainments, horses and activities of the royal family. Kendall took the lead with his suave manner guiding the badinage. Cecilia was proving to be the more dominant of the two sisters, although it was readily obvious both girls were well schooled in the social graces. Radcliffe quickly took to Diana and began participating in the conversation but following his brother's lead.

A tea cart was rolled in during the get acquainted session. Unobtrusively the maid served finger sandwiches and a variety of small biscuits, colorful tarts with fruit fillings and squares of decorated cakes, all on French china.

Kendall guessed that Cecilia was older, possibly nineteen, while Diana appeared to be a year younger. Both were attractive and used paint skillfully to highlight their features. Each was perhaps five feet four or five inches tall, both of slim figure, and their dresses were designed to give the right accents. Their father, Sir Alfred Isham, it developed, was on the king's counsel and an expert in finance.

As the afternoon faded to evening it was becoming evident that the girls were enjoying the newcomers. They had expected country provincials from the shires and only reluctantly accepted a request from Mr. Ross to meet sons of one of his best clients. They were finding both men, especially Kendall, to be socially attractive, physically alluring and pleasant as companions. Now past the accepted hour of tea time, the girls were reluctant to have the men depart. Sensing this, Kendall asked if they could meet again, possibly for riding. Arrangements were made for the afternoon the next day.

"Well, Radcliffe old boy, it appears we made a couple of conquests. How would an Isham in the Roche family suit you, court connections and all?"

Radcliffe considered his brother's question and was piqued sufficiently to read values for them. He saw money in the arrangement, power with a court connection, and fine living in London. He might possibly get a position in the firm of Ross, Byers and Millersly. "I shall have to give that thought further consideration."

"Which one?" Kendall laughed aloud.

"Possibly Diana. After just one meeting it seems to me she is more mature, more my type."

"Interested?"

"Perhaps."

"Don't pass up an opportunity that has been handed to you. We'll have many times to be with them during our stay in London. Think about it while we are with them. Who knows? With your business skills you might land a post on the king's counsel."

The idea was more appealing as Kendall pursued it. Suddenly Radcliffe laughed out loud.

"Are you pushing me onto Diana so you wont have competition for Carinna?"

"Then we would both be winners, you more than I." Kendall felt pleased with the development.

Radcliffe did give thought to Diana and all benefits that would accrue to him through marriage and he noted to himself that, "it would be well to court the girl, meet the father and use Mr. Ross to encourage the union."

The next afternoon was ideal for riding. Sun continued to shine warmly, unusual for June. The brothers procured excellent mounts at the exclusive riding club to which they had been referred. There they met Diana and Cecilia, both dressed in current fashionable riding habits, long skirts, buttoned vests over long sleeve shirts, and jaunty narrow rimmed bowlers on their heads. Both were excited. "Oh, boys, we are in luck. We have been invited by the Duchess of Kensington to join her party and the Duke of York will ride today. We must hurry."

Kendall saw to it that Radcliffe was paired with Diana while he stayed close to Cecilia as the four trotted through street traffic to the edge of St. James Park, the designated meeting place. The four dismounted to mingle with other arrivals, the girls making introductions and guiding get-acquainted conversations.

A coach rolled to a stop, a magnificent roan tethered behind. Footmen assisted a beautifully attired lady to alight followed by her entourage of three young men who immediately hovered over her. She waved them aside to permit her guests to pay respects. How delighted we are to have two young men with us in London," she smiled in greeting after Cecilia made the introductions. Her eyes roamed over Kendall, apparently taken with him. "You must talk these two charmers into bringing you to my soiree this Saturday. We must get better acquainted."

She mounted her roan and guided her riding party to the main lane leading into the park.

Late spring provided a profusion of color, flowers shining brilliantly in broad clusters across the park. Trees, newly dressed in a variety of green shades, provided welcome intermittent shade. The lake was glass like, the only ripples being created by swans gliding serenely, mostly in family groups, their cygnets, many losing their gray baby down, following parents obediently.

The gait was slow since the purpose of the afternoon outing was to be seen. Groups of riders met, intermingled to chat, then rode on. The custom permitted Radcliffe ample time to pursue his own purpose. Deliberately he imitated Kendall's charm and attempted the first steps of courting. Diana was beguiled by Radcliffe's demeanor and in response practiced her own charms.

Kendall kept Cecilia away leaving the two on their own as much as the interplay of groups permitted.

The duchess maneuvered members of her group so as to bring Kendall to her side. "Are you enjoying London?"

"I am fascinated by all the beauty, this park, this day, these ladies, and, he hesitated to gain her eyes, "by you especially, Madame." His eyes lingered on hers and he let his voice convey an intimate meaning.

Elizabeth, Duchess of Kensington, intrigued Kendall, prompting him to think of the first woman with whom he shared a bed, the woman in York who introduced him to the ways of love making. "I wonder if this one would be as good," he considered to himself as he rode next to her.

He had not been with an older woman since that first time but he never forgot the expertise of her arts.

The duchess was well known in court and social circles. She was the second wife of the Duke of Kensington, cousin to the king, and a wealthy landowner. Younger than her husband by more than twenty years, the marriage was an arranged convenience, for her father whose limited income could not support his land holdings or his manner of living. The alliance saved his status but provided little love for her. At the duke's death she inherited not only a substantial income but considerable property. She was, therefore, a wealthy member of nobility, one who enjoyed spending and entertaining in a royal manner. Not yet thirty and still an enchanting woman, she was sought after by many, but her interest was reserved to a very few.

Like so many others, Kendall was quick to recognize her physical beauty. With auburn hair swept up to hide under a bowler, the carved features of her face were revealed. Most notable were high cheek bones which gave emphasis to emerald eyes that created an unusual alluring effect which she used expressively. Her lips were full and rich, frequently employed in a smile which revealed pleasantly formed teeth and a slight dimple in either cheek.

Seated erectly on her steed, Kendall admired her straight back and squared shoulders which thrust her chest forward to accentuate well rounded breasts which he considered wishfully, "are ready to be cupped and enjoyed."

"You intrigue me, Madame. You manage your mount with great skill. I can see you are an accomplished horse woman. It is evident you enjoy the sport making it a pleasure to ride with you."

The duchess eyed this young man somewhat taken aback, not expecting such polished charm from a provincial. "Tell me about Yorkshire. Is it all moors?"

'They are only one of our natural assets. We have features equally beautiful." He described briefly but enthusiastically the River Dale, the landscape beyond, the abbey ruins, Moncton Tor with its sweeping landscapes. "Oh, yes, we have moors, but we have much more."

She liked the lilt of his voice, the Yorkshire accent, and especially the way he held his body as he rode. She undressed him as he rode.

Her lusting was broken by the approach of another riding party. Immediately she became the Duchess of Kensington, dignified, graceful. She smiled affectionately as the roan under her expert hand carried her next to the approaching Prince of the Realm.

George Hanover, heir apparent, was still a youth, but he made an impressive figure on horseback, riding erect, squaring his shoulders and returning in kind the smiles directed at him.

The duchess raised her hand for the prince to accept and he took it to his lips. "Madame, you are fetching as ever, lovelier than this enchanting day."

"Your Highness is too gracious. May I present one of your loyal subjects from Yorkshire, Mr. Kendall Roche."

"Your Highness." Kendall spoke clearly and made a bow from his saddle.

"And his brother, Mr. Radcliffe Roche"

Radcliffe who had been beckoned forward by the duchess, bowed and said, "Good day, your Grace."

"You know Sir Alfred Isham's daughters, Diana and Cecilia." The duchess continued her introductions. Kendall winked at his brother in praise of their accomplishment in meeting the prince, and Radcliffe felt a flow of satisfaction, stimulating him further to consider Diana and a life in London with her. His contemplation on the subject led him to peer ahead in time. "The Prince of Wales will be king and if I use my opportunities to advantage, I could be part of his reign."

He smiled, pleased with his future prospects. Immediately he turned to speak to Diana for he reminded himself that it would be through an alliance with her that his future would unfold. His plan, instantly formulated, called for meeting her father and especially for making a favorable impression on him.

That night at the inn the brothers talked over supper. "I noticed the duchess discarded her escorts and favored you, Kendall. Careful. Diana tells me the noble lady is a widow and surrounds herself with young men."

"That might not be so unpleasant. She is an attractive woman."

"Too old for you, but her wealth is something to consider."

"Perhaps, but money is secondary. It's love that counts. That in my judgment is where it begins and ends."

His brother's comment disturbed him. He knew he had to ask the question about his feelings toward Diana but he did not wish to face it. He calmed himself with an inner statement, "Later when I know her better I can consider my feelings. Then I can decide if I love her. Anyhow, love grows after marriage." In the back of his mind was his fear of love making.

A note arrived addressed to Radcliffe and Kendall. It was signed by both Diana and Cecilia and invited the brothers to meet at the Isham home Saturday at seven and drive with them and their parents to the Duchess of Kensington's party.

"The opportunity is handed to me," Radcliffe smiled to himself. "I am to meet Sir Alfred." Any thought of affection for Diana was pushed to the background. Making an impression on Sir Alfred was paramount.

Myriads of candles set the Kensington mansion aglow and music from the salon welcomed the duchess' guests as they arrived. She greeted each arrival in the receiving room, chatted a moment, then suggested they visit "my pub where libations await you." Fifty guests had been invited including the king's brothers, William, Duke of Gloucester, and Henry, Duke of Cumberland, with their wives. Some members of the king's counsel were also present. Diana and Cecilia saw to it that Radcliffe and Kendall were properly introduced, then they joined a group of younger people dancing in the salon.

Radcliffe was pleased that Mr. Ross had been invited. The presence of his mother's agent gave him instant entree to his plans for the evening, for as they talked, Sir Alfred joined them. "My boy," he announced in a booming, jovial voice, "Diana is well taken with you. She finds your company stimulating. Tell me about yourself."

Radcliffe blushed momentarily, surprised by the sudden opportunity to present himself. He recovered quickly to attempt a reply, but before a first word was out, he was interrupted.

"Ah, Sir Alfred!" Mr. Ross was exuberant. "Let me respond for our young visitor. He is much too modest to praise himself. I assure you he manages skillfully at his tender age a large estate in Yorkshire and he is clever enough to make it a very profitable business. This young man, Sir Alfred, shows great promise. He is in London to learn about the more technical aspects of the wool business."

"That is a worthy recommendation indeed. I would like for us to become better acquainted, Radcliffe. Meet me for lunch on Monday. Make it the Cheshire Cheese. Say one o'clock. Just the two of us."

"Why, thank you, Sir. That is very kind of you. I shall anticipate our meeting with pleasure."

Sir Alfred took his leave and Mr. Ross looked at Radcliffe. "That, my boy, is unusual. I would guess that Diana spoke very highly of you to her father. Sir Alfred must be looking at you as a possible son-in-law otherwise he never would have given you the time of day. Diana is his treasure and he will be doubly sure of the man who wins her. Marry into the Isham family and you will have a bright future."

"Diana is a lovely girl, Mr. Ross. She does interest me even though we just met. I am grateful to you for introducing us. Kendall and I are having a rousing time. We never supposed we would be enjoying London so much."

"A pleasure. I wanted the two of you to have a good time. Now we must talk business. I scheduled a block of time Wednesday afternoon. Be at the office with Kendall at one thirty and we shall enlighten you on the mysteries of the wool business."

Kendall continued in the salon where Cecilia kept him dancing. He was intrigued with her friends and she doted on the attention he gave her. The duchess entered and he bowed. Immediately she was at his side. "Cecilia, my dear, I beg privilege of the hostess. May I take Kendall from you for this dance?" She slipped her arm though his and they joined a line.

He was charmed by this woman whom he recognized was beguiling him. Her wiles were polished, honed to perfection, and he wanted her to captivate him. She was beautiful to behold, dressed in white with a bodice that revealed too much cleavage, her glistening auburn hair coiffured to enhance her allures, and her features were painted softly to emphasize her attractiveness. He wanted to seize her.

"Walk me in the garden, Kendall," she invited. She led him through French doors into an English garden lighted by candles placed in effective locations. She kept her arm clasped around his and guided him along paths outlined by small carved hedges. They chatted easily, she leading the badinage that drew from him his past, his interests and his plans for the future. Willingly he revealed all, enjoying her company and feeling for her body so close to his. "I didn't spend all my life in Yorkshire. Radcliffe and I attended Oriel College at Oxford where we had a rousing few years away from home. Radcliffe won all academic certificates and I collected extra curricular awards, the ones that remind me I had an exhilarating time of it."

The duchess had been following his story and laughed at his mirthful interpretation of his past. "You are an attractive young man, Kendall. I would like to know you better. Come to supper on Wednesday evening. How is seven?"

When they returned to the salon, the duchess handed him back to Cecilia. "You have a fine young man, my dear."

Precisely at one twenty-five on Monday, Radciffe entered the Cheshire Cheese. The pub was crowded with business men drinking and eating. A waiter approached. "Mr. Radcliffe Roche? Come with me, sir." The waiter guided a climb up a short flight of stairs then motioned him to enter a small private room. "Sir Alfred will be here shortly."

Sir Alfred Isham was a portly man of medium height, dressed in the proper style by London's leading private tailor. He maintained a serious demeanor, a reflection that he was one of England's ranking financiers, eminently successful in business and commanding a sizeable income. Formerly a counsel member, he now gave service to the crown by advising the king on financial matters. "Good day to you, Radcliffe. I see you keep your appointments on time. Shall we order and then we can talk." The door was closed by the waiter as he retired.

"As I told you, Diana is enamored of you. This is the first time she has felt so strong about any young man, although I am aware you have just met. What are your intentions?"

"Why, sir." The question came unexpectedly and Radcliffe had to pause to weigh his reply. "I am exceedingly fond of Diana. Because we just met we are still getting acquainted . I would hope we could have a life together if we find we belong to one another." He looked directly at his interrogator fearing he had spoken the wrong statement and that all his thoughts for the future were dashed.

"Well stated, my young man. I was fearful you were a seeker after fortune and that my daughter was merely an entree to my wealth. I am pleased you respect the fact you just met and of course you could not have made up your mind on marriage. Good. That relieves me. I shall tell her ladyship." He puffed. "Diana is very special to me and in no way can she be hurt. Her young man must place love as first priority, above all else." He patted the table to give emphasis to his view. "Now, what are your financial prospects?"

"Sir, I am heir to Rochedale Manor estates, a sizeable tract in Yorkshire that produces sheep and cattle. Mr. Ross can attest to our income. Wool brings a good profit."

"Mmmmm. How can you court my daughter and become better acquainted if you are in Yorkshire?"

"I shall have to be in London oftener, and, if you please, sir, perhaps Diana may visit me at Rochedale Manor."

"How is your business sense?"

"I think it is very good. I have almost full responsibility managing the estate, with my mother's approval, of course."

"I might arrange a place for you in one of my firms if your relationship with Diana dictates. That would make it easier for you to be in London. How long will you remain in London this time?"

"My brother and I plan to be in London about three weeks, sir."

"Very well. I shall report to her ladyship. I am sure she will arrange some suppers or other such so you can get acquainted."

Sir Alfred continued to probe. Radcliffe remained the perfect gentleman, ever aware of the purposes of the questions and keeping his own goals clearly in mind.

As they departed Sir Alfred shook Radcliffe's hand and expressed pleasure in their meeting. "You lead me to believe Diana has made a wise choice."

Radcliffe smiled as he walked toward Temple Bar, confident he had made a favorable impression and he saw his future brighten substantially. As yet he gave no thought to Sir Alfred's first requirement for his daughter.

Mr. Ross, Radcliffe and Kendall sat around the large oak table in the firm's conference room. The fourth person was Roger Ellersby, chief clerk for the firm. "Gentlemen, I have asked Roger to join us since he directs the workings of the office and has full knowledge of all transactions. I want to discuss with you the business principles that guide our working relationships with Rochedale Manor, how wool prices are set, the charging of fees and other aspects of interest to you. Roger will review the books, records and other accounting procedures we follow to aid our clients."

Mr. Ross began by reviewing current business conditions enlarging on those aspects that were affecting the need for wool, the function of supply and demand on both need and prices of wool, uses being made of wool by various enterprises and speculation as to what the future portended for the use of wool. He then talked about prices, the movement up and down a scale, factors affecting prices, particularly at the moment, the role of middle handlers and how he saw the future of prices. He summarized, finally, the services his firm gave clients in marketing their raw material and how his fees were determined.

There were questions and these were discussed at length. Radcliffe impressed Mr. Ross by using Squire Gunnings suggestions in his comments and questions, and by the manner in which he participated in the pursuit of subjects. It was evident the young man had a good background of understanding and was only in need of detailed instruction. Mr. Ross recognized that his basics were sound and that he had a natural bent for business and finance.

The chief clerk then conducted the brothers on an information tour of office procedures. Rochedale Manor books were examined and explained. At this point, because of his Wednesday evening appointment, Kendall took leave, but Radcliffe remained, obviously captivated by all he was learning.

At day's end Roger and Radcliffe were still engrossed. "I regret the need to terminate our discussions, but we must close the office. If you would like we can continue at my place," the clerk suggested. "My housekeeper will have enough supper and we will not have to eat out."

It was a short walk to Roger's bachelor quarters on a street near St. Bartholomew's church, a section of the city that survived the great fire. Supper over, the two continued talking although the subjects were no longer related to business. Radcliffe was taken by this young man who had risen to the responsible position of head clerk in a short time and who, it was evident, commanded the respect of the firm's owners.

Roger in turn was impressed by Radcliffe. They felt a mutual warming of friendship and experienced a genuine pleasure in the other's company.

Suddenly Radcliffe was aware of the late hour. Time had gone unnoticed and he was shocked by the lateness.

"It is very likely you will not find a cabby in this part of the City at this hour," Roger noted. "You are welcome to stay on and leave in the morning. It is not wise being on these dark streets considering the times."

Radcliffe mulled the invitation then accepted. He was shown the bedroom and both men prepared to retire. Candles were blown out and Roger slipped into bed beside Radcliffe, their bodies touching. Radcliffe did not withdraw. He was aware of Roger moving, adjusting his position so that his body now curved about his own. Roger's arm moved over his shoulder and caressed him. He enjoyed the sensation.

Kendall made special preparation for his appointment. He bathed, scented his body, brushed and combed his hair with care and dressed in a new suit. He took time to assess himself, making sure he was presentable. He had been looking forward to this evening since the duchess spoke the invitation.

At seven he raised the door knocker and let it fall. He was shown to a sitting room where he stood admiring several small framed pictures on the walls. In concentration he did not hear her enter but he felt her hand on his shoulder and tingled at the touch. He remained as he was, staring at a picture, then suddenly he turned and enfolded her in his arms. "Got you!" he called out.

"Now, Kendall." She tried to reprimand him for embracing her. She struggled slightly and he let her go.

"You are lovely tonight. Let me look at you." His greeting was full of boyish enthusiasm. He took a step backward to behold her beauty. She, too, had made special preparation in her grooming. A heady perfume had already begun its wizardry. He smiled in appreciation and said softly, "You are enchanting me." He took her hand and raised it to his lips.

"Our full moon makes the garden a paradise. Come, walk with me." She let him keep her hand as she guided him outside. There were no candles. A light breeze was blowing and he detected a shiver. Quickly he dropped her hand, placed his arm around her shoulders and pressed her to him. Her bare flesh was soft but firm. He felt excitement instantly.

"You are a sorceress," he complimented her. He wanted her to stop but she kept to her slow stroll. She would stay in control as long as possible, for she knew the moment she allowed him some freedom, his command would be dominant, completely. "You invited no others to your dinner," he added.

"How can I know you better if there are others taking my attention? It is you who interests me tonight."

"Tonight?" His question was spoken in a tone of disappointment. "Tomorrow your interest will be given to someone else." He stopped and turned her toward him. He looked down onto her lovely face. "I am for one night."

His inference displeased her. He saw her anger flash across her face, her eyes spitting fire at him. "You think I am a wanton, directing traffic across my bed. Is that your impression of me?"

Her challenge stimulated him. He grabbed her and crushed her against him. When she threw back her head to protest, he covered her lips with his and pressed hard. She relaxed in the pleasure of his attack.

"Come," she directed breathlessly when he finally released her. "It is best we have supper now." It was the only thing she could think of saying to regain control.

Supper was served in the French style with a different wine for each serving and delays between. There was time for her to guide their conversation to learn of his background, to entice a description of his experiences, to encourage statements of his interests, to speak of wishes for his future and this she did skillfully. He was aware of her intrigue but did not protest. She had captivated him.

Brandy topped the supper but not at the table. It was served in a small drawing room where a love seat was the only accommodation. Slowly they sipped and talked, but now it was he who questioned. Under the influence of liquor she revealed more than she intended, facts about her marriage that were decidedly unsatisfactory, particularly in intimate relationships, her fear of remarriage since her suitors were interested mainly in her wealth and the joy she had in entertaining. "You no doubt believe as many of those who don't know me that I am a titled courtesan who pleasures only in bed romping. Is that what you believe, too?"

"I think only that you are a delightful lady, astonishingly beautiful, and a joy to be with." He stopped there for he did not wish to declare additional thoughts about his intentions.

"You are a boy with stardust in his eyes." She placed a hand on his thigh as if to emphasize her remark then poured a second brandy for him. Her touch sent a ripple through him. He peered beyond an opened door that revealed a small portion of a piece of furniture. Quickly he gulped a portion of the brandy then immediately consumed the rest. He rose without speaking. Instantly she felt disappointment to think he was taking his leave. She was unprepared for his quick action. He picked her up in his strong arms as he would one of his ailing lambs.

She, grabbing his back, felt the interplay of well developed muscles as he carried her through the door and into the next room. He discovered an oversized chaise longue topped by pillows and at its foot a fur rug.

Gently he placed her on the longue and knelt beside her. His hands cupped her face and he kissed her gently, brushing his lips across hers. She started to rise but he placed a hand on her shoulder to restrain her. "I need to shed the stardust of boyhood and become a man, "he whispered.

He kissed her again, full on the lips, forgetting gentleness this time. His passion was beyond control. He sent his tongue probing her lips as he directed his hand about her breasts and down the cleavage. She sighed, and as she did so he sent his tongue into her mouth. Responding now, her tongue challenged his, stabbing then retracting. She felt her bodice loosen and her breasts opening to freedom. He left her mouth to find her ears, exploring first the lobes and then her chin. Her breasts became engulfed in a flood of kisses. As a baby he suckled her nipples. Passion was mounting in her own body, and she encouraged him to continue. She released some catches and the waist of her dress opened. He pulled at her gown until it left her. Somehow her under garments appeared on the floor. She lay before him disrobed, her chest heaving.

He leaned backward on his knees, his eyes shining in delight as her nakedness spread before him. "Fascinating enchantress!" he exclaimed aloud.

She heard his delight expressed and moved to make room for him. He accepted the unspoken invitation, stretched out beside her, flesh to flesh, hers soft, satiny, his firm, hardened by his active life. His arms caressed her and he moved his hands about to know her better, then more completely. Fearfully she anticipated what he would do to her. She felt him leave her for a moment then he appeared over her. She prepared herself, but the terror she expected did not materialize. She scarcely felt his entry and the skill of his machinations created pleasure for her. She began her own movements until the harmony of love was complete.

They lay side by side exhausted, she resting her head on his chest, he providing comfort with his arm about her. In time he rose, placed the rug over her, dressed, then lovingly took his leave, his kiss lingering on her lips. Her happiness was beyond expression. It was the first time she had lain with a man since her husband died.

Elizabeth Farnsworth was a spirited girl, bright eyed, physically attractive with a winsome personality that lured a string of suitors with romance on their minds. Her popularity won invitations to numerous London social functions, some in the best homes where she met influential people including those within the royal circle. It was on one of these occasions that she was introduced to the Duke of Kensington.

Instantly charmed by this blithe spirit, he saw in her a substitute for a wife who long since had ceased to be a matrimonial companion. Past fifty, he presented a figure that showed the ravages of time that had not been too kind. A portliness acquired from excessive living and lack of physical exercise had developed about his frame, and his face, now pudgy, was marked by reddened pin stripped veins. He dressed fashionably in rich brocades and silks of French design to hide obesity and to add height to his average stature. He saw fit that Elizabeth received invitations to parties he attended since he recognized that should he ask to be her escort before she knew him better he risked the embarrassment of refusal.

His plan was carefully devised. At each party he engaged her in conversation, danced with her, and by skillful design became more frequently her companion for suppers. At group riding parties he invariably rode at her side and for picnics she sat next to him in his carriage. His infatuation for her grew stronger with each association. The plan for conquest matured when she received an invitation to be presented to the king, the most prestigious event of the social calendar.

Being of the blood royal, a cousin to the monarch, the duke took advantage of an opportunity to impress the object of his affections. Thrilled beyond belief as he knew she would be, she accepted his invitation and instantly fell under his aegis. He arranged for her presentation gown, an exquisite creation by a French couturier, bespeckled with jewels, and shortly before he called for her she received a diamond necklace with matching tiara. His conquest was complete when, before the assembly of ranking peers of the realm and a multitude of notable guests, he escorted her down the avenue of onlookers to kneel before their majesties.

A short time later the Duchess of Kensington was found dead, having expired, it was reported under extenuating circumstances. Her passing left the duke free to pursue his infatuation, and as soon as it was expedient to do so, he requested permission to call on Elizabeth's father.

Mr. Farnsworth was completely cognizant of the duke's impassioned feeling for his daughter and saw in it the possibility of making an agreement that would relieve his own critical financial situation. He received the duke who requested the privilege of courting Elizabeth. The two talked at length and by the time the last glass of brandy had been consumed, a deal had been struck. Mr. Farnsworth saved his estate but lost his daughter.

Once his plight was explained, Elizabeth accepted her father's agreement. He gave her away in a fashionable wedding at St Margaret's next Westminster Abbey.

Unprepared for marriage as she was, she did not understand that the duke's performance in bed was other than natural. He slobbered about her person committing a variety of vulgarities, and to compensate for his own physical incompetentcies he employed devices of his own making. Publicly he was a devoted husband who fawned on his wife, dressing her in gowns that set the fashion, smothering her with gifts ranging from simple lockets to furs and ultimately to diamonds set in gold and platinum mounts for every purpose. He gave her a London town house and a country estate. He took to calling her "Doll" and treated her as one, showing her off at parties, receptions, royal functions and the theater.

The Kensington racing stables were well known throughout England and he spent much of his time with his hobby. Elizabeth accompanied him and, recognizing her interest, he provided training. In time she became an accomplished horse woman.

The inevitable occurred. Women talk resulted in the realization that her husband had yet to bed her properly. Mortified to disgust, she looked about and felt attracted to men her own age. The duke rebelled. Angered at a misinterpreted over solicitous action by a young admirer, the duke challenged the innocent man. Although dueling was outlawed, seconds made the necessary secreted arrangements, guns were fired and duke fell. It was established the duke fell by accident.

Elizabeth inherited vast wealth and became instantly a sought after widow.

Wise now to the ways of the world, she kept her own council, permitted no transgressions, entertained lavishly and despite common gossip, was the proper Duchess of Kensington, proper that is until she met Kendall.

Radcliffe walked from St, Bartholmew's church to Chelsea. He wanted time to think about the night just passed and to determine what it meant to him. It was the first time he had bedded with a man and when he left Roger he did not know whether to abhor the experience, forget it as another adventure in the ways of big city life, accept the guilt that bothered him and remained with him now as he tried to sort it all out, admit that he felt pleasure in the event, or deny it ever happened.

No matter how he thought, the nagging fact persisted that he enjoyed Roger. It was different from being with a woman, yet it was not. The physical act had the same result, the body touching was the same although the feel of a woman was softer, more sensuous. At first Roger's actions revolted him, but with arousal and the encouragement to relax, the emotion changed. Cooperation and initiative developed.

At no time during the stay with Roger was there the excruciating head pain that always accompanied an affair with a woman, and there was not that fearful, compelling drive to put his hands on Roger's neck as there was when he was with a woman. He would have to think more on it.

His meditation turned to Sir Alfred and Diana. "How does this affect my future? He said that love for Diana came first, above all else. That statement bothers me. I don't know if I love Diana. I enjoy being with her and she is a charming person. I could love her, I think. I need to be with her more, alone with her to determine the extent of my caring, to learn if I love her.

Recognition of the need to be alone with her caused apprehension. "To be alone with her. How can I manage that? Kendall is so skillful with women. But I . . . . . ." Fear surfaced. "What if that pain in my head starts when I attempt to make love to her?" Again he tried to analyze himself. "What causes that pain? Is it because I am afraid to love? Is it fear that causes the pain?"

Doubts consumed him, doubts about his ability to love, doubts about himself, doubts about the night with Roger, doubts about himself as a man, doubts about his future. The doubting troubled him deeply and such was his depression when he entered the inn.

"Radcliffe, there you are. I could not find you." Kendall noticed at once that his brother was wearing the same clothes he had on yesterday.

"I took a lengthy walk to do some thinking. How was your evening with the duchess?"

"Ah, now there is a woman, a complete woman. What a joy!"

Kendall's exuberance made Radcliffe cringe. What his brother had, he lacked. "What is it that makes the difference?" he considered. Aloud he asked, "Have you had breakfast?"

"No. I have been waiting for you. I am famished. Let's eat."

The two reviewed their meeting in Mr. Ross' office and both agreed they had not only learned more about the business but felt the price fixing for raw wool they questioned was completely fair.

"Have you given any more thought to your meeting with Sir Alfred?" Kendall's inquiry renewed Radcliffe"s worry.

"Indeed I have. I think there is a promising future here for me. With you managing Rochedale and I working under the patronage of Sir Alfred, we could build an empire. In time we could rise to his level."

"No, it is not 'we,' Radcliffe. It is you. You have the business brains. I can manage Rochedale alright, but it is you who will have to manage London."

"It isn't London that bothers me. It is Diana. Sir Alfred said that love for her must come before any other consideration. I'm not sure of my love for her."

Kendall thought a moment, recalling the night in the Peterborough inn when Radcliffe refused to participate in his escapade. "It is training. I had an excellent woman one night in York. All you need are a few instructions and Diana will be clay in your arms. How about a go at it?"

Radcliffe's first reaction was one of revulsion, but the notion occurred to him that if Kendall could become a master with proper training, he could, too. "Very well. I leave it to you."

"Leave it to me. Tomorrow evening we go to Mr. Ross' men's club," Kendall announced. "He has arranged for supper and a social evening. It will be formal dress and we need to bring no ladies. This is a side of the business world we haven't seen and it could be interesting." A wink gave interpretation to the word.

Mr. Ross met his two young guests, introduced them to some of the most influential men in the world of finance, talked privately to Kendall about final arrangements for the evening while Radcliffe was involved in discussions elsewhere. Kendall saw to it that Radcliffe had brandies as they talked.

At a prearranged signal from the club master, Kendall took his brother in tow, followed the master to a part of the club they had not seen, and ascended a flight of stairs to a series of apartments. In one small salon two beautifully gowned women, perhaps in their middle twenties, greeted the young men, served brandy and guided a clever repartee that was particularly pleasing to Radcliffe. At a precise moment one of the hostesses rose. Politeness required the two young men to rise also and as they did, she placed her arm around Radcliffe's waist and guided him into an adjoining room, closing the door behind them.

A master at her trade, she began practicing her skills instantly. He was entranced as she involved him in undressing her, fondling her and taking her to bed. She guided his hands over her body and maneuvered him to assume dominance. He was responding actively, enjoying the thrill of love making and for the first time playing the completely masculine role.

When she had aroused him to his zenith, he coupled with her, their bodies writhing. She saw his eyes become glassy and she felt pleasure that her assignment was being filled successfully. His arms released the firm grip they had about her and his hands began a steady move across her chest and onto her neck. She saw his eyes become watery. This action was not strange. It had happened before. Men had a variety of ways of expressing their involvement before a climax. She continued her efforts to bring him to fulfillment. His hands roamed about her throat, and she felt them tighten, now tighter, tighter. Her breathing became difficult. She began fighting him, fear mounting as no air reached her lungs. A massive blow from her clenched fist to his head startled him and he let go. Quickly she rolled him off her and stood up.

He looked at her in amazement, questioning, both hands holding his head. "What is wrong? What happened? Why did you leave me?"

She stared at him, bewildered. His eyes cleared somewhat but his skin was sallow. "Are you well?"

"My head is pounding. The pain. The pain!"

Quickly she covered herself with a robe, poured a brandy, told him to drink it, and left the room. Kendall was just leaving the room opposite. They met in the salon.

"Your brother is ill. He complained of a painful headache. He was enjoying our go when he tried to choke me. He doesn't recall doing that."

Kendall entered the room and found Radcliffe about dressed. In reply to a questioning stare, he explained, "I don't know what happened. I was having an amazingly good time when she left me." His speech was slow, measured and somewhat slurred. "Anyhow the pain is not so bad now."

"She said you had your hands about her neck. She could not get her breath."

"That is rediculous! She was masterful with me, Kendall. I was having an amazing experience. All of a sudden she was on her feet looking at me."

"You get dressed. I'll meet you in the salon."

Kendall spoke again with the woman. "Tell me exactly what happened." She repeated her story with more detail.

"He doesn't remember a thing about choking you." Kendall left a sizeable bill on the table. He knew the event would not leave the salon.

When the boys left London, Radcliffe had a firm commitment from Sir Alfred. On a return to London latter in the summer a formal announcement would be made of his engagement to Diana..

Chapter Nine

"Well, Mrs. Esterham, you selected the right day. It is beautiful! The sun is out brightly and we are warm. All seems in readiness for our big day." Mrs. Roche's expressed joy was due in large measure to the return of her sons. The boy's arrival only two days previously had been a welcome surprise and they shared with their mother the enjoyment of their trip. A laugh was spontaneous as each told about their experiences with the highwaymen. "Damn those men," Kendall summarized. "They made you, mother, pay for our horses after all."

"Yes, and they will probably enjoy our hospitality by arriving today for our carnival," Radcliffe broke in. "Well, if they do I'll be alert. Give them credit, though. They had the last laugh."

"First guests are arriving," warned Mrs. Esterham. A few wagons, buggies, carts and a carriage were forming a line in the parking area at the edge of the meadow. Other vehicles were approaching on the manor lane.

A carnival troupe had appeared the previous day and organized their equipment between the abbey and the river. Their living quarters had been set up along the river, fireplaces formed of rocks sending up whiffs of smoke and temporary clothes lines flew a few dish towels in the gentle breeze. Animals were penned, ready for the children's entertainment.

"I am glad for our young people. A warm day means they can go in the river. Did you go wadding as a child, Mrs. Esterham?"

"Oh, yes, Mrs. Roche. "That was one of the delights of summer. Here comes the Willowby wagon full of kegs."

Willowby guided his horses expertly to park his wagon near the carnival. He had it figured that most of the people would spend a good part of their time there, and the day being warm, he would be ready to dispense quantities of ale. The more the better. Mrs. Roche would pay him by the keg and party day always meant a good take.

Kendall appeared at his mother's side. "I just talked to the manager of the theater group. They will present a play early this afternoon and in the late afternoon. He wants to use the great hall. I think that will be fine, better than making a presentation in the abbey with people milling about and the carnival being so close. Since there will be no rain we will serve all the food outside and let them have the hall. What do you think?"

"That is fine with me, son. How think you, Mrs. Esterham?"

"I would everyone eat outside. The inside will be easier to clean tomorrow. That means we need to serve between twelve and three."

Radcliffe met with the gypsy lady and they decided to place her booth near the flower garden, the quietest part of the area assigned to the day's activities. As her husband and son put her moveable house together, Madame Zorkina inquired if Radcliffe was the son of the house. Learning that he was, she invited him to have his fortune told. "A wise man rules his fortune. I can tell you enough so that you can be a wise man."

Radcliffe entered the booth prepared for a bit of sport. He chose card reading, shuffling as she directed, and making three piles. He watched her as she sat opposite, eyes closed as if in a trance, quietly preparing herself. When she opened them to look into his eyes he wanted to laugh. She picked up the deck revealing his past and quickly analyzed the cards. She did the deck revealing his current history. "You are happy and sad, no, worried. You are successful in your work and that brings you pleasure, but you are not successful in love." She studied the cards one by one, moved them about to different locations then looked at him. "Sometimes the cards wont tell me all I seek, but they tell me you have an illness. It appears only at times. I cannot tell when. Is it when you make love? Don't answer me. I don't want to know. You know. That is enough."

He stared in disbelief, no longer wanting to laugh.

She picked up the deck of the future. She spread the pile of cards on the table, studied them, changing the position of some to form a variety of geometric designs "Mmmmmm. Interesting. You are preparing to make a change in your life. It is a change in business. But you are not sure what you want to do. There is something that holds you back. A girl. You are not sure about her. You will have girls seeking your heart. Be careful. It appears you will have problems. Love or is it the lack of it. That may be a problem. Or is it money? No. It will be . . . . .do I see scars, perhaps some blemishes on the skin? You will make a decision. You will choose one girl. I see a big party. Yes. Is it a wedding party? I cannot tell." She remained quiet as she studied other cards. "There is something strange here. I cannot make it out. I see you with a girl. Is it a fight? Are you fighting over a girl? She picked up one from the table and waved it, flipping it in front of him. "I see a gun but I cannot tell who has it. Is it in your hands? You must be careful of a gun. It will mean serious trouble for you. There is blood."

The sport Radcliffe intended to have with the reading did not materialize. He was astounded by the violence in his future. "Can you tell me why there is a gun? Perhaps I can prevent blood spilling if I know the circumstances surrounding the gun."

After studying the card again, the gypsy admitted, "It is not clear. I think there has been a murder, but I do not want to say. It is best you stay away from a gun. You have my warning. Remember, a wise man rules his stars."

Radcliffe stared at the single card still in her hand. When he rose he placed coins in a dish whose location she identified with a sweep of her hand.

By noon more than three hundred persons were enjoying the Roche's hospitality with the carnival theme being to everyone's liking. A dancing bear attracted much attention and children and adults alike laughed at the antics of a monkey. He leaped on people, doffed his hat and performed a variety of tricks. Chief source of revelry was the carnival itself with its rides, games, and special features, all free, all in constant use.

Squire Gunning arrived with Carinna and Flora. Kendall watched both alight from their buggy and he was instantly at their sides. He gave greeting to all then properly asked Squire's permission to escort Carinna for the day. The two bounced off gleefully leaving Flora to search for Radcliffe.

Nothing had yet been said of Radcliffe's engagement plans except to his mother. They had agreed to keep this development a family secret for the time being. She was surprised, however, at her sons's association with Sir Alfred Isham and his family. Radcliffe reviewed in detail the benefits that would accrue to him by a union with Diana as well as the values to Rochedale estate. Mrs. Roche was more conservative in her evaluation since she would prefer having her son at home. She asked for time to think about his plans. Meantime they all concurred that these unexpected developments from the London trip should not be made public, at least for the present.

Radcliffe watched Carinna place her arm in Kendall's as the two headed across the meadow for the carnival attractions. While he could no longer pursue a courtship with Carinna, there was Flora to enjoy. "She may be the more interesting anyway," he concluded, "and Diana would not mind my friendship with her on such a day."

"You are thinking about me, Radciffe Roche." A voice was at his shoulder and he turned to face Flora.

"I was indeed." He smiled in greeting. The girl looked fetching in her light colored frock brightened by ribbons passing through eyelets about the collar and waist. A matching ribbon tied her hair into a tail down her back. She was enough to make him forget Diana. "Aren't you going to ask permission to be my escort for the day?"

Her coyness left him without a way to say no. "Do you know I was looking about the meadow for you? Shall we go?"

She slipped her arm through his immediately and directed him toward the carnival. She strutted as if she had conquered the world and spoke to everyone, friends and strangers alike, letting them know she was being escorted by the heir to Rochedale Manor. "This will cause some tongues to wag," she gloated to herself, but more important, it put Radcliffe on record as preferring her above all girls, including Carinna.

Constable Ormand came into view. He stepped up to Radcliffe, nodded to Flora, and said, "I shall want to speak to you. I am continuing my study of Emma's murder. I delayed meeting with you since your return because I knew you were involved with all this, but I shall come calling."

"Please do, constable. I'll be glad to speak to you."

When he disappeared into the crowd, Flora looked at Radcliffe with a concerned expression. "Is he going to charge you? Why the idea. If he does I'll tell him what I know. Emma told me who was coming that day. But she made me swear it as a sacred trust. I wont hold it as a trust if he bothers you."

"If you know something, you should tell the constable. He has to solve Emma's murder."

At that moment the monkey leaped onto Radcliffe's arm. Fortunately he had a brief warning and caught the animal squarely. The crowd following the monkey's antics had a jolly laugh over the adventure particularly when Radcliffe played too roughly with it and received an angry show of teeth in reply. Flora took the little fellow and soothed it with gentle strokes and comforting words.

"I shall wager a farthing I can best you at darts," the young man challenged.

"You are on for one shilling. Show your money," she threw back the challenge.

The dart booth was operated as a fund raiser for charity by the men of Tosten, five throws a shilling. Being a popular sport, darts commanded a large audience, mostly among men, who played the game in all seriousness. Flora tossed first and surprised everyone with a score Radcliffe did not better and he took a good natured ribbing from the onlookers. Her score was posted on a chart for women and to that moment it led the rest.

"Now see here, Flora. You are an expert at darts. Not only do you win a shilling from me, but you stand to win a pound if your score holds up. Wherever did you develop such a good eye?"

"I play with father and you know how exacting he is. He makes sure I learn all the skills and he sees to it that I practice."

The loud clang, clang of a noisily clashing gong attracted their attention. They approached an area where a man was gathering an audience before his booth which was designed as a theater.

Children were being seated on the ground in a semicircle while adults stood behind. Their gleeful chatter waned to silence the instant curtains parted and marionettes appeared to begin their captivating performance. The story of a beautiful princess imprisoned in a castle by a dreadful dragon enchanted the audience, and the prince who saved her was shouted on to victory by loud cheers from everyone.

"That princess got her man, now how about learning if you will get yours," Radcliffe quipped. "What do you say to your fortune? Mother asked the gypsy woman down the river to do some reading. Game?"

"Of course. But don't tell father. He doesn't think much of soothsayers and less about gypsies."

After a wait, Flora entered the booth. She chose cards for her reading, but because of the number of people interested in her skills, the gypsy was telling only the future, nothing of the past or present. "You will continue to seek romance, but you are seeking also wealth with it. Be careful. You have a dark card. The dark card tells me you will have problems with your romance."

Wide eyed, Flora asked, "What kind of problems?"

"It is not clear but I see you fainting, no, more than fainting. There are hands on your neck. Be very careful of the man you choose for romancing."

Flora was shocked at the gypsy's accuracy, but it wasn't the future that was being related to her. It was the past. Flora recalled instantly the hands Radcliffe put on her neck and the scarf she had to use to cover the blemish. "The card that reported all that must have gone into the wrong pile," she thought.

"This card gives me a warning about you," the gypsy continued. "You have some information someone wants. The card says do not tell. Keep your secret. There will be trouble if you tell, trouble from someone you don't suspect. That is all I can tell you." The gypsy paused. "No, wait. What is this showing?" Study of a card continued. "Oh, here is something. I see a journey. A journey for you? I cannot be sure, but there is a journey. It will not be a good one. Be careful of it. During the journey or after it you will be in danger."

"When is the journey?"

The gypsy traced the card with her forefinger then raised it to her breast. "It will be within four to six weeks, perhaps. For your safety, don't go."

Flora rose and left the booth. "What is it?" Radcliffe placed his hands on her shoulder and looked into her face. "You are pale. Are you feeling well?"

"I am alright. Only a little weak. Let's sit down in the garden for a moment." She took him by the arm and clenched it tightly. "She frightened me. Do you think she knows the future?"

He brushed a kiss across her forehead.. "Now don't be upset. If she did she would be running the world. Do you realize what a line of people would be outside her booth if she could tell the future. She's part of the carnival to provide entertainment for our guests. Don't take whatever she told you so seriously. Didn't she tell you anything happy that would please you?"

"No. What did she tell you?"

"That I am successful, but that I should be alert to a gun accident." He paused a moment. "Now that is a good example of a gypsy's prediction for the future. How many people use guns and how many gun accidents are there? Anyone who handles guns can have an accident. These fortune tellers always speak in broad statements, never in specifics. Don't worry about it. Let's have some ale then join the dancers."

Just starting as Carinna and Kendall approached the carnival area was a performance of trained dogs, a motley crew of mixed breeds of various sizes. On command they jumped through hoops, did somersaults, walked first on front legs then hind legs, formed pyramids, played dead, "counted" objects, leaped over barrels and received jubilant applause for all their tricks.

More challenging was a presentation by a magic specialist. The man was clever in making objects disappear, producing articles from incredulous locations, and changing the colors of pieces of cloth. He asked Carinna to assist him in some of his capers and willingly she climbed onto his platform. He drew a bird from her hair, an egg from her hand and a string of beads from her neck. She laughed excitedly with each prank and won accolades from the audience for her participation. She was pleased, for all could see Kendall assist her down from the platform and he gave her a big hug for her sportsmanship.

Just beyond was a snake charmer holding his spectators in awe. His reptiles were exotic specimens, caged until ready to show. He had children from the audience volunteer to assist and they were entranced when the snakes entwined themselves around their arms and legs. The serpents were foreign to England and created more interest when they were placed on exhibit.

Three lively acrobats were uproarious as they performed, yelling commands, shouting cadence, emitting grunts and shouting in satisfaction when they completed a feat. Dressed in outlandish clown suits, they attracted a large gallery and were not disappointed as they leaped, danced, skipped, vaulted and gamboled through various routines.

"I must get you to the archery field," Kendall alerted himself. "Will you come with me?"

Competition was scheduled for one o'clock. "I haven't pulled a bow string in months but I am going to enter. Will you support me?"

"Of course, Kendall. Anyhow, you should. It is your party and the men need to see you taking part in the competition."

A long line of contestants waited for the action to begin, for several prizes were worth their efforts: yearling calves and lambs from choice Rochedale herds. A row of targets placed on bales of hay was set up one hundred feet beyond the archers. Kendall had seen to it earlier that bows and arrows were made available, but most competitors brought their own. The judges had determined that half the competitors in each round would be eliminated, that five arrows would be shot with the best and poorest being cast out and that a score would be based on the middle three efforts. It was obvious from the beginning that archer experts were numerous, some men having practiced all year intent on a prestigious victory. The winner was considered by all concerned to be the best archer in North Riding.

Kendall reached the second round. "You are very good," Carinna complimented him. "With practice you could compete with the best of them."

"I need an ale after that. How about you? Then I must see to the serving. Will you go with me?"

The excellent weather made serving the large number of guests very easy. Mrs. Esterham's crew of women had worked diligently preparing for the event and under her skillful direction all was ready. Buffet tables were arranged at the corner of the house near the kitchen and she told guests they had two responsibilities, "Bring your own plates and forks and eat to your full."

Kendall was shooed away when he asked to help, but it was obvious he was not needed. Ladies had placed on tables quantities of mutton, beef, meat pies, a variety of vegetables, piles of fresh bread, and collections of scones, biscuits and cakes. No one would leave hungry.

The two chatted as they awaited their turns. He held her hand and looked down at her attractive face. "You haven't told me you would accept me, Carinna." She caught the seriousness of his statement.

"Ah, but you have not asked father if you could speak to me."

"Is it necessary to be so formal?"

"Let's hear what the gypsy says." She pleaded, putting an end to his pursuit. The two waited their turn then she entered, leaving him to talk to others in line.

Carinna chose to have her palm read. "You have strong lines, easy to read, and this one tells me you are happy in the pursuit of marriage. But you are not aware of a problem. This line crosses the marriage line to tell me that all is not well, perhaps competition for you. Is there a girl who is trying to take your man from you? Ah. You don't know. I advise you to beware."

The gypsy became silent to continue her study. "Are there two men who interest you? You could make the wrong decision in deciding on a choice. Select the one where the heart is. But heed my warning. You stand to lose all if you make the wrong decision."

Tracing another line, she said, "I see a journey. A journey for you? I cannot be sure but there is a journey for you or for someone close to you. It will not be a good one. Be careful of it. During the journey or after it you will experience sorrow."

Carinna was thoughtful when she looked at Kendall outside the booth. "What is it?" he asked placing an arm on her shoulder.

"She told me something that is bothersome. I'll be fine. She is waiting for you."

Since Kendall had not talked to the gypsy during preparations for the party, she did not know him. "Your lines tell me you are a happy person by nature. Good lines. You enjoy life. You take life as it comes. I don't think you know you have a problem. But you have some." She drew some figures on his palm with her forefinger then commented, "I advise you not to make a quick decision about marriage. There is something developing now, something you are not aware of. When you know what it is, think carefully about it before taking action. Your whole life will be affected by your decision."

She studied further. "This line bothers me. It is warning me but all I can see is trouble. Someone will get you into trouble. You know the person but I am not able to tell you the trouble. A relative? I am not sure. It is to happen before long. You cannot prevent it."

He put some coins in her dish when he left. "Well that was interesting," he commented when he met Carinna. "Someone is going to get me in trouble and there is something brewing about my marriage. What are you up to?"

"You don't seem to be bothered by what she told you."

"No, but you were. You look better now. Whatever she told you, it was upsetting."

"She said something about a decision for me."

"I bet she didn't tell you exactly what decision to make."

"No."

"Of course not. It is always something general, but she is safe in saying it. Every person has problems, decisions to make, dangers to face, and young people face difficulties in marriage. So she talks about the truths of life and she catches all of us. It is entertainment." He patted her hand.

"Speaking of entertainment, I would like to see the play." Carinna's suggestion piqued Kendall's interest. "Let's do. By the time we eat, the second presentation will be starting."

When they served themselves Carinna and Kendall joined Flora and Radcliffe in the shadows of the abbey, for the direct sun was still warm and the breezes were cooler in the shade. Radcliffe had to hurry his meal since he was making awards to winners of several competitions. He invited Carinna to join him and Kendall was surprised by her instant acceptance. "Meet us in the gallery for the play," Kendall called out.

After the two departed Flora begged Kendall to talk about his London trip. "Especially the plays. I think I would be dazzling to act on a stage and receive applause."

Kendall described a farce he attended at the Savoy Theater and to entertain Flora, he embellished the plot, glamorized the actresses, and was fanciful about the audience, especially the tributes of flowers and shouts of approval paid to the leading actress. She was enthralled by the description.

In his usual accomplished style, Radcliffe presented prizes to winners for archery, darts and bowling and was thanked in return by the men's club chairman on behalf of everyone present for providing so much pleasure on another party day at Rochedale Manor.

"Radcliffe, you are so masterful in front of a crowd. You speak so well and know just the right words to say." She looked up into his face. "You have made this a wonderful day for everyone." Carinna was vibrant in her compliments. "It is a joy having you home again. Did you like London?"

"Oh, yes. There was so much to do, so much going on, and people were very gracious to us. Kendall and I were included in so many socials and activities."

"We missed you and you haven't called on us at Compton Health since your return."

"Forgive me for being negligent, Carinna. With all the catching up to do after the long absence, and the details to care for in presenting the party, I haven't had much time for myself. You do understand?"

"Indeed I do, but when this day of over, I shall expect your call. You do remember you spoke to father?"

The reminder of his obligation to Carinna struck him with guilt, for it was this very duty that had kept him from Compton Heath. "But how can I call on her when I am avowed to Diana," he pondered to himself.

Carinna appeared lovely to him, the white frock giving her freshness and the sun brightening her face with a sweet glow of youth. Her eyes glistened at him, questioning. He could not refrain from touching her chin and lifting her face upward. He kissed her gently. "I shall be at Compton Heath."

Carinna was stimulated by his impulsive expression of affection. "It is so unlike Radcliffe to give way to his emotions, particularly when people are near," she noted to herself. "I am sure of his love for me." She slipped her arm though his and they started toward the house. Radclliffe's closeness caused her to think again of her choices, and at this moment she was drawn to Radcliffe. "On a day such as this, I want to be Mrs. Radcliffe Roche. If he should ask me now, I would say yes." She entered the great hall pretending she was mistress of Rochedale.

The most dominant feature of Rochedale Manor was the great hall, a huge room adapted from the dormitory of the old abbey. Rising through two stories it had been enhanced in the last century by a magnificent hammer beam ceiling of finely carved natural oak. The walls were of squared and polished granite stones covered in part by Flemish tapestries, and surrounding the gothic fireplace were mountings of swords and shields, some dating from the War of the Roses. Oriental carpets covered the floor. Sofas, chairs and other furnishings had been moved to the wall to permit the majority of the audience to sit on the floor.

At a mezzanine level on the south wall was a gallery, a protruding, carved wood platform which was used by musicians. Here had gathered Flora and Carinna, Radcliffe and Kendall.

The troupe had curtained off a small portion of the room to provide a dressing area and a stage where a few props were placed to suggest a scene. A man in a long, loose robe faced the audience and announced that the troupe would present a shortened version of MACBETH, a play by William Shakespeare. He gave a brief synopsis.

Three women made up as hags entered the stage. One stirred the contents of a caldron.

To the last child there was silence, faces wrapped in wonder, for most of the audience was viewing their first play.

Macbeth! Beware Macduff;
Beware the Thane of Fife.
Be bloody, bold and resolute; laugh to scorn
 The pow'r of men, for none of women born
Shall harm Macbeth.
Macbeth shall never vanquished be until
Great Birnam wood to high Dunsinane Hill
 Shall come against him.

As the play unfolded the audience began to see a relationship between the words of the gypsy and the fate of the main characters in the play. The witches were like fortune tellers. Many of those who had a reading from the gypsy wondered about the words she told them of their futures, particularly the four in the gallery. "Can it be the gypsy knows?"

The murder of Duncan renewed anxieties for some in the audience, particularly parents, since Emma and Otley's deaths had not been solved, and many of the safeguards the constable suggested for the protection of young people, although still in effect, had been relaxed. Furthermore they knew the constable had no leads to identify the murderer.

The play ended to generous applause. The four young people went to the food tables for sweets and sat on the edge of the meadow to enjoy their repast together. The sun was low and already many guests, particularly those who lived at a distance, had left. The carnival was being dismantled, ready for early departure in the morning and Mr. Willowby's ale cart was gone.

"I never should have gone to that gypsy. Of all the happy activities here today, I should be leaving with gladness in my heart, but I am not. I blame that gypsy." Carinna's tone was angry. "I see she is gone. I think if she were still here I would be tempted to tell her."

"Careful, my dear," Kendall laughed. "In the telling you may reveal to us what she told you."

"Oh, I can't do that. What she said involves us." Instantly she saw her error and put her hand over her mouth. The rest laughed.

"Come now, Carinna," Radcliffe urged. "You have told us part now tell us the rest."

Flora interrupted. "I'll tell you, at least a bit. The gypsy said I seek romance and wealth." She cast a longing glance at Ratcliffe.

"Well, do you get it?"

"That is the part I can't tell." Flora covered the fact that the gypsy did not comment on the success of her effort.

A Strangeness

Squire Gunning appeared. "I have paid my respects to your mother, Radcliffe, Kendall. Girls you run and do the same. Meet me at the buggy immediately."

By night fall all was quiet. Clean up would take place the next day. The boys sat with their mother discussing the day, pleased that all went so well.

"I am afraid the gypsy caused too much concern." Mrs. Roche did not look pleased. "Some of the ladies were especially critical and the vicar agreed with them."

"I for one liked the idea, mother." Kendall gave her support as usual. "The gypsy probably told them something that touched them too closely. Did you go for a reading?"

"No. I was too busy with guests." Mrs. Roche thought it wiser not to tell of her prior meeting. Looking more disturbed she added, "Constable Ormand told me he would be stopping in to talk to both of you."

In the silence of her bedroom, Mrs. Roche's thoughts were not on the joys of the day that had brightened the hearts of her numerous guests. Rather they recalled the words of Lady Macbeth:

My hands are of your color, but I shame
To wear a heart so white.
What, will these hands ne'er be clean?
Here's the smell of blood still.
All the perfumes of Arabia will not
Sweeten this little hand.

In horror she sat on the edge of her bed thinking of Otley and looking at her hands, palms up, trying to shed the memory of those moments in the abbey.

Chapter Ten

"I have decided to accept Radcliffe when he asks me to marry him." Carinna made the announcement to her father and sister as they sat around the supper table.

The remark caused Flora to halt her fork in disbelief. It had been weeks since Radcliffe had spoken to her father for permission to see Carinna and he had not been to the house since. She assumed his absence meant he had reconsidered his intentions toward Carinna and that she herself had replaced her sister in his affections. "After all," she concluded privily, "he did spend most of party day time with me. He held my hand and kissed me." Aloud she challenged, "Why, Carinna, I thought it was Kendall who took your interest."

Knowing she had the upper hand, Carinna glanced at her sister a moment then smiled sedately. "Kendall is a dear boy, full of life and a charmer, but it is Radcliffe who has the characteristics I seek in a man."

"I believe you have made a wise choice, my dear," her father smiled in support. "I am pleased. And if you do as well, Flora, I shall be equally assured that both my girls will be well cared for. When may I expect his request for your hand, Carinna?"

Squire Gunning had expected Carinna's announcement, only he supposed it would have come sooner. Of course Radcliffe was shy when it came to girls, he had recognized, and some concern had developed when the young man did not visit Carinna after he gave him permission to speak to his daughter. But there were the facts that he did go to London for a prolonged visit and preparation for party day did take his time.

"It should be very shortly, father. I saw Radcliffe only yesterday on the lane. We just happened to meet and he said he would be visiting Compton Heath Saturday afternoon. I invited him for tea."

Flora returned her fork to the plate and with great effort held her composure. Suddenly she lost all appetite and wanted to leave the room. She knew better than that, however. Her father never permitted such a violation of etiquette and the act would reveal instantly her alarm and invite a scene. Instead she struggled with herself and made the comment expected of her. "Carinna, I am so happy for you. Have you thought about a date for the wedding?"

Squire interrupted. "It will not be immediately. We shall be proper with at least a six month engagement and the banns must be read appropriately. Remind Radcliffe of propriety when he asks you. It would be just like him to want to marry post haste."

"Of course you will wear mother's wedding gown." Flora forced herself to appear excited, but her father's comment about a six month engagement took her concentration and she did not hear her sister's reply. Six months gave her some working time and instantly she considered how to use it. She became aware of her father's voice speaking an admonition to her.

"After tea on Saturday, Flora, see to it you take a polite leave of Carinna and Radcliffe. It is well we give him an opportunity to be alone with your sister. I would like this settled on Saturday, Carinna. Too much time taken to make a few decisions will give other girls a chance to catch his fancy."

Radcliffe let his concerns consume his thoughts while he sat erect on his horse, giving his steed freedom to walk leisurely on the path to Moncton Tor. When he reached the summit he dismounted and walked among the boulders. He was aware of noises and subconsciously identified them as horses hooves on rocks. He remained stationary, listened intensely, then peered around a rock to see who was coming. He saw Flora.

She dismounted and walked to a part of the summit that presented an unbroken view of the landscape below. The rains of yesterday had cleared the air so that objects in the far distance stood in sharp relief. She waited, pretending to enjoy the magnificent scene, but she was alert for footsteps she knew would tell her of his approach.

Flora had been sent on an errand by her father and was returning home by the River Dale lane when she spied Radcliffe. Recognizing that he was walking his horse rather than hurrying, she knew instantly that he was not on business. She followed at a distance, crossing her fingers, hoping he would take the cutoff to Moncton Tor.

"Flora. How nice to see you. You on Moncton Tor is a delightful surprise."

She swung around, brightening her smile, and with joy in her voice she beamed, "Why, Radciffe. It is you who surprises me." She took his hand and pulled it to her breast. The action drew him to her.

"I was just thinking about you," he confessed. He did not intend to say that but the look she gave him was captivating.

"I am pleased, Radcliffe. I want you to think about me often. You are in my thoughts constantly. What do you think of when you think about me?"

"This!" He could not help himself. The taunting eyes compelled him to pull her close to him, crushing her body against his, and she molded her curves into his. Her head fell backwards. He kissed her passionately. She fought to hold her lips on his, pressing, prolonging. She roamed her hands around his back then down his sides. He had to end his kiss to catch his breath.

She grabbed his hand and led him a distance to the cavern entrance. She pulled him down and he followed her inside. "Strange," he thought. "I have seen the opening for years but never thought to look inside."

Flora had known about the interior for years and recently she saw Kendall and Carinna enter the cave. She knew what went on inside. She had watched as much as she could through the opening. It was enough. Now she was inside with Radcliffe. She would do what she had seen those two do.

She drew Radcliffe to her, took his hands, guided them over her curves, stopping to release catches. In no time she was disrobed. She helped him divest his clothes then flung herself at him, placing her breasts in front of him and pressing his face into them. She continued to arouse him by running her hands about his person, down his back, along his sides and over his chest. He followed in kind. Gently she lay down and pulled him with her, placing herself beneath him. Completely aroused, he found her, she helped him couple. Together they became as one. His eyes became glassy as he enjoyed their togetherness and he felt the beginnings of a head pain. His hands crawled upward, over her breasts and onto her neck. Instantly she grabbed his wrists and with great effort forced his hands to her sides as she continued to gyrate her body to his fulfillment.

As they lay next to each other in silence, he kissed her. It was the first time he had demonstrated so completely his manliness.

"You were marvelous, Radcliffe. You make me very happy. We could have this enjoyment forever, just you and I, as man and wife."

She allowed the force of her statement to linger, then she spoke softly, "Kiss me then take your leave."

"Strange," Radcliffe considered as he rode alone down the hill, "the pain in my head began when I loved Flora. I can't recall what happened after that but I feel fine now. She said I made her happy, that I was good, good as a man!" The realization that he must have performed well pleased him and he felt encouraged, proud, especially that Flora paid him such a compliment. He started to sing a tune. He broke it off when a new thought came to mind. "She said we could have the same enjoyment forever, that we could be man and wife. Maybe she is the one for me. She makes me feel good that I am a man, that I can perform as a man." Singing started again. He sang the rest of the way home.

Flora mounted her horse feeling confident that the unexpected development had aided her plan. "This is the best thing that could have happened. Being Mrs. Roche is in my future."

Saturday turned wet and cold. Heavy clouds formed rapidly and by noon rain was pelting down. A strong wind whipped trees and rippled meadows. Radcliffe preferred to stay home but he had made a commitment and he was prepared to keep it. Bonnie greeted him in the stable, but even she decided the rain was too heavy to venture out.

By the time he arrived at Compton Heath he was well soaked. A fire was warming the sitting room and he stood before it continuing to dry out. The housekeeper had removed his coat and shirt and he had toweled himself well, but his pants were still damp. The robe squire had loaned him was small, making it difficult to keep it closed about his large frame.

Tea was served but Carinna encouraged him to remain standing by the fire. It was awkward drinking and eating the small sandwiches but he managed. "I have not had adequate opportunity, Squire, to thank you for preparing me so well for meeting our London agents. Because of your generous help I was able to question intelligently and discuss pertinent issues with considerable aplomb. In fact, I made a noticeable impression on Mr. Ross and received his compliments."

"It was my pleasure to help you, my boy. I assure you I am ready to assist you in any manner." He cleared his throat, testing the attention of his daughters to the praise just awarded him.

"Do you intend to go to the York meet this year, Squire"

Gunning talked about possibly attending the York racing meet scheduled for the first part of October. "I am registered to participate but I am having trouble selecting the two horses I agreed to enter." The two men discussed horses for a time them Gunning departed.

Graciously Flora found an excuse to leave.

"I did not ask your father, Carinna, but do you plan to go to York with him?"

"He has not discussed York with us. I would like to go but he does not approve of all the social life. Will you be going?"

"Kendall wants to go and you know tradition. We have never missed a meet. Mother says no to his encouragement, but I have a notion she will go. I shall go, too. I do need to return to London before long, however. Probably before York."

"To London? Already!"

"Yes. I have a very fine offer for a business position. I am interested in it."

"Does that mean you will be working in London and not living at Rochedale Manor?"

"Probably." Radcliffe was seeking a way to take leave without approaching the subject of his courtship with Diana, but he had not found a way. He sat down on the love seat next to her. As he did so his wrap opened exposing his bare chest. Immediately he was embarrassed and tried to cover himself but the robe was too small to stretch across his person.

Gently Carinna put her hand on his bare skin. "That is no matter. Stay." She had made up her mind that if he did not express himself at this meeting she would take the initiative. She moved her hand across the curly mat of hair on his chest and let it rest on his right breast. Playfully she manipulated a nipple. She did not know what to expect either from herself or from him. Her experience with Kendall gave her some background but with him she followed his lead. Now she was the aggressor.

He stared at her in disbelief. "Carinna. Sweet, gentle Carinna. What has besieged you?" He murmured as a shudder passed through his body. He placed a palm at the back of her head and drew her to him. Instead of taking his kiss as he intended, she lowered her head and directed her lips onto his breast, her tongue taking the place of her fingers. He felt he was being possessed by this angel who had in a passing moment become a demon. "Carinna! Carinna! You must be mine! Forever! Forever!! He felt the beginnings of a head pain.

She heard his words and stopped her aggressiveness. She looked into his eyes, now glassy, and mumbled softly, "Yes, Radcliffe, forever."

She rose, walked to the fireplace and poked the embers until they reddened, tossed a log onto the heap and stared at the flames until they took hold. Her face had a determined look. "Like the flames, I won." she thought. "I have his commitment. I am the new Mrs. Roche."

She turned to face him. He rested as he was, still in ecstacy from her unexpected treatment, eyes now closed, his chest still bared.

Carinna went to the sofa silently, approached him from the end where his head rested on the upholstered arm, and gave him a kiss. His eyes opened. He looked surprised. For a moment he was not aware of his location. He sat up instantly, became cognizant of his appearance and tried to cover his chest. "Forgive me, Carinna, if I offend you. I regret this unseemliness."

His comments puzzled her, but she said quietly, "I understand. It is alright. I shall get your shirt and your coat from the drying room. When she returned he was standing before the fireplaced, his back to her, obviously embarrassed.

"May I have your leave to dress?"

She left the room. On her return he was groomed but appeared shamed. "I apologize for this accident. I trust you will forget it and let me return."

"There is no problem whatsoever. I shall expect you anytime. Please do return, tomorrow if you have time."

The rain had let up to a light drizzle by the time he reached the lane and in the approaching darkness he could see that skies were clearing. "I somehow got through that meeting without a scene. I just could not tell her about Diana. It was apparent she expected me to speak about an engagement, but fortunately she did not pressure me." He felt relieved but he knew the avoidance was only temporary. Until the time was right to announce his engagement to Diana, he would have to fulfill the demands of protocol and see Carinna again.

Mrs. Esterham intercepted Radcliffe as he entered the house. "Constable Ormand is here to see you. He is in the waiting room. Kendall is having brandy with him and has been keeping him company until your return. Your mother is in the study by herself."

"Good evening, Constable. Forgive my appearance. The rain and I had a very wet meeting. Would you please give me time to change?" He took more time than was necessary for he wanted to prepare himself for the coming discussion.

Kendall poured his brother a brandy and the constable began an interrogation with a few opening amenities. "Your party day was an outstanding success, Radcliffe, and I compliment you. The community is grateful to you, as you know, for continuing the long tradition and for providing so much pleasure. I am sure everyone recognizes all that is involved as well as the amount of organization necessary to put on such an event. It was particularly helpful to me for it brought the community together and helped push the murders to the background.

"They are not forgotten, however, and I must move forward on them. Radcliffe, tell me again about your actions the morning of Emma's murder."

Radcliffe's response was consistent with his former statements which emphasized that his activities had taken him far afield from the abbey.

"Now tell me about your actions leading to the discovery of Otley."

He reviewed his actions leading to the finding of the boy. He did not refer to his lapse of memory, however.

"Was Otley dead when you found him?"

"I think so but I cannot be absolutely sure of that."

"Mmmmm." The constable pondered a time then began again. "Kendall, tell me about your movements on the morning of Emma's death."

The young man retraced his activities consistent with his prior report.

"Did you go to the abbey?"

"No, sir, I did not."

"I have reports you were seen in the abbey."

"I am aware of that, constable, but those reports are incorrect."

"What proof do you have that you did not go to the abbey?"

"I have none. I doubt if anyone saw me after I left the house."

"Where did you go?"

"I went to Moncton Tor."

"Were you alone at the Tor?"

"Yes, sir."

The constable observed Kendall carefully during the questioning to any display of nervousness or hesitation. He could detect nothing. His responses were immediate and they were delivered in a matter of fact tone. He did not volunteer any facts, however. "Were you meeting someone there?"

"Carinna Gunning told me that if she could get away from Compton Heath she would go to the Tor. I was hoping to meet her there. It would be a chance meeting, but she did not arrive."

"What time did you return to the house?"

"Not until well after tea."

"Where did you go after you left the Tor."

"I went back to Stilliston Meadows."

The constable made a mental note to speak to both Carinna and Tenley about the veracity of Kendall's statements. "Your mother said she saw you in the meadow the morning of Emma's death."

"Mother told me she did. She said I had on my heavy coat. But, Constable, at no time that day did I wear that coat. It was hanging in the back entry where I leave it. Mother said she saw my back. She could have seen someone else. That coat is similar to coats worn by most farmers and herders in Yorkshire. She said she did not see the face of the man who wore the coat."

The constable recalled the details of Mrs. Roche's statements to him and Kendall was accurate in reiterating them. He had not revealed to the young men that other persons, those who passed through the abbey on the way to market, had reported they had seen Kendall in the meadow. They did say they did not see him in the abbey. He could not accuse Kendall of murder on the basis of people having seen him in the meadow."

Radcliffe listened to the questioning of his brother but could find no way to provide an alibi. He thought he detected in the constable's questioning and demeanor a hint that Kendall was being considered as the prime suspect.

"How well did you know Emma, Kendall?" the constable continued.

"I knew her very well. I frequently took packages to the Minshall home, packages cook prepared. The three of us talked often. At town socials we met and danced and talked. She was a nice girl, friendly, a pleasure to be with. She seemed older than fifteen, more mature for her age."

"Did you ever call at the Minshall home just to see her?"

"No, Constable."

"Were you ever alone with her?"

"Yes. A few times old John was not at home when I delivered cook's packages."

Ormand wanted to ask if Kendall knew her as a woman but reconsidered. "Not now," he cautioned himself. Instead he asked, "Have you seen or met her in the abbey at any time?"

"I may have seen her about the abbey. I don't recall but I never met her there."

"Did you see Otley the morning of his death?"

"Yes."

"Where?"

"On Moncton Tor."

"What was he doing?"

"I believe he was there to pass the time of day, but I can't say for sure. He could not tell me."

"What time did you see him there?"

"It was midmorning, I think."

"Did you bring him down with you?"

"No. I left him there."

"Why?"

"It did not occur to me to bring him down. I gave it no thought."

"Could he have walked from Moncton Tor to the abbey between the time you left him and the time Radcliffe found him?"

"I don't think so, Constable. Otley could not move very fast and it is some distance from the Tor. It would be faster coming down for most people but not for Otley."

"Are you telling me you think someone helped him down, possibly to the abbey?"

"I can't say that, Constable. It just seems to me he could not have made it to the abbey on his own without some help between the time I saw him and the time Radcliffe picked him up.

"Mmmmm," Ormand thought. To himself he added, "Kendall is tied somehow to both Emma and Otley. I don't have all the facts yet. He could have been the last person to see Otley alive. If he killed Emma he killed Otley, too. I agree with him, though. Someone brought Otley down from the Tor or at least some of the way down. Was it Kendall? The clue is in his relationship with Emma. If I knew that, I could complete the story."

Radcliffe looked at his brother. He saw no sign of concern on his face, but it was obvious that Ormand had about made up his mind on Kendall.

"Thank you, boys," the constable said as he rose. "If you think of anything be sure to tell me. I shall be talking with you again. Goodbye."

At supper her sons reported on the meeting with Ormand. Mrs. Roche was concerned for Kendall and asked him again, "Did you go to the abbey?"

"No, mother."

"That is what we shall have to prove," she sighed, "but how?"

Kendall rose. "Are you telling me I am about to be charged with Emma's murder?"

"No, Kendall," Radcliffe reassured him, "but I do believe the constable is looking for more evidence to involve you. He just doesn't have enough now."

"My word doesn't mean a thing."

"Oh, yes, it does!" Mrs. Roche was firm. "We must somehow find support for your words."

Carinna felt exultant. Her meeting with Radcliffe went better than expected. Her goal had been achieved. In his way he asked her to marry him. No, it was not in the manner she expected, but that was not important. What was important was his proposal. At their next meeting they would have to set a marriage date, select a honeymoon site and decide on the manner in which she would live in Rochedale Manor.

At supper Carinna made her announcement. "Radcliffe proposed to me and I accepted."

"My dear, I do congratulate you." Her father smiled broadly, his pleasure mounting.

"This calls for a brandy. Drink with me."

Flora was shocked but covered her surprise with some flowery words of congratulation. She accepted a small glass filled with brandy and joined her father in toasting her sister amid wishes for much happiness and long life. She watched her father kiss Carinna and she added her own seal with a peck on her forehead.

"What is your date" he inquired.

"We did not discuss that. I am aware of your wishes, however, and when Radcliffe returns to discuss details we shall allow at least six months from now, probably next spring."

Flora could barely hold her anger until she entered her room where she let go with expletives that would have infuriated her father, invectives that were reserved for the stables. "That man! That man!" Pillows flew across the room. "How could he select Carinna?"

After she had vented her anger, reason returned and slyly she set up her alternatives.

"I shall be a Roche. That much is definite. It is either Radcliffe or Kendall. I prefer Radcliffe. She does not have him yet. He is fair game until the ring is on her finger." She sat on the edge of her bed and reconsidered her plan, now modified because of their sharing in the cave, and listed her methods of attack.

Chapter Eleven

The annual October racing meet in York contained a tradition whose origin was lost in antiquity. People of the north country looked on it as a vehicle for enjoyment, socializing and horse competition, while for the host city it was a boon for the local economy. Although races were scheduled for three days, pre and post activities stretched celebrations to more than a week, but individual participants began preparations months and even years in advance.

Montague Gunning belonged to this group. To associates Squire said nothing about his plans for the York meet. To trainers he only gave directions but he supervised their work carefully. For himself, however, he evaluated horses with objectivity, selected only the most promising flesh for breeding, sometimes introducing new seed from proven stock owned by other stables, then he developed a program of training that would produce a winner at York. His horses had crossed the finish line first often enough to establish his entries as formidable participants, but more pleasing to him was the respect acknowledged by his neighbors and breeders in North Riding for his accomplishments. He paid for this recognition by not only spending excessive amounts of money, for cash awards at the track were nominal, but he gave time to his enterprises that could have been given to more lucrative adventures.

Neither Carinna nor Flora knew their father's plans for York since he did not discuss them, and for some years it was the middle of September before he told them they could attend with him. He did not participate in some meets if he thought he did not have a reasonable chance of winning, and he was known to have declared his entry or entries then withdrawn them just before meet time.

This year was one of doubt for Squire. He had two good horses, each a possible winner. He had paid entree fees on both, but neither was showing their original promise in late sprints.

Disappointment led to indecision. As it turned out, the deciding factor was Radcliffe's proposal to Carinna. Squire was fully aware that the Roches always attended the York meet. It was a tradition for them. They did not enter horses since they did not fancy raising racing flesh, but they did enjoy the competition, placing bets and especially attending social functions. "For Carinna's future I'll go," Squire finally concluded. "Radcliffe will escort her to socials, they will be together frequently and resulting therefrom he will want to set a wedding date. If I can't always win at horses, at least I can win some of the Roche wealth through my daughter."

In a rare instant he laughed aloud. "Think of it. My filly Carinna coming home a winner."

That evening he made an announcement to his daughters. "I have decided to enter two horses in the York meet and I believe both of you should attend. That means of course I must leave Compton Heath ahead of you to care for the various and sundries prior to the races and remain after the meet to see to some post racing business. That also means you need transportation to and from York as well as escorts while you are there.

"Carinna, I want you to invite Radcliffe to tea. I want you to explain to him that I shall have entries in the meet and that you and Flora will be attending. I want you to let him know that you will expect him to escort you to the socials." He paused.

"On second thought, the invitation should go to Kendall as well and, Flora, you must be present at tea. You will need an escort, too, and he is available." It was the first time he had spoken of his wishes for Flora. "It would be fine for me to have two Mrs. Roches. Furthermore, both of you will need transportation. Get a commitment out of them that they will take you there and bring you home."

The written invitation was received by the young men with mixed emotions. Kendall was pleased and showed it. "I enjoy going to Compton Heath. Carinna gets more beautiful by the day." He stared out the window of Radcliffe's room. "I do believe I will ask for her hand. Can you imagine being married to that one, holding such loveliness. I shall of course talk to mother about a marriage and then I shall have to speak to Squire. What a system. Before I speak to Carinna I must speak to my mother and then to her father. After all that suppose she doesn't want me."

Radcliffe heard only half of what his brother was saying. The invitation prompted him once more to consider the predicament caused by the London trip. He walked to the window and stared across the meadow to the abbey. "Before I took that trip to London, it was Carinna," he mused. "Then London gave me Diana. Now it is Flora who intrigues me. That one. She took me with conviction. But she did something else. She showed me I can perform." He smiled in satisfaction then his face turned more serious. He turned and faced his brother. "Kendall, I have been considering. I really should see Diana. I have been away from her too long, and you know what absence does to a young heart. I need to go to London. What would two or three weeks do to your plans?"

"Not a thing. If you left now you could be back in time for York. Go ahead. I am planning on Diana for a sister-in-law and I would not want to lose her. After all, once you take Diana you leave Carinna without competition from you."

"Very well, I shall speak to mother. And as for the invitation to Compton Heath, attend for me, too, and pay my respects." He relaxed a bit for finding a way to avoid meeting with Carrina. "But I ask that nothing be said about my purpose for going to London."

Kendall replied to the invitation at once, accepting for himself but including regrets for Radcliffe.

Consternation at Compton Heath was the immediate result. Squire saw his plans take a jolt, Carinna was devastated and Flora was miffed. She saw her chances for nabbing Radcliffe flounder for she knew she had to seek him actively after the cave episode. But a second thought calmed her. She saw Radcliffe's absence as an excellent opportunity to begin a pursuit of Kendall. She considered how she might do it.

Kendall prepared carefully for his visit. He bathed, brushed his hair vigorously, combed it with more than sufficient strokes and dressed in the riding habit he had purchased in London. He stood before his mirror, swagger stick in hand, assessing his efforts. Making some minor adjustments he assured himself he had done all he could to gain Carinna's favor. Radcliffe had all but cleared the way for him by chasing off to London. He mounted his horse feeling confident.

"Carinna is mine!" he shouted at a gallop. "She's mine!"

Kendall entered the drawing room, a bounce to his step and his face beaming. He was greeted warmly enough, but there was something lacking he was not immediately able to identify. "Radcliffe sends his regrets," he announced immediately. "The poor fellow had to go to London but he would much rather be here."

"He will return in time for York, I do hope." Carinna's statement was more of a begging question.

"Indeed he will. Are you attending?" Kendall's eyes went immediately to Squire Gunning.

"Yes, son." Kendall was taken back to the point of being shocked. Squire had never before used that word in addressing him. It was even stated, he thought he noted, with an inference of endearment. He looked at Carinna for a clue and interpreted her smile to mean she was looking favorably on him and concluded that her father approved of their match. He felt elated.

"I have decided finally to place in competition two of my horses. That means I will be going to York some days early and will remain some days following. I would like to ask if you and Radcliffe would take Carinna and Flora in your coach when you go and bring them home when you return."

"Why that would be a pleasure, Squire. A great pleasure." He had visions of escorting Carinna and of the numerous opportunities to demonstrate his desire for her. The thought of her being so close for so long was almost too much to comprehend. He grinned at her with a boyish appreciation.

The housekeeper rolled in a tea cart and Carinna presided. Squire volunteered some facts about his entries that prompted Kendlal to jibe, "Do they warrant some handsome wagers?"

"I would not have entered them if I did not believe they would come in." The comment was without humor. "But I do expect considerable competition. I have been informed that the overall quality of horses will be the best in years."

Squire found an excuse to depart giving Flora an encouraging nod as he left the room. She had her plan but it required Carinna's absence. If her sister did not leave him to her, she would leave.

The three talked for time, mainly about York. "Do you know on what day you will be leaving for the meet?" Carinna inquired, not really caring, more to make conversation. She still found Kendall attractive but she did not in any way want to compromise her relationship with Radcliffe. "Strange," she thought, "Why hasn't he commented on Radcliffe's proposal. Radcliffe certainly told him about us."

Kendall had been studying Carinna since her father left the room. He found her enchanting today, so feminine in her tea frock, and her hair seemed to have a delicious sheen as if set on fire by sunbeams coming through the windows. He wanted to put his hands on her but her sister's presence hindered that move.

Flora eyed them both. Since the day when she spied on them in the cave, she knew of his attachment for Carinna. It was this fact plus her own transgression with Radcliffe that so astonished her when she announced his proposal. There was something strange about that. Could her sister have made up the whole proposal story just to protect a first claim on Radcliffe? Possibly. "Why is it that Kendall hasn't spoken of the proposal? If he knew he certainly would have said something." A thought occurred to her and she stood, excused herself, and left the room. Carinna did not notice the door was not completely closed. Flora remained behind the door and observed the sofa.

Kendall could contain himself no longer. He stood, strode to the sofa and sat next to Carinna. Instantly he took her hand to his lips where he held it letting his tongue play on her skin.

The sensation created a tingle and she shivered. "Kendall," she admonished him. "You must not. I am bespoken."

Her statement stunned him. "You are what! Who?"

"Speak to your brother."

"My brother! That is impossible. Why he is al . . . . . . " Instantly he recalled the pact with his mother and Radcliffe to keep Diana a secret. "So that is it," he nodded to himself. "It had to be London.

Radcliffe had to see Diana. So he proposed to Carinna, kept it a secret, then hurried to London to salvage his business prospects."

He stood. "Very well, Carinna. Adieu." He strode out the door and was almost to the front door when he felt a hand on his arm restraining him.

"Please stay, Kendall." Flora looked up at him, her eyes pleading. She let her hand trail down his arm until it enfolded his. She led him to a sitting room and closed the door. He sat then she sat next to him. "It is obvious. You do not know. Radcliffe proposed to Carinna. She accepted him."

He looked at her, surprised and hurt. "Thank you for telling me." He wanted to say more but something cautioned him. He spoke as he rose, "I shall let you know when we plan to leave for York."

"Don't go. Compton Heath is always open to you and I am here. Please come in when you ride by. I enjoy your company, too."

"You are considerate, Flora."

"I would be happy to ride to Moncton Tor with you. Now. If you like."

He looked at her and wondered at her invitation. A smile was on her face as if she knew something.

"Thank you. That is not necessary. I shall speak to your father on the way out."

Events of the afternoon left Kendall puzzled, and he could not put the pieces together, try as he may. He let his horse have his rein, for the route home was well known, leaving himself free to concentrate on the bewildering facts. "There is something strange about all this. Why didn't Racliffe tell mother and me of his proposal? He knows my interest in her. I don't understand why he proposed to Carinna when he had already made a commitment to Diana. Did he go to London for the purpose of terminating that alliance? It isn't like Radcliffe to keep all decisions to himself. We have always talked openly.

"Strange, too, the way Carinna acted, as if she was hiding something. Could she feel guilty about our romp in the cave? She knows my love for her.

"Flora was too anxious to have me stay. She is aware of my interest in her sister and now she wants my attention.

"It looks like the Gunnings have a plot going. Radcliffe for Carinna, Kendall for Flora, and Squire asking us to escort them to York as a push for both. Not bad for him to have both Roches for his daughters. But I have no interest in Flora. This is all something to be straightened out when my brother comes home."

Flora watched Kendall pass through the gate. She was unhappy with herself for not being able to hold him. "It is because he was shocked by Carinna. Strange that. He could not have put on an act that well. He really did not know. Why didn't Radcliffe tell him? Perhaps he did not want to hurt his brother. He knows Kendall likes Carinna." She thought of the cave. "Well, Kendall is mine to take. But I wont wait until York to catch him." She watched him disappear down the lane.

The ride to London had given Radcliffe much time for contemplation. He weighed carefully all his options so by the time he arrived he knew exactly what he wanted and what needed to be done to get it. He had made up his mind that he would marry Diana. He established quarters and went immediately to the Isham house. "Strange, isn't it," he thought to himself as he waited for her in a small reception room, "how conflicts resolve themselves. They only have to be faced and decisions made. Kendall can marry Carrina, they will have the house and he can manage the estate. My future is in London."

Diana rushed into the room. He opened his arms and she fell into them. He kissed her gently first, then he raised his head and looked down on her, his eyes exploring her face. His lips fell on hers again, pressing violently, his ardor telling her he wanted to ravish her. "Oh, Radcliffe, you have been gone so long. I have missed you so," she mumbled through his lips.

When he set her free, he confessed, "You have never been out of my mind. I had to return just to see you, to hold you.,"

"When can we marry? Let's speak to father."

"Immediately."

"He will be home this evening. Stay. We shall have supper."

"Whatever you want, my beloved."

Sir Alfred expressed a friendly welcome, shaking Radcliffe's hand and calling him son.

Radcliffe was surprised at the warmness, but he was further astonished when over a supper brandy Sir Alfred asked, "When do you plan to be in London permanently? I have a position, an excellent position, arranged for you in the financial house of Barnes McCreedy. It wont wait indefinitely."

"I have given great thought to my move, sir, but I have hesitated making a decision until I know how this visit develops."

"If it is Diane you are wondering about, don't be concerned. You are all she talks about. Her mother and I are very pleased she chose you, and if agreeable, we can discuss an engagement announcement date and a wedding date. We are members of the established church."

"I am as well, sir. I would like to return home with both dates firmly set so I can make the necessary adjustments at Rochedale Manor."

Over supper the talk was light with Diana and Cecilia reporting on their social activities, affairs of the royal court and their plans for the remaining days of summer. "And you must join us for every party!" Diana pleaded.

"Nothing would please me more," Radcliffe smiled, "but I have a commitment with my family to attend the York racing meet, a tradition that has not been broken since the dark ages."

"Isn't that about the middle of October?" Sir Alfred asked.

"I recall that social activities begin the second week but horse racing is scheduled for the third week with more activities following."

"Mmmmmmm," Sir Alfred responded, tapping his cheek with his forefinger.

Before he said goodnight, Radcliffe had two dates. Diana asked for a spring wedding and she selected fifteenth of May with the ceremony to take place in St. Margarets next to Westminster Abbey. Their engagement announcement party would open the London social season in the spring.

Several small parties were organized quickly so Radcliffe could either renew acquaintances made during his first visit or meet for the first time more of Diana's friends and relatives.

The Duchess of Kensington was a frequent guest, and at each function she made it a point to converse with Racliffe about Kendall. "Of course he will be at York with you?" she inquired each time they met.

Feeling depressed over Carinna's engagement, Kendall took to riding at will across North Riding, going wherever fancy directed and frequently with no purpose at all. He had received two notes from Flora asking him to visit, but he had no interest in her and sent regrets citing the press of duties due to Radciffe's absent.

Flora did not take his refusals lightly. She had made up her mind she was to be Mrs. Roche and she was determined in her purpose.

Since her father's words of encouragement, she started a program of pursuit. Failing all else she had her threat, the statement Emma had given her. "One way or the other I shall be Mrs. Roche."

No, Radcliffe was not beyond her grasp but for the present he belonged to her sister.

"Failing Kendall, I have the cave hanging over him. My pregnancy will make him mine." She thought often of this possibility but preferred not using it. "It is there, however, just in case."

Flora remained alert. She saw Kendall riding his horse on two occasions and each time he was on Rochedale land. Purposely she watched for him and was not denied. She surprised him one afternoon walking his horse along the Dale. Bonnie was with him. "Why, Kendall! What a pleasant surprise." Her greeting was forced with charm and she noticed he was taken aback by her presence.

"Hello, Flora." His tone was flat. "You must be on an errand. Don't let me detain you."

She caught his rejection but ignored it. "For once I am riding just for pleasure. Aren't you?"

"Yes and no. I have a problem to resolve and I find that getting away and riding in the wild gives me a better chance to think."

"Father says that when you have a problem, talk it out. I have a good ear. You can respect my confidence."

"I am not ready to talk it out. I just want to be alone and do my own thinking."

Again his snub was recognized but deliberately she disregarded it. She dismounted and came to his side. She put her hand on his. "Kendall, I can help you. Let me." She squeezed her hand into his.

He withdrew it. "When I need your help, Flora, I shall seek it." He started to move on but her hand on his arm restrained him.

"We have always been friends. Why are you unfriendly now?"

"I don't intend to appear unfriendly, Flora. It is just that I want to be alone."

"It is Radcliffe's proposal to Carinna that has upset you. It was a surprise to me, too. I thought she was keen on you and I know you are keen on her." She ran her hand up and down his arm and looked directly in his eyes. "But you have me." Deliberately she stretched up on her toes and kissed him.

"I am not ready to think of anyone else."

His quick response, spoken with so much intensity, infuriated her. She believed she could beguile him easily since he was rebounding from the loss of Carinna and that he would fall into her arms. Her failure immediately was manifested in anger. Without thinking she vented her wrath. "Think twice about me, Mr. Kendall. I know who Emma was expecting to see in the abbey the morning of her murder."

He stared at her in amazement. "What is that supposed to mean?" His eyes drilled her with sharp intensity as he spoke with rancor.

Recovering from her own astonishment at making such a statement, she added quickly, "It is a secret I had with Emma. She swore me to secrecy. It will never be told. I hold it as a sacred trust."

"Then I shall tell Constable Ormand you have information about Emma. He is looking for anything that will contribute to solving her murder. Come, let us go to him. Now!"

"No, Kendall, it is of no importance. Will you see me home? I do not always feel safe when I think of what happened to Emma."

Glad to end the unwanted encounter that terminated in anger for both of them, Kendall agreed. He assisted her to her horse, then he mounted. At the gate to Compton Heath, Flora invited him in for tea but he declined and departed.

"Damn," she swore lustily. "I made a mess of that. Never mind. The next meeting will be better." She met Carinna at the door.

"Didn't you invite him in?" she challenged as she watched Kendall ride down the lane.

"I did. He is not very happy. I suppose he is miffed by Radcliffe's proposal to you. Or should I say of your acceptance of Radcliffe."

Carinna felt a twinge at her sister's comment, a reaction prompted by guilt. She had been bothered ever since the tea by Kendall's strong negative response to her inference of Radcliffe's proposal. She assumed Radcliffe had told Kendall of her acceptance and was surprised he did not know. "Had I guessed his ignorance, I would have handled the situation differently. Despite all I do not want to hurt him. He has my heart, but this he shall never know. It will be difficult being near him, being my brother-in-law, living, at least until he marries, in the same house. Somehow I must manage that. Father wants him for Flora. He is not Flora's type, but I shall help her win him."

Carinna returned to the drawing room, sat in the love seat where Radcliffe had proposed, and in the quietude thought again of his words. "No, he did not say, 'Will you marry me,' but that is what he meant. What he said carried the same meaning. 'Carrina, you must be mine. Forever!'"

The more days she lived beyond the moment of his statement, Carinna had to work harder to convince herself that his words were tantamount to a proposal. She arose and went to the window. The garden she tended was lovely in the sunshine, flowers blooming in a variety of colors, giving her a sense of security. Her thoughts, though, did not.

"I cannot fathom Radcliffe. He proposes to me but he does not return. I have not seen him since I accepted him, then I learn he went to London. Why did he not come to Compton Heath to tell me himself? Why, not even a note has he sent. Strange that. But in York I shall be in his company. We shall have many opportunities to talk, enjoy each other, to make plans. I shall have to work to understand that man of mine."

When Kendall returned home he found Radcliffe talking with their mother. Guy gave him a greeting with a swishing tail and he kissed his mother. "Welcome home, Radcliffe!" The brothers embraced and patted each other's back. "How was London? No highwaymen this time, I hope."

"No. All went well. Sit down. I just started telling mother the developments, but I can start over."

"Have a brandy. You must be tired."

"That would be fine. I stayed in the inn at Great Thirkston last night so the journey was not too long today."

"How is the Isham family?"

"Fine, and the girls particularly send their love. I had long talks with Sir Alfred and of course Diana. Sir Alfred has arranged for me to take a fine position with a top financial firm in London, an assignment that will allow me to earn a good salary."

"That means you will be leaving us," Mrs. Roche interjected. "I want you here, Radcliffe."

"I know this is different from your plans, mother, but it is an outstanding opportunity for me, one that will result in time to a higher position, ties to the court and possibly a title. You wont be alone. Kendell will be here. He is very capable of running the estate and I wont be gone permanently. I shall want you to visit in London."

Her displeasure was revealed on her face but she said no more.

"Also," Radcliffe continued, "Sir Alfred accepted me as a son-in-law." Kendall's face blanched. "Our wedding date is set for fifteenth of May next year at St. Margaret's. So, mother, you will be going to

London in the spring. After Diana I want you to be the belle of the city."

Mrs. Roche was reserved in accepting her son's announcement. She realized that the marriage would take him from her.

"Oh, another development. Before leaving London Diana told me she was encouraging her father to attend the York meet. If he can manage, he and Diana and Cecilia will be there, and, mother, you will meet your daughter-in-law to be.

"Some special news for you, Kendall. The Duchess of Kensington asked continuously after you. She definitely will attend York. She has relatives there, Lady somebody, I can't recall the name, and she is looking forward to seeing you. What did you do to attract all her attention? Careful, boy. A wealthy widow is a dangerous siren."

Kendall was left aghast by his brother's report. By the time he recovered, Mrs. Esterham rolled in the tea service. She was invited to sit and Radcliffe had to repeat most of his story for her. Her reaction was the same as Mrs. Roche's except she added, "That young thing will just have to give up London life and live in North Riding. You have enough to keep you busy here, and she can learn to be a proper mistress at Rochedale Manor."

The discussion continued with pros and cons until Mrs. Roche introduced the need to consider an engagement announcement party at Rochdale. "Word will get around soon enough and we must do what is right. Since Diana has come as far as York, perhaps she can come here after the socials and meet our friends."

"That would be fine with me," Radcliffe agreed.

"Very well. I shall send Sir Alfred and Lady Isham an invitation. Mrs. Esterham, are you up to such a party?"

"Oh, yes! We may not have the king and queen present but Radcliffe will be proud of what we do."

As soon as he could get Radcliffe away from tea, Kendall asked to speak to him at once and directed him to his room. "Do you realize what you have done?" His tone was challenging and brought a confused look of shock to his brother's face. "Carinna has made it known that you proposed to her and awaits a wedding date, and now you report your engagement to Diana."

Abashed, Radcliffe's mouth fell open. "Why, I did not propose to Carinna. Why would she report that?"

"It must have happened when you were at Compton Heath for tea, before you left for London. I doubt she would announce something as serious as a proposal unless it occurred."

Radcliffe remained thoughtful. "You know I was caught in the rain the day I went there. Squire provided a robe for me while my clothes dried. Tea was served despite my disarray and Carinna was left alone with me. We talked then I took my leave. I would not propose to her. I was already avowed to Diana. Why would she say I proposed?" He hesitated and looked at Kendall. "We were alone. I cannot prove I did not say it."

Kendall studied his brother's face. Radcliffe was never one for telling lies. Even as a child a white lie was beyond him. It was always the truth at all costs albeit the truth often got him into difficultly. "I believe you. Could it be Carinna made up the story to be sure you did not get away from her? Could it be she wants to be Mrs. Roche, not Mrs. Kendall Roche, second best, but Mrs. Radcliffe Roche, mistress of Rochedale Manor. Could she have guessed you had interests other than business in London. Did you say anything about Diana to anyone hereabouts?"

"No."

"Radcliffe. Could you have proposed and you do not now recall that you did?"

He turned and walked to the window. He looked at the abbey sitting in dusk. "I don't know." His voice was shallow as if he was not sure of himself. He turned to face his brother. "I thought I was improving. I have not been forgetting." He paused, feeling insecure. "Yes, I could have forgotten. Or, Carinna made up the story. I do not recall saying one word she could misconstrue."

"The fact remains she believes she has received a proposal."

"What is to be done? I could see Squire Gunning."

"He has already gone to York. We are taking Corinna and Flora with us in the coach when we go."

The two considered several alternatives and finally concurred. "Yes, I do believe it is the most gentlemanly course to take," Kendall summarized. "As far as I know nothing has been said about it in Tosten. Carinna may be waiting your return to discuss it further. If so, you will not be too late to stop her notions. Would you like to have me with you when you speak to Squire?"

"I think I should handle my own affairs, but on the other hand with you as a witness, there will be no further opportunities to report untruths."

"In that case, let's say nothing about the proposal to either girl, or to anyone for that matter, until you speak to Squire. Furthermore, I think you should proceed with your life as if this thing did not happen."

"Thank you, Kendall. You are always a rock."

In his own room Kendall considered his predicament. Radcliffe's denial would make Carinna available to him. He was still in love with her. The cave had determined that. "But do I want her for my wife now? She made a choice and I was not selected. Well, first things first. Let Radcliffe clear the situation."

Chapter Twelve

"It is only right that I should go to York although I don't feel up to it. But since Radcliffe's friends will be there I must. It is necessary that I meet my future daughter-in-law and I don't want Londoners to think we are just mere country provincials. Sir Alfred particularly must know we are cultured and have background. The Roches do go back to the conquest and that could be more background than he has. Now Mrs. Esterham, we must get to preparing the house. I don't know how many visitors will be coming here after York but we must be ready."

"We shall be ready, never fear, Mrs. Roche. While you are in York all bedrooms will be cleaned, the silver polished and I'll take on another girl to assist the visitors." The two women remained in the study to finalize plans for housing and feeding their guests after the boys withdrew.

"I wonder about entertaining but the boys will have ideas. We'll discuss that subject during supper."

As usual all dressed for the evening meal. Mrs. Roche raised her question. "Yes, mother, I would like a few socials. Diana is always going to some party or activity. Even if it turns out that she is the only visitor, I want her to meet our friends." Radcliffe gave no indication of concern about Carinna although he could not remove the worry from his mind.

"She loves to ride. What would you think of a riding party to Moncton Tor?" Kendall suggested. "If the day is right a picnic would be ideal."

"Of course riding, but I was thinking of a dance in the great hall for when it is decorated no room is more impressive. To me it is more striking than all the salons we visited in London."

"How long will our guests be with us?" his mother inquired. "If long enough it just might be she would like to go to Harrogate Spa. You could plan a few days there." Memories of her own honeymoon came to mind. "It is fashionable and more like London."

"I was thinking of holding Harrogate as a possible honeymoon site, mother, but I have not discussed this question with Diana. I shall ask if she would like to go there."

"After all the socializing in York, she and others who come may want a quiet period." Kendall introduced a new thought for consideration. "We can show them the estate and our countryside, and if they are interested in our abbey ruins, we can take a trip to Rivaleaux Abbey. That would make a wonderful one day outing with a noon rest and meal at an inn. No dress up, few people and not a lot of preparation."

More ideas were presented so that by the end of supper there was an ample list from which to arrange a busy social schedule.

"Do you know where the guests will be staying in York?" Mrs. Roche inquired.

"Sir Alfred has business ties. He said housing would be no problem if he decides to go. I did tell him that rooms were at a premium during the meet but he was thinking of a private home.

"The Duchess of Kensington, if she comes, will stay with a relative. Do we have accommodations?"

"Yes, son. Our inn held our usual rooms until they heard from me. Squire is there now and Carinna and Flora will be housed there as well."

The mention of Carinna's name forced the concern he faced to surface. His mother knew something was bothering him, but now she saw the worry on his face. "What is it that is troubling you, Radcliffe? I have noticed it throughout supper. Tell me."

"I have a problem, mother. Kendall reported to me that while I was in London, Carinna told him I had proposed to her."

"Did you?"

"Of course not."

"Have you talked to her about it?"

"Indeed not."

"I think we should have a meeting with the Gunnings as soon as possible after we get settled in York. I shall speak to Squire. Who else knows about this?"

"As far as I know," Kendall volunteered, "only the Gunnings and the three of us. I have been in Tosten several times since this developed, but I heard nothing being discussed there about a proposal. I am sure if something had been said, word of it would be around not only Tosten but all of North Riding."

"How did you learn of it, Kendall?" His mother was intent on getting at the facts.

"The day I went for tea at Compton Heath. Flora said Carinna told her that Radcliffe had proposed to her."

"Strange," Mrs. Roche commented. "That is not like a girl who has just received a proposal. In my day a bride to be could keep no secret like that. She told all her friends immediately. I wonder if Carinna misunderstood something you said, Radcliffe, something that was less than a formal proposal. She may be waiting for you to speak to her again. I suggest you do not see her privately until this matter is clarified." Mrs. Roche assumed a businesslike tone and both young men recognized her final statement as a direction. "I think Squire will agree there has been a misunderstanding after our discussion with them."

Kendall glanced at Radcliffe and recognized instantly an expression of relief. He had not been sure how his mother would react to the problem, but he smiled to himself. "I should have known she would take hold and set about to resolve it. She is not one to procrastinate. It should be an interesting meeting."

The Roche coach stopped in front of Compton Heath at the appointed time. The girl's travel trunk was placed on top by stablemen and Carinna and Flora were helped inside. The driver skillfully maneuvered the team of four out the gate for the return run to Rochdale Manor.

Roche travel trunks were stored next to the Gunning's, cook arrived with two baskets of her specialties, and Mrs. Esterham inspected the coach's interior to make sure all was prepared for the passenger's comfort. The Roches appeared and there were greetings all around. Since it was the first time Radcliffe had seen Carinna, she put her plan of entrapment into effect. The brothers prepared for the encounter by placing Radcliffe on the seat facing forward next his mother. That maneuver put Kendall between the girls with their backs to the front.

"It is very kind of you, Mrs. Roche, to take us to York. It is because of your generosity that Flora and I get to go." Carinna was sincere in her expression of gratitude. "And our thanks to you, Radcliffe and Kendall, for escorting us. Father said that unless the Roche boys looked out for us we could not go. Responsibilities require so much of his time that he cannot take us to many activities."

"We shall be glad to help as much as possible," Radcliffe responded. "I shall be entertaining friends from London and I expect to spend time with them."

It was obvious Carinna was shocked by the statement spoken so matter of factly, and Flora was equally startled. "Does that mean you will not be taking us to the socials?" Carinna found it difficult to speak.

"On the contrary," Kendall reassured her. "We shall see that you attend as many socials as you like. You will be meeting new friends and having a grand time."

Mrs. Roche listened with interest. "It is obvious," she thought to herself, "that all this has been carefully planned by the boys. Clever of them. Kendall is so supportive of Radcliffe. And I know what this problem with Carinna means to him. He has had his eyes on no one else."

"Your London trip seemed like a long absence, Radcliffe. I trust we shall have time to talk while we are in York. There is so much to discuss, preparations to make, dates to set."

"We must meet with your father as quickly as possible. I intend to speak to him the first time I see him. It is important that we set a time for a meeting." Mrs. Roche was definite.

The coach driver stopped his team at the Inn of the Ring and Fleece to rest the horses and to provide a noon meal for the travelers. An ale was ordered by Radcliffe for everyone. By this time the early tension had dissolved and was supplanted by light banter. All recalled good times from the past and Mrs. Roche told stories of the York meet when she was a young woman. "King George ll was present one year for the opening ceremonies, and the reception that evening for His Majesty was on a grand scale." By the end of the meal a comeraderie matching that of party day was reestablished and continued until they passed through the Roman walls and into the city.

The inn used by the Roches was indeed fashionable, catering to the upper class, and providing comforts well beyond those in a public inn. Separate rooms were assigned to each of the Roches while the girls were placed together. Two envelopes were presented to Radcliffe by the inn keeper. Opening the first, he announced instantly with obvious pleasure, "Sir Alfred has already arrived with Diana and Cecilia. They are guests of Lord and Lady Ashford."

Mrs. Roche reacted with raised eyebrows as she recognized the name. The Ashfords were regarded as the leading family in York if not in the entire shire.

"Lady Isham had commitments she did not wish to break," Radcliffe continued. "The Ashfords would like us to join them for a small supper this evening. Are you up to it, mother?"

"Of course. Pen our acceptance at once."

"Ah, Kendall. The second note is from the Duchess of Kensington. She is a guest of Lady Brownley. She enclosed this sealed bit for you."

Kendall read silently and smiled. "The duchess asks if we can call for her and Lady Brownsley this evening and convey them to the Ashfords for supper." He did not report the rest. His mother probably would not understand.

A maid assisted Mrs. Roche to unpack then she went to each of the brother's rooms to arrange their wardrobes. Hip tubs were brought to each room with pitchers of hot water and thick, fluffy towels. By six thirty all were refreshed, rested and aboard the coach.

"How do you know this Duchess of Kensington, Kendall?" Mrs. Roche's curiosity could be contained no longer.

"Why, she is a friend of the Ishams, or rather a close personal friend of Diana and Cecilia. Her husband died leaving her a very wealthy lady, rich in land holdings. She also has strong ties to the court. The girls introduced us to her and she invited us to several of her socials. She is a bewitching lady, mother."

Mrs. Roche was impressed with the duchess as soon as they met. She and Lady Brownsley, both beautifully groomed and bejeweled, took seats opposite in the coach. Striking Mrs. Roche first was the duchess' beauty, a light face paint complimenting her best features, but it was her demeanor that quickly became more dominant once her friendly, engaging personality was demonstrated. The women chatted amiably leaving the brothers in silence until the coach arrived at the Ashford mansion.

Not able to contain herself within the bounds of etiquette, Diana rushed to Radcliffe as soon as he alighted the coach and fell headlong into his arms. Their embrace lasted over long, leaving the responsibility for assisting the ladies to Kendall. He found it convenient to demonstrate his own feelings by an embrace of his own when he helped the duchess down the coach steps. "You surprised me by your visit to York. Are you prepared?" he warned.

"It depends on what you have in mind," came the challenge.

"Only what two minds have in common."

"You can be cheeky. You tease me deliciously." Her laugh conveyed her understanding.

Radcliffe took responsibility for introducing his mother to the Ashfords following his introduction by Diana, and to Sir Alfred, Cecilia, and the nephew of the Ashfords who was Cecelia's partner. Mrs. Roche vented her charm, which was considerable, and soon she was making her own impressions on the Londoners.

Supper was served in a small dining room under a crystal chandelier. Some of the talk was about the racing meet, Lord Ashford advising wagers on horses he knew to be winners, and about many of the people who would be at the races. William Henry, Duke of Gloucester, had arrived in York to represent his brother, the king. Lady Ashford reviewed all socials that were scheduled, and they were numerous. "But most important, of course, is the reception for His Highness, the Duke of Gloucester and Maria, his duchess. Since Lord Ashford is chairman, I have seen to it that all of you receive invitations."

After supper Diana whisked Radcliffe away and the duchess monopolized Kendall. Cecilia and her young man departed leaving the seniors to themselves.

"You are most kind to include the Roches at your party, Lady Ashford. You have made it a delightful evening."

"Thank you, Mrs. Roche. Tell us about Rochedale Manor."

Sir Alfred was greatly impressed by the wool production of Rochedale and Lord Ashford confirmed the abundance of high quality wool from the region. "You see," he explained, "my financial interests are centered in wool and I know what comes to market from Rochedale."

By the time evening ended and the coach was called, Sir Alfred had established a bond with Mrs. Roche. "May I ask you, dear lady, since my wife cannot be with me, if I may act as your escort for the meet?"

"You are kind to offer, Sir Alfred. I would be most honored."

The next morning Radcliffe found Squire Gunning at breakfast. Following greetings and the required amenities, Squire exuberantly leaped into a monologue about horses. "A fine collection of racing horses is here. Stables as far south as Kent are represented. This should be a smashing meet, excellent competition, but my two entries should do well. I am spending much of my time talking to trainers and learning about new techniques. Ideas for improving my program are numerous."

As he continued, Radcliffe wondered about the change in characteristics. "It is so unlike Squire to say more than a few sentences at one time about anything. He doesn't rant like this at home." At first opportunity the young man said, "It is very necessary, Squire, that my mother, Kendall and I meet with you, Carinna and Flora as soon as possible."

Instantly Gunning concluded that the long awaited date for Carinna's engagement announcement was in the offing. He beamed happily. "Of course. What would you say tonight following supper. In fact, why not the three of you join the three of us here at seven and afterwards we can talk. I'll arrange for a private room. With the races beginning there wont be much time. Best we get to it quickly."

"Fine. May I wish you good fortune with your entries. I shall have some pounds on your horses and expect to become richer."

Kendall's attraction to ecclesiastical architecture began as a boy when he played among the ruined abbey of St Clement le Mer next to his home. On his own he had visited the more impressive ruins of Fountains Abbey and Rievaulx Abbey in Yorkshire, but always when he went to York he spent a part of each day in its magnificent minster. At the Ashford supper he talked about the massive structure to the duchess and she was impressed by both his knowledge and his appreciation for the minister. It was because of her request that he was calling on her to escort her on a tour of the edifice.

"You are lovelier than ever I saw you in London." His greeting was sincere and he expressed his feelings in a squeeze of her hand.

Her smile was radiant as she responded to his compliment. She had taken great care in preparing for this meeting for she wanted to present not only her best physical appearance but she wanted to impress him with another side of her character. She had recognized an aestheticism in his nature that he obscured by a bravado facade. "He would like his friends to know him for his lightheartedness, his love of a good time, his readiness for riotous adventure, but underneath he is a sensitive person. He admires beauty and finds it in nature and in the supreme works of men. He is attracted by physical loveliness of a woman but it is the beauty of her character that holds him." It was because of this perception she prepared herself for him today.

He raised her hand to her lips and she was charmed again by his manner. She had always enjoyed gentlemanly attention paid to her, but too frequently she discerned in their actions an ulterior motive that related to her position and wealth. She did not react so to Kendall. Since that night in London when he made love to her she felt a growing fondness for him, a response no man had ever evoked in her, and she was using the York meet to determine how much of this was infatuation for a young attractive man. She had planned purposely to come to York and she was testing her feelings.

They entered the superb structure of York Minster and stood in awe at man's imposing accomplishment. Before them was the interior splendor of early English gothic, a series of massive colonnades, piers of clustered shafts soaring upwards, the spaces between filled with a rhythmic pattern of pointed ribbed arches. Sunshine filtered through stained glass of the clerestory windows to color the nave with rosy tints. He held her hand. "Do you know that this magnificent building was begun it the thirteenth century and took two hundred fifty years to complete. What a legacy they left to us." Slowly they walked down the nave until they faced the exquisite choir screen whose niches were filled with half size statues. "These are our monarchs, all our kings from William the Conqueror to Henry V1. Did I tell you that the first Roche in England arrived with the Conqueror?" She caught the pride that filled him at this moment.

He guided her into the north transept where they stopped to wonder at one of the supreme glories of medieval art, a five panel stained glass window. "It is called the Five Sisters. It doesn't seem possible that artists put all this together in 1250. At the bottom of the central panel is a scene of Daniel in the Lions Den. This window was used as a text book for people of the middle ages since so few people knew how to read. Priests brought their parishioners here to tell them Bible stories. Come. You be my pupil." He guided her in finding subjects for other stories.

His guidance took them to the crypt below the high altar. "This is the oldest part of the minster, all done in romanesque. Do you know that even in Anglo-Saxon times there was religious activity on this very site."

"You are well versed in history," she complimented him. "I am just beginning to recognize a different side of Mr. Kendall."

"I find pleasure in my heritage, that is all. Are you ready for a little sustenance after all this walking?"

"If you like."

"Do you mind walking a little distance into the old city? There is a little place to have tea."

"Lead on, but don't lose me."

He guided her to the Shambles, a picturesque collection of medieval timber framed houses and shops, the second stories of some overhanging the narrow cobbled stone street. He opened a black oaken door and assisted her to a table for two in a small alcove lighted by bottle glass placed in leaded window squares. They were served tea, scones and small cakes.

"May I say you are a pleasure for company." Kendall reached across the table to take her hand. "You make me feel important."

"Thank you, Kendall. May I return your compliment. You make me feel very much a woman. I enjoy being in your presence, especially when you convey your thoughts through your touch as you do now. You communicate sensuously better than an author does with words."

"Tell me what I am saying now."

"You tease me."

"Then I shall tell you. May I escort you to the races and to the reception for the duke?"

"You are a dear. I am invited to attend opening day with Lady Brownsley and her party but I believe I could take the liberty of asking you to join us."

"Thank you. I realize my request is late but I did not know you were coming to York. I do want much of your time while you are here." He paused to look into her eyes. "And I hope I can be in your presence without the usual number of people about you. Are you aware I have been alone with you only once?"

She smiled. "I remember it well. It does not take your word to prompt a recall of that time."

"May I have a private time with you then?"

Fearing he may think her to be the storied promiscuous widow, she gave a squeeze of her own to his hand and replied, "Let's not plan ahead for each moment of our days. Wouldn't it be better to share our time with others, to enjoy the activities of the meet with our friends and let the joy of our companionship result from all we do together? Please."

"It is as you wish for now. But I shall not give up my quest."

"Kendall, I must speak about something that bothers me. It is best to get it on the table before our relationship progresses further."

"Of course, my dear. I do not want you troubled."

"You are a young man starting out in the world. I have lived a bit longer than you."

He reached across the table, clasping her hand tightly, smothering it in his. "You are telling me you are older than I," he interrupted her. He smiled affectionately. "In a lifetime a few years are meaningless. What matters then if I am younger? It is love that makes all else insignificant.

"A lifetime of love knows no bounds, no difference, no ages. What we share, we share as lovers. We are equal, equal in the giving and equal in the taking. I am not interested in years. You are what interests me. You. My Elizabeth."

Supper with the Gunnings proved to be a pleasant affair sparked by Carinna's conviction that Radcliffe was ready to follow up his proposal with date setting. Squire, having agreed with her, was unusually jovial all during the meal. Flora, jealously hoping against hope, decided to await the discussion.

When remains of supper had been cleared, brandy was served. It was planned that Radcliffe would present the problem and that his mother and Kendall would take part as necessary depending on reactions by the Gunnings.

"Thank you, Squire," Radcliffe began, "for an excellent supper. We appreciate greatly your hospitality. I asked to meet with you to discuss a serious question that has arisen. When I returned from London, Kendall informed me that I had proposed marriage to Carinna." Looking directly at the smiling girl across the table, he added emphatically, "I did not propose marriage. The fact is I am affianced to a young lady in London, and was at the time I was supposed to have proposed to Carinna."

There was a deadening silence. Carinna sat as a statue, stunned, completely. Her smile changed to an expression of awe. Not only did he deny his proposal to her, he announced he had selected another. At first she was mortified that he called her a liar, then as the reality of her situation clarified, she felt humiliation.

Squire could not believe what he heard. Instantly he saw his main hope for a Roche connection disintegrate, the money he anticipated for increasing his racing stock go like a lost wager.

Flora remained composed. The main hazzard to her own ambition was dissolved in a sentence. She still had a chance for Radcliffe despite his avowed status, but better was the open track to Kendall. "He wont pursue Carinna any longer," she considered instantly, "now that she passed him over for his brother."

Carinna was the first to poke a hole in the silence. Meekly but without tears she said, "But Radcliffe, you were very definite in your statement. You said, and I shall never forget the beautiful way you murmured those words, 'Carinna, you must be mine forever, forever.'"

"When am I supposed to have said that?" he snapped in a challenge.

"We were alone. We sat together on the sofa. You spoke with great furvor."

"Did I say any words that sounded like, "I want you to marry me?"

"No, Radcliffe." She became dramatic. "You did not have to. It was plain to me that what you said meant marriage." Her voice lowered to affect humility, the hurt one. "How else was 'you must be mine forever, forever' to be taken? No other way than the way you meant me to take those words." At that moment she decided she was absolutely right and would not give in.

Kendall cut in. "Why, Carinna, you did not tell me of Radcliffe's proposal to you. When I began making love to you the last time I came for tea, you stopped me and said, 'Speak to your brother.' Why did you not tell me then? I had to learn from Flora that you had received a proposal. The fact is, Carinna, you did not receive a proposal from Radcliffe. You only thought you did because you wanted one." His words were spat at her with contempt. The love he did indeed once have for her had ebbed to nothing since she passed him over, and he let his wrath fall on her.

"See here, Kendall, you are speaking to my daughter and I expect you to show courtesy." Gunning had recovered from his daze and aired his ire for the whole situation on the young man. He was on thin ice, he recognized. It appeared Carinna jumped to conclusions too rapidly and, should Carinna lose her attachment to Radcliffe, his only hope for Roche money was through Kendall developing an interest in Flora. In no way did he want to interfere with that possibility. He relaxed noticeably and added quietly, "We are trying to resolve a difficult problem and it is best done by speaking without fury."

"You are right, Squire." Mrs. Roche spoke with dignity, sitting erect in her chair, one arm on the table, her hand clutching a handkerchief. "We have been friends too many years to let a misunderstanding interfere. It seems to me there are two wrongs involved and they do not add to a right. Being already avowed, Radcliffe should not have spoken such words to Carinna. And Carinna should not have interpreted the words to mean a proposal although the circumstances might have allowed the interpretation. I think the central factor is Radcliffe's intention. Since he was at the time pledged to another, he did not intend marriage to Carinna."

Instantly Radcliffe saw his clue. "Forgive me, Carinna, for causing this hurt. I do apologize."

First shocked by the sudden turn of the meeting, she quicky realized the discussion was at an end and that she was the loser. Tears began to flow. Mrs. Roche gave her the handkerchief she had been clutching, and Flora placed an arm around her sister's shoulder, speaking consoling words.

"We are here for a good time," Mrs. Roche declared. "Tomorrow night Lord and Lady Ashford are hosting the royal reception. They extended invitations to all of us. There will be young men and dancing and gayety. Shall we say seven o'clock for departure."

"And races are about to begin." Radcliffe laughed aloud, an expression of the relief he felt in resolving the predicament with Carinna. He would find that Flora would be a more formidable threat.

Carinna lay in bed, her disturbing thoughts preventing sleep. Tears could not change the fact that she had lost Radcliffe. Thoughts of Kendall gave her further fright. "The way he spoke to me. Never have I heard him speak like that. Never! Have I lost him, too?" In a sudden move her hand covered her startled face. "The gypsy warned me!" She had not thought of the cautioning remarks from the fortuneteller since party day. She had no reason to. "I thought they were merely words, a bit of the entertainment as Kendall said they were. He was wrong. I should have given heed. 'I advise you to beware.' Yes! Those were her exact words. 'Competition. Beware of competition.' If I had only believed her. I could have beaten my competition. I could have planned for it. I could have taken action. I could have won. I could have had Radcliffe right now." All that could have been passed through a scrambled mind suffering the disaster of loss.

What Carinna did not know was the competition her sister had already started to provide.

Tears flowed gently. "Yes, I remember her advice. 'Select the one who has your heart.' She knew. I heard but I didn't give her the time of day. Kendall. My heart was and still is with Kendall. I made a foolish mistake. I wanted too much. I should have been satisfied with love, not position."

She thought for a time. Tears stopped. A determined look replaced her tears of grief. "The gypsy said I would lose all if I made the wrong decision. Well, I don't intend to lose all. I am warned. I intend to make the most of York." Her plotting began.

Flora entered the bedroom she shared with her sister, soothing her and sympathizing with her for her unexpected loss. All was not sincere, however. She was close enough to Carinna to regret the devastation she saw in tears and a trembling body, but she was very much aware that the proposal denial removed the only barrier to her own pursuit of Radcliffe. As sobs continued to rack the body next to her, she renewed her plotting. There were two avenues open to her she recognized. First there was Kendall. Despite his treatment shown her at their last meeting before York and the words he so meanly spoke, she convinced herself that all was not lost with him. "If I am clever I can snare him. There is that secret I can use." The smile was knowing and reassuring.

"Radcliffe is the superior catch. Being number one Mrs. Roche is far better than number two. So he is avowed. So! Carinna accepted a proposal from him and look what came of that. That girl in London can find her proposal ending the same way. No. Radcliffe is not lost. He is still fair game." She reviewed her plot. "Failing all else there was our tryst in the cave. I can tighten the snare." She smiled at the thought.

Gunning withdrew from the diningroom with his daughters and saw them to their room. In sympathy he verbalized reassurances to Carinna, but he was angry. He had seen his strongest alliance with the Roches fall at the post. He gave vent to his frustration with a furious smack on a table that reddened his palm. "How could she bust up the best chance she had of financial security! She could have been the leading lady in our parts and I could be assured of a better stable. Well, it isn't all lost." Before retiring he gave concentrated thought to the futures of his daughters. "Tomorrow we shall talk."

Mrs. Roche and her sons remained in the diningroom. "Difficult as it was the meeting went more easily than I expected," she admitted. "I am convinced Carinna misconstrued your words, Radcliffe, but she gave me a clue. I do believe very much that she wants to be a Mrs. Roche. The days ahead could be difficult ones for both of you, for Flora may have interests, too. Be watchful. I don't object to either girl. I like them. But being a woman I know women's wiles. Take heed. Be alert." She eyed each son in warning. "Now I must to bed."

"What does all this do to your relationship with Carinna, Kendall?" Radcliffe asked after his mother had gone. "I know how much you care for her."

"I confess I was upset when Flora told me you had proposed. I thought she would choose me, so sure that I delayed making my proposal. That was foolish. If I had proposed when I should, all this would not have occurred. But since she declared for you, I shall not call on her." He paused for a thoughtful moment. "Do you remember the gypsy hired for party day? At first I thought she was a bit of the entertainment, but I have recalled many times her warning as she read my palm. She had more influence on me than she knows. Maybe it was her caution that kept me from proposing when I should have. Anyhow, the gypsy looked directly at me and said, 'I advise you not to be quick about marriage. Something is developing.' Well, I believe a new interest is emerging."

His brother smiled knowingly. "I hope it works out for you." He paused to become more serious. "I agree with mother. Carinna may not give up easily and Flora has shown an interest in me. We could still face some difficulty. Let's make an agreement. If either girl makes an overture to you or to me, we shall inform the other."

"Agreed."

Chapter Thirteen

As they promised, Radcliffe and Kendall called on Carinna and Flora to take them to the race track. Both girls were cordial in their greetings and neither let on there had been any disagreement. Instantly they initiated the plot suggested by their father. Flora's arm went through Radcliffe's and Carinna reached for Kendall's hand. As they stepped into the coach, Flora took a facing seat and Carinna the opposite forcing the boys to sit next to either one. The girls talked of the good time they would have being together for the day.

The moment they entered the social room at the track they were greeted by two fashionably dressed young men. Radcliffe introduced them to the girls as Lord Ashford's grandsons. Almost immediately one suggested that they have some refreshments. It was as if they acted on cue, for that is how Radcliffe orchestrated the meeting.

As the young men guided the girls in one direction, the brothers walked in the opposite, the older to join the Ishams and the younger to meet with Lady Brownsley's group.

It appeared that all of York was attending opening day at the races. A large crowd milled about greeting friends, discussing horses, seeking tips and planning bets. Women were showing off their finery, sharing social news and seeking to be seen. Radcliffe forced his way through the morass of people only to be recognized by Diana who first hid from him. As he passed her hiding place searching for her, she furtively approached from behind, throwing her arms about his waist.

Startled momentarily, he turned and she fell into his arms. He kissed her lovingly on the forehead then stepped back to hold her at arms length. His eyes smilingly roamed about her. "You are beautiful, like an array of stars that glisten in the heavens." He pulled her to him and kissed her firmly on the mouth completely unaware of the spectators whose stern stares found the performance unseemly.

Pulling her by the hand, he plowed a passage through the crowd, paid his respects to Sir Alfred and the Ashfords then joined the throng, seeking friends and introducing Diana. As he hoped he encountered Carinna and Flora with their young men. Enthusiastically he purposefully involved the girls in conversation. He noted anger in Carinna's eyes and a curtness that snapped her sentences. Even Flora showed scorn for him, a display that was not part of her plan for snagging him. Their reactions made him wonder if he should have been so bold in flouting Diana.

The Duchess of Kensington received Kendall warmly, introduced him to Lady Brownsley's other guests, and then suggested they stroll. She put her arm through his to move him out of the immediate crowd and into the flow of people. He was soon introducing her to his friends including Carinna and Flora who were still walking with their young men. "These dear friends live close to Rochedale Manor, Duchess. Their father is racing some of the best horses in the meet."

Carinna's ire rose as Kendall continued talking. At first irked by the blatant act of shoving her and Flora onto two dull boys, then angered by meeting Diana, she was riled completely by the introduction of a duchess. She thought it was obvious to all that Kendall was over solicitous to his London friend, but she interpreted his actions to be intentional just to belittle her.

Flora's face became livid. Her upset was such that she could not speak. She sensed that Kendall had more than a passing fancy for this woman and instantly the duchess became a threat to her own chances for him. More and more she had considered her plan for entrapping him but now it seemed that Emma's secret would have to be told.

Believing he had made his point with both women, Kendall moved off only to encounter Constable Ormand. He was presented to the duchess and the three conversed briefly. "Our constable is endeavoring to solve two tragic murders, both young people in our community."

They chatted for a bit then the constable took his leave.

"Do you plan to place some bets?" Kendall was getting anxious to try his luck.

"Of course. Let's go."

The horses' stalls were open to view but the number of people interested in evaluating the entrees had congested the aisles making the task difficult. There was as much socializing as there was inspecting and movement of people was slow. Fortunately there was time for both. The two weighed the merits of several horses recommended to them. He knew she was a horsewoman who rode skillfully, but her considered comments surprised him. He made notes when they were in agreement and these would be guides to their betting.

A bugle call gave warning that wagering was open. Kendall took the numbers of their favorites to a bettor and presented his money. He was given cards in return. "Now we'll see how good our luck is," she smiled when he returned to her.

"I don't have to wait for a race to find that out, my dear. I know my good luck is right here. It started the moment I learned you were in York." He brushed his lips across her forehead. "And it improves each time I am with you."

She smiled appreciatively. The more she was in the company of this youth, the more she felt his presence on her emotions. She had to admit that he affected her as no other male had and for the first time she was considering a man seriously. She thought of her age. "Twenty-eight," she admitted. "I am older than he but he doesn't mind. At twenty-two age may not be that important to him. What will be the case as we both grow older?"

A bugle sounded, calling horses to the post for the first race. It instantly triggered a hubbub and all interest went to the track. The running oval was drenched in sunshine, outlined by white fencing. The infield was green, a clipped grass whose softness eased the intensity of the sun. The horses paraded before the crowd then assembled at the post. At a signal they took off, their riders guiding them into position. Shouting from the multitude began instantly and did not stop until the lead horse crossed the line.

Kendall smiled at the duchess. "You have a winner, my dear. This is the reason I respect your knowledge of horse flesh." He called a waiter and asked him to collect her winnings. "What number do you recommend for the second race? Will the notes help?"

She studied the paper he handed her and stated the number. "It is luck, you know," she laughed. "I make judgements on what I see, but when the horses run the unforeseen happens. It could be a horse leaves late at the start, the jockey misjudges, or a favorite can be hemmed in and can't break out of the crowd. Any number of problems can develop and always do."

"You have all the luck now. I'll bet with you this time." When the waiter returned Kendall tipped him then gave him money to place a bet on the duchess' number. "My luck began the day I met you. You were riding a roan horse in St. James Park. I was jealous at once of the young men attending you."

"I remember it well. It was your first ride in London. You made a pleasant impression on me." She looked at him with taunt in her eyes. "You always make an impression me."

He was struck with her sincerity. Impulsively he kissed her.

"Kendall," she rebuked him. "We are surrounded by people."

"Good! I want all the world to know I love you." His voice was louder than was necessary for a conversation. Stares came from those nearby for his transgression of social acceptance and instantly she suggested they walk.

"Forgive me. I do not want to embarrass you but I do love you. You must know that."

She prepared herself for his kiss but it did not come. She wanted him to kiss her, even in a crowd. She felt disappointment. The feeling amazed her. She wanted him to ravish her. Now.

"Kendall, please take me to Lady Brownsley's home."

"Are you ill?" He put his hand on her shoulder and turned her so that she faced him.

"No. But please." Her eyes revealed the urgency.

"Immediately." He called for a hackney. When they were admitted to the Brownsley mansion he explained to the housekeeper that the duchess was ill and to please bring water. "Where is her room?"

"Up stairs, second door to the left."

Kendall picked her up and carried her to her bed where he lay her down. He gave her a drink of water when it came and closed the door after the maid left. He sat on the bed next to her.

"You play the ruse well, Kendall," she smiled. A wicked thought appeared in his eyes and she received his kiss ardently. Quickly he sent his tongue exploring her neck. So involved was her response that she was not aware he had freed her breasts from her bodice until she felt his tongue.

His action was tempered with experience and served to arouse her inner passion. She moved her body to help him remove her clothing. Quickly he disrobed and lay beside her stroking her sensitive parts and directing has hands wherever they wanted to roam. Her legs moved to invite his pleasure but he teased her rapturously with gentle pecks. Suddenly he moved to place himself for entry, unable to harness himself further. After, when he lay beside her, he made his proposal. "You know I love you. Marry me. Let me care for you. I want you near me, always. I want your loving. Be my wife."

"I am yours. Forever."

Stimulated by her enthusiastic response he made love to her again, raising her to heights supernal, knowing every part of her until she collapsed. He left her sleeping with a radiance glowing serenely on her face.

That night when he called on her to take her to the Duke of Gloucester's reception, she looked luminous, reflecting still the pleasure of her afternoon. She was dressed exquisitely in a light blue taffeta gown which complimented her auburn hair. Jewels fell from her ear lobes and others rested prominently on her bosom. It was evident she had taken great care in preparing herself.

Kendall kissed her lovingly and she was no less adoring in her response. His proposal had given her life new meaning and she conveyed her ecstacy in the unspoken language of touch. In the coach he pressed her to him and she rested her head on his shoulder. The closeness gave confidence that the words of love he whispered in the afternoon were not merely those flowing from his ardor of the moment. "I do love you, my darling," she heard him say and she reacted with an affectionate nudge of her body. "Is there someone I must speak with to obtain permission to marry you?"

She giggled girlishly. "You might try the king!" Her mood changed suddenly and she considered his question. "When my husband died he left me without immediate family, my parents having died shortly before his death. They had no other children. So you have a problem, my sweet. Perhaps I was speaking in jest, but your request should be presented to the king after all. I am his cousin by marriage. I carry a title that is inherited by blood royal. Shall we ask the duke about it this evening?"

"Why not?"

They entered a beautifully decorated reception hall alive with movement, music and mirth. Vivid bunting floated across the ceiling while festoons of flowers, some in hanging baskets, added varied colors. Clusters of potted plants and trees gave a cooling relief to sparkles of light shed by spangles of crystal prisms hanging from chandeliers. The great room was already crowded with people, women dressed in exquisite gowns boasting sparkling jewelry dancing with partners to the music of a small orchestra while some men sought spirits from a barkeep in an adjoining alcove.

Kendall guided his duchess about the hall meeting many of the same people who were at the afternoon races.

The music stopped then struck up a regal air for the Duke and Duchess of Gloucester who entered the hall accompanied by the Lord Mayor of York. A receiving line was formed and all in attendance made obeisance to the royal couple.

At an appropriate time, Kendall and his duchess approached the duke, she made a polite courtesy and received a warm greeting from her cousin. She presented Kendall who, after bowing, spoke confidently, "Your Highness, may I respectfully ask a question?" Receiving permission, he continued, "It is my intention to marry the Duchess of Kensington, but I am in a quandary as to whom I should address a request for permission."

The duke replied after a pause for consideration, "Why, young man, I suggest you address a note to the king requesting permission to speak to him. State your purpose." He turned to his cousin. "My dear, may I be the first to congratulate you both and to wish you unending happiness."

Both withdrew and Kendall announced enthusiastically, "I shall write this very night."

He no sooner made the statement when Flora appeared at his side. He reintroduced her to the duchess but Flora ignored her obligation of acknowledgment. "Kendall, Carinna and I are very angry and so is father. Neither you nor your brother appeared to escort us to this reception. Father had to bring us."

"That is unfortunate. I understood Lord Ashton's grandsons would escort you."

Furor was blatant. "We dismissed those two children after the races today. Kendall, I wish to speak to you privately before this evening is over." With that she spun on her heel and walked off.

"Forgive the outburst, my dear. She came to York hoping to be feted by my brother and me and she is bitter. May I ask for a dance?"

Flora was wretched indeed. She had expected to be escorted by either Kendall or Radcliffe to various activities and felt keen humiliation when the Ashford boys appeared on the scene. "Dumped we were on those two mere infants." She thought again about the manner in which Radcliffe and Kendall walked off leaving her and Carinna with those boys. She continued to search for Radcliffe. "It will be different after tonight. They will come crawling to me." She caught sight of Constable Ormand and smiled.

Radcliffe, Flora noticed, had spent the evening with Lord Ashford's party in the company of Diana. She watched them dance and socialize happily, "but never once has he acknowledged my presence. This Diana he introduced me to, who is she? He gives her all his time." She joined a group on the fringe of the Ashford party and began talking to a young lady to whom she had been introduced at the races. "Who is that attractive couple?"

"That is Mr. Radcliffe Roche and she is Diana, daughter of Lord Isham visiting from London. They announced their engagement very recently. Would you like to meet them?"

"Thank you, but not at this moment." She walked away stunned. "Engaged! How could he!" Hatred began to surface. "He gave no thought to me. He forgot too quickly our little cave. But he is not married yet. I can begin my game now."

She saw Kendall leaving the dance area with the duchess. She approached him and requested, "Kendall, may I see you. Alone." He spoke briefly to Elizabeth then followed Flora to a corner where she turned to face him. "Kendall, you have been despicable to Carinna and to me. I find it an affront to both of us that you continue to ignore us. And after leading us to believe that you were interested in marrying one of us. Now I must know. What is your intention toward me?"

"Why you little snipe. If you think I have an interest in you it is because you wish it. You tried hard enough to nab me, but I see nothing about you to attract my attention." Kendall spat out the words.

Momentarily taken aback by his verbal attack, she recovered and smiled at him. "Think twice before you turn away, Kendall Roche. Unless you agree to escort me and pay me some attention, I intend to tell Constable Ormand about Emma's secret."

"You threatened me before with that so called secret. Well you just go right ahead. In fact, I shall accompany you, now, and you can tell the constable in front of me."

"Your duchess might miss you. Go back to her. But be warned."

She watched him turn and leave, the disgust he felt evidenced in his manner as well as in his words. The fact that the threat meant nothing to him prompted her to search for Ormand.

Her mind was made up and her decision was firm despite a warning the gypsy had given her. Each time she made up her mind to tell, the gypsy's admonition flashed before her. "'The card says do not tell. Keep your secret. There will be trouble if you tell.' Father does not hold with gypsy fortune telling but that one may know her business. What if I tell my secret and I do have trouble?" She wondered if Kendall would do anything to retaliate. "Well I am going to tell because I am sure I have lost him so what difference does it make anyhow," she encouraged herself. "It is he who will be in trouble for killing Emma."

Her search for Ormond ended when she found him talking to a group of men. She approached and made motions with her hand to attract his attention. He came toward her.

"Constable, I have something to report. I need to talk where we cannot be overheard." He guided her to a quiet area off the main room. "After I tell you what I know please don't be angry with me for not speaking sooner. I was sworn to secrecy by Emma. She said it was a sacred trust. Well, Emma and I were good friends. Just before the day she died she told me she was to meet Kendall."

"Where were they to meet?"

"In the abbey."

"Do you know why Emma wanted to meet Kendall?"

"Yes. She said she was going to have his baby."

Ormand instantly read into the statement the motive for Emma's death as well as the proof he needed to tie Kendall to the murder. He needed to ask one more question. "What were the exact words Emma used about Kendall?"

"She said, 'I am in love with that handsome beast and I am going to marry him.'" Suddenly Flora felt faint. Her heart palpitated rapidly. "What have I done? I told him that Kendall had Emma pregnant. That is the kind of story I am going to tell to get Radcliffe. That will be too much, and the constable will be suspicious. He wont believe me. No one will believe me."

"Did she name Kendall as the man she meant to marry?"

"Not exactly, but she meant Kendall. He is the handsome one. Better looking than Radcliffe."

"Are you sure she could not have meant Radcliffe?"

"Constable, she could not have meant Radclliffe."

"Why are you so sure?"

"Because she often spoke about Kendall. I don't recall she ever mentioned Radcliffe. Emma told me once that Kendall made love to her."

"Could she have just been saying that?"

"Not Emma. She didn't tell lies."

When she left him, Ormand stayed to evaluate the information just given him. "My hunch is proving itself. I just know Kendall killed Emma and Otley."

Ormand returned to the main room and located Kendall in the Brownsley group. He kept an alert eye and when Kendall moved away from his friends, the constable intercepted him. "Kendall, may I have a moment? Come with me to where it is quiet."

"I know. You are going to tell me that Flora spoke to you. I encouraged her. She keeps threatening me that unless I give in to her demands and agree to be her future husband she is going to tell you something Emma told her."

"Oh. Do you know what that something is?"

"Only that it is a secret trust as Flora calls it."

"Be honest with me, Kendall. Did you know Emma as a woman?"

"Yes."

"When?"

"More than a year ago."

"Not since."

"No."

The constable saw one of his theories dissolve. "If Emma was pregnant, it was not Kendall," he commented to himself. Aloud he said, "Thank you, Kendall."

Left alone he weighed Flora's purpose in speaking to him. "It appears the young lady is showing disappointment by telling on Kendall. Still, her story needs investigation. It could be that Emma was meeting Radcliffe, not his brother. She could have thought Radcliffe was the handsome one."

Satisfied she had done her worse on one brother, Flora proceeded immediately to spin her web about the second. Radcliffe was easy to locate. He was still standing next to Diana enjoying a conversation with a small group of friends. Flora joined in, finding a place next to Radcliffe. She was introduced to all then asked if she might whisk him away for a few moments. He excused himself then followed Flora to a site on the fringe of the crowd.

"You have been very haughty, Mr. Radcliffe," she began. "You had me believing I was the woman in your life. Now I understand that you are engaged to that London woman. Well, you can't forget our little play in the cave on Moncton Tor. I wont let you forget. I had a beautiful time with you, so beautiful you have me pregnant. I am expecting your child." Her stare at him was intent.

"Your what!" His voice was loud in disbelief, loud enough to attract attention from those standing nearby. Aware of his shock, he fought to control himself. Instantly he saw his world crumble. In pieces lay his entire future, his promising business opportunity, his chance to build a financial empire, the possibility of gaining royal favor, a marriage into influence. All had disappeared in one statement. He had no words, so unlike the Radcliffe who could always control any situation. "Flora, this is very serious," he finally said. "I must talk with you further but not here."

"What is there to say? You must marry me."

"There is much to say. It is impossible to talk now or tomorrow. Perhaps tomorrow evening."

"Only if it is to talk marriage."

"Let us meet. I shall be in my room after supper."

"Very well." She walked away, a smirk on her face, confident she had become Mrs. Roche, Mrs. Radcliffe Roche.

Radcliffe stood as he was, stunned. He struggled to control his emotions and to overcome the fear that dominated him. On rubbery legs he returned to Diana, trying to cover his distress.

Instantly she noted his distress. "What is it? Please, let us sit down."

Seated he felt better. "I just received some distressing news that may make it necessary to return home for a short time. Would you mind if I have to be away from you for a time?" A plan had started to formulate to remove Flora as a problem, but the details were missing.

"Of course not. If you have to be away, I shall understand. But don't make it too long. Is it something that Kendall could handle?"

"No, dear. It is something I must see to."

Alone in his room, Radcliffe agonized. He was about to leave for a walk to relieve the tensions he felt when a rap was heard on his door. His brother entered.

"This is not the time to talk but we agreed to report to each other if either Flora or Carinna made advances. Well," said Kendall noticeably upset, "Flora went to Ormand tonight and told him that Emma planned to meet me at the abbey the morning of her death. Ormand asked me if I had known Emma as a woman and I confessed I had." He paused. "This makes it appear that I am even more of a suspect in his eyes."

Radcliffe started to report Flora's charge of pregnancy but instead replied, "She is a demon, a cat with claws venting her spleen."

"Well there is one bright spot to my life. I asked Elizabeth to marry me and she consented."

Radcliffe grabbed his brother and they embraced. "I am so happy for you, Kendall. You will be very happy. We should have a brandy but there is none."

"We'll celebrate later. I haven't seen mother yet to tell her, so don't mention it. I want to tell her first. Get a good sleep. Goodnight."

Radcliffe could not sleep. He wrestled with a variety of alternatives that surfaced as he considered his dilemma. "I have to believe her. I could ask Dr. Poole to examine her but she would refuse. There is no way I could force her to accept an examination. If I spoke to Squire he would demand I marry her instantly. My mother would think likewise. Kendall should know about her accusation, but he would take strong action immediately and word would reach Sir Alfred and Diana. It is better I keep my own counsel and work it out my way. It is imperative I do not lose my opportunities in London."

Sometime during the night he slept but only after he reached a decision. In the morning he reviewed the steps he would take, satisfied that what he had decided to do not only was practical but necessary.

"You are in such deep thought, Kendall," Elizabeth smiled. "I have lost you already to a mysterious reverie."

"No. You have not lost me. Never."

"Have you spoken to your mother about our promise to each other?"

"No, my dear. I haven't seen her yet. Sir Alfred has been her constant escort and he has not given her a moment to herself. I shall try to see her this evening if she isn't involved in more of his plans. I am surprised she has the energy to keep up with him."

"How are you betting today?"

"I am going with Squire Gunning's horses. At least I know the man and I have a lot of respect for his training program. He feels confident of his entries and his mounts."

"He is Carinna and Flora's father as I recall." She thought seriously a moment then added, "After Flora spoke with you last night I saw her speaking to Constable Ormand and later she had Radcliffe cornered. He looked pale when she left him. Is she a trouble maker?"

"I must confess I don't know her that well. She was always Carinna's little sister but suddenly she grew up. I had eyes for Carinna and until you entered my life I had planned to ask her to be Mrs. Roche."

"Ah. A rival."

"No. That is past tense. You have no rival." His voice was gentle and sincere. He bent over to kiss her. "Elizabeth, will you return to Rochedale Manor with me after the meet? I want so much for you to see my home and how we live. It is not like London but we can arrange a social or two. I want you to know my mother and we must talk in quiet surroundings about our marriage plans and ....

Aware of someone near, he looked up to find Ormand waiting for his attention. "Hello, Constable. You remember the Duchess of Kensington."

"Of course. Good day, madame," he bowed. "May I speak to you privately, Kendall?"

"Excuse us, my dear."

Kendall followed the constable a distance to where only a few people mingled. The two faced each other and Kendall waited. "I must pursue a question. It is not clear why you think Flora wants you involved in Emma's murder."

"Flora asked me to marry her and when I refused she said she would tell you about a statement Emma made to her."

"Oh," The constable put a knowing look on his face.

"Any problems?" Elizabeth asked when he returned.

"The constable has new information related to one of the murders he is investigating. He wants to discuss it when we return home. You did not tell me how you are betting."

"You are so sure of the Gunning entree. I'll go along with you."

Kendall called for a waiter to place their bets. As he did so Radcliffe and Diana approached. He noticed his brother looked a bit haggard but withheld comment. "We are about to place bets on Squire's horse. Will you join us?"

"Of course." It was a routine reply. "Diana will be returning home with us, Kendall. I invited Sir Alfred as well but he must return to London."

"Wonderful! It will be a pleasure having you in our home, Diana." He turned to Elizabeth. "Now, my dear. Will you join Diana?"

"Please, Elizabeth," Diana added enthusiastically.

"You leave me no room to say no. If your mother is agreeable I shall accept your invitation."

A bugle call to the post was sounded and interest swung to the track. It became obvious to Kendall that something other than Diana and horses was taking Radcliffe's interest.

That night the two young men and their mother had supper together. "This is the first time since I met Sir Alfred that I have had a quiet moment. He has so much energy and he is so popular. He insists on me meeting his friends and joining all the activities with him. I pleaded a night off so I could recover. I haven't seen either of you. How did your fortunes fare at the track?"

"I am doing alright. Squire's winner today recovered my losses today so I am ahead," Kendall volunteered.

"I can't match you," Radcliffe added. "I have not been at all lucky. I'm afraid my concentration has been elsewhere."

Kendall was about to question but decided against it. 'My concentration has been elsewhere, too," he smiled. "Mother, I have asked the Duchess of Kensington to marry me and she has accepted."

"Oh," her response was one of surprise.

"Now don't ask me why I didn't get your permission first. You have not been available. I have seen almost nothing of you since we arrived."

"Well, that is true. I did not know you were interested in her as a wife. Is it sudden?"

"I suppose you could say so. She captivated me completely. I have invited her to come home with us so you can know her better."

"Diana is coming, too, mother."

"Good. We shall all get to know one another and make wedding plans. The York meet of 1770 will be memorable for providing me with two daughters-in-law. I must say, though, that you modern youths take things into your own hands. In my day. . . . . . "

The three laughed and continued their conversation, making plans and looking into the future.

It was Kendall who introduced a somber note to change the tenor of the conversation. "Mother, Ormand spoke to me at the reception last night and again today. It seems Flora told a secret to Ormand. It is to the effect that Emma expected to meet me to keep an appointment with her in the abbey the morning of her murder."

Immediately fearful but holding herself under control, she looked up at her son and inquired, "Did you have an appointment?"

"Why, no, mother. It is just a ploy played by Flora to get me to marry her. For some time she has been playing up to me, especially since Carinna announced Radcliffe's proposal. She must be thinking she can frighten me into marrying her."

Radcliffe felt the sting of Kendall's statement and he paled. "Just exactly what did Flora say to Ormand."

"The constable did not want to talk about it. He merely said he would see me after we returned home. Can you believe Flora, that sweet innocent child who matured very suddenly into a vixen. The gall of her trying to entrap me."

Radcliffe opened his mouth to tell of Flora's charge against him but instantly had second thoughts. He would have to admit his involvement and he was not ready to face the aftermath it would cause. Instead he commented, "It appears the Gunning girls want to be married into the Roche family by any means."

He took his leave and entered his room still not sure how he would meet the challenge flung to him by Flora. She would be knocking on the door shortly and his inability to arrive at some decision made him nervous to the point of being unable to think. He took to pacing the floor. The plans he made the night before did not look so promising the longer he considered them. His conclusions remained the same, however. "I shall not lose my opportunities in London!"

He heard the expected knock on the door.

Chapter Fourteen

Flora braced herself for the coming meeting with Radcliffe. "He is a shrewd one." she warned herself. "I know his way with words. He will try to work some ruse on me but it wont work. He is going to marry me. There can be nothing less than that."

She thought of the gypsy's caution to her. "Oh, yes. I recall. She said a trip would have bad results. Well, she was wrong, wrong like the bruise on my neck. She said that in my future I would be bruised, but that happened last spring when Radcliffe tried to choke me. Instead of being a journey with a bad ending it is working out splendidly. I am going to be Mrs. Roche. I agree with father. You can't believe what gypsies say. They don't know. Who does know the future? No one. I am going to make my own future."

She scanned her image in a mirror and made some adjustments to her attire and to her hair. Looking directly at herself she said to her reflection, "Get him, Flora. Don't give in. Stand firm. He's yours for the taking."

Flora's haughty attitude preceded her into Radcliffe's room. She lingered in the open doorway letting her arrogance dominate him as he stood aside to await her entry. When she passed him she gave him a flick on the arm with her finger. "I am just thinking how it will be married to you, Radcliffe," she grinned as she turned to face him.

"Sit down, Flora." It was a quiet, calm voice making it obvious that he was trying to control himself but underneath was a surging of bitterness he was fighting to master. "Tell me, are you feeling well?" His words referred to the baby she was carrying, but it took a moment for her to realize he was not referring to her general health.

She took the chair he offered. "Well enough. The baby will give me no trouble for a while. I want to know when you plan to marry me. We must not wait too long, you know. I shall be showing and then tales will be told. It would soon be around Tosten that Radcliffe Roche had put Flora in the family way. You know what would happen."

"How do you know you are pregnant?"

"That is insulting. Any woman knows when she is pregnant. There are certain signs and feelings. I have the signs and the feelings. These are not topics for conversation with men. Gentlemen. You are I trust a gentleman. I wont discuss the signs with you." She searched as she spoke for the words she had heard when women talked about pregnancies, but she could not recall any of them. She warned herself to get off the subject for she realized she knew nothing about it.

"Have you talked to Dr. Poole?"

"Of course not. It is only while I was here in York that I got the signs and the feelings." She began to be fearful of his questioning and that he would try to trap her into confessing her lie. A meeting with Dr. Poole would destroy any opportunity she had to marry.

"Will you see Dr. Poole?"

"Absolutely not. A lady does not get pregnant until after she marries, but you could not wait, Radcliffe. I am not going to talk to Dr. Poole or to anyone and say I made love to Radcliffe Roche. That is embarrassing for a lady. As a lady I refuse. After we marry I shall see him so he can guide me through the birth."

"Will you talk to my mother?"

"She is the last person I will speak with. The idea! No! I shall speak to no one about my condition and that is firm."

The more she talked the more he became convinced she was using her pregnancy story to trap him. It had been used on him before by someone less sophisticated than Flora. The memory of that whole affair sickened him. He had tried making love to the girl after she begged him to take her. "It happened last April. Winter was suddenly brought to an abrupt end by a beautiful warm day. I was riding just to enjoy the sun and the loveliness of creation. She was walking on the lane. It seemed so natural to have a lovely girl complete the picture. We walked together for a time. Then she put her hand in mine and pulled me close to her. Suddenly she stepped in front of me and reached up to kiss me full on the mouth. As we kissed she put my hand on her breast, hugged tightly, and rubbed her body over mine. She pulled me to the ground, and as she did so she raised her dress. She directed me over her. Her hands aroused me as they roamed over my body. Despite my effort I could not reach fulfillment. When I gave up she said, 'Radcliffe, why did you try to choke me?' Startled, I said I did nothing of the kind. Later she asked to meet me. It was then she said she had to have me. As I made love she said she was pregnant by me and that I had to marry her."

He looked at Flora. Here was a formidable foe, a woman he knew could prevent him from attaining all he wanted in life just to achieve her own goals. Details of a plan he sought to combat her with were beginning to form as they talked.

"Flora, I cannot speak to you about a marriage date until I review your condition with my mother. It is best we get you home for she will want to see you as soon as I tell her about the pregnancy."

"I do not want to speak to your mother. I am not marrying her." In all of her planning Flora recognized that Mrs. Roche was the only person who could not be controlled. "Of course she will want to know the signs and feelings and then she will involve Dr. Poole and my father," she told herself.

"If you do not see her, we cannot marry. It is as simple as that." Radcliffe saw for the first time a weakness in her attack and he thought of a way to work on it. "York is not the place to speak to mother. When are you thinking of going home?"

"You tell me. You brought me to York and you are to take me home. When am I going home?" She snapped her words.

"I'll see to it that you and Carinna are taken home. In fact, I shall conduct you myself. The races end tomorrow. Can you be ready the following morning?"

"Yes."

"Be ready then. I shall speak to your father to inform him of our leaving. Now, Flora, listen carefully. When I take you to Compton Heath, change to your every day clothes. Tell Carinna you are going for a walk or that you need some exercise after the long ride, or what ever you want. Just get out of the house. Take the lane to the manor. I shall meet you to take you to Rochedale. I shall have told my mother of my intentions by then and you two can work out the necessary plans for our marriage."

He paused to note the effect of his own entrapment. Flora was watching him intently, following every word and agreeing with him. He pressed on. "The more I picture you as my wife, the more I know you are the right one for me. I am glad of our cave adventure, Flora, for that wonderful tryst made you mine. It took you to see it, though, and I shall be forever grateful to you for that."

"Oh, Radcliffe!" Her tone changed instantly. "I am so happy. Kiss me." She rose and walked to him, her arms open. He received her in his arms and kissed her on her forehead.

"Does Carinna know about your condition?"

"No one. I have spoken only to you."

"Good. Say nothing to anyone. We shall have all this taken care of day after tomorrow and you shall be mine. Now run along, my sweet."

"Oh, Radcliffe! I am so happy!"

She returned to her room glowing with the satisfaction she had captured the heir to Rochedale Manor even after he became engaged to someone else. Her lie would be known to no one else. "He shall get me pregnant immediately after our marriage anyway, so even he will not know. Carinna is going to be surprised. Her little ruse did not work after all, but mine did." Joyously she did a polka down the rest of the hallway.

Radcliffe closed his door and leaned against it. His plan had matured almost without effort, and as he reviewed the steps he would take to materialize it, he smiled in satisfaction.

Feeling better than at any time since Flora announced her pregnancy, he went to his brother's room. "Kendall, I feel an obligation to take Carinna and Flora home. Will you escort Diana to Rochedale with mother and Elizabeth? I plan to leave day after tomorrow, early in the morning. There is no need for you to leave at the same time, however. Stay through the last days of the socials if you like. I'll explain to Diana."

"Of course. But I would rather get transportation for those girls and send them off. You are too honorable, Radcliffe."

"Well, we must live next door to the Gunnings and neither girl is happy with their substitute escorts." He laughed. "I shall have opportunity to alert Mrs. Esterham of Diana and Eliszabeth's visit and we can make the necessary preparations for them. I'll tell mother."

Mrs. Roche was relieved when she heard Radcliffe's plan for, "It may calm Flora and she wont bother the constable further with stories about Kendall, and Mrs. Esterham will be pleased to know ahead of time about our guests. But don't tell her about the weddings. I want to surprise her."

Radcliffe spoke to Gunning about his plan and Squire expressed his gratitude. "I do thank you, my boy, for forgetting about our unhappy disagreement." Not only was he pleased with the proposal, but he felt confident that the suggestions he made to his daughters for snarling Radcliffe had been successful and that the young man would yet be his son-in-law.

"I want to thank you for your victory yesterday. Kendall did very well on your horse and both of us wish you a first again today."

"The better horse ran yesterday but Compton's Choice is capable of winning. If you plan to bet be conservative."

The last day of racing brought out the largest crowd of the three day meet. Radcliffe passed on Gunning's advise to Kendall and he bet accordingly, advising Elizabeth to do the same. Flora and Carinna walked up to them unescorted and purposefully, Kendall surmised, stayed, much to his chagrin. He and Elizabeth had agreed not to mention their betrothal until he received a response from the king granting permission to marry. Flora no longer acted the hurt maiden, in fact it appeared to Kendall that she was unusually friendly and buoyant in her demeanor. She brought a smile to his face as she spoke to Elizabeth, putting on exaggerated airs and affecting a London accent. He could not determine the cause for such a change in attitude. The last time he saw her she was demanding that he marry her. Now she made no reference to her demand or did she show any anger toward him.

Carinna was equally charming.

"Are you placing bets on Compton's Choice?" He asked the two girls. Flora replied instantly . "No Kendall. I no longer see charm in racing." Her affected speech was rediculous.

She fluttered a handkerchief. "I am ready to return home and prepare for my future."

"I am betting father's horse to win," Carinna broke in. "I think he has a good chance."

"We are with you," Elizabeth spoke out, ignoring Flora. The girl had become boring to her and she preferred at least that Flora leave. Recognizing that would not happen, she made a suggestion. "Kendall, shall the two of us accept Lady Brownsley's invitation for lunch."

Kendall read the comment as intended and agreed. "Come, Elizabeth. Good day, Carinna. We hope it is a good day for Compton's Choice." He ignored Flora. Along the way he placed his bets, all of his cash going to Squire's horse in the fourth race. Elizabeth chose another horse for her bets.

Lady Brownsley had invited a large number for lunch. "It is the last day for the horses, and we must eat," she said to Elizabeth. "I like your young man the more I see him. Nab him. Take him home to London and lock him up. You will loose him if you don't. My. He is a handsome brute."

"He is special. I'll consider your advice." Elizabeth watched Kendall as he moved about talking to people, laughing with them and enjoying their company. She was pleased she had come to York. What she sought she found. She had to know if her feelings for Kendall were deep enough for marriage or were only an older woman's infatuation for a youth. "I made the discovery. I am sure of his love for me. We shall have a good life." The inner joy was exhilarating and very satisfying. Together they enjoyed the races, making side bets and jibbing the other over his or her losses, but it was the comeraderie itself that brought them pleasure.

A call for the fourth race brought them to the rail. The horses passed the first turn in a mob but three broke free on the far side. By the last turn Compton's Choice was running neck and neck with a challenger that would not give in. Together they crossed the finish line in a dead heat.

Early the next morning Radcliffe was accompanying Carrina and Flora through the Roman wall and into the countryside. The sun of the past few days was blotted out by a heavy blanket of clouds and the weather looked threatening. The hired driver moved his team rapidly over the moors now appearing more somber under leaden skies, not even animal life being noticeable from the window of the coach. Conversation among the three passengers was limited to the races, success of the Gunning stables and an occasional reference to social activities. Radcliffe reserved his participation to responses, spending most of his time developing his plan in silence. A mist began falling shortly after a rest stop and by the time they arrived at Compton Heath rain was falling steadily.

Quickly travel trunks were removed from the top of the coach, adieus were spoken and Radcliffe continued on to Rochedale Manor where he was greeted lovingly by Mrs. Esterham. After he paid the hired driver and saw him off, she ushered her boy inside to a warm fire. "You returned alone. Are the others staying on?"

"For a day or two to enjoy the closing socials. I brought Carinna and Flora to Compton Heath since our coach would have been too crowded. We are to have guests. The Duchess of Kensington and Diana Isham are returning with mother and Kendall.

"Only two guests. That will be no problem. I expected more. The guests rooms are ready and the larder is full. Now tell me, did you have a good time?"

Radcliffe reviewed in detail his participation in the York meet, highlighting social events, the reception for the Duke and Duchess of Gloucester and Squire's success. He was watching his timing and at an appropriate moment, he rose and said he had to go to Tosten. He purposely chose a great black cape to protect himself against the rain, stopped in the kitchen to greet cook and in the stable he spoke to Bonnie. He sent the only attendant on an errand that would keep him away for some time. Bonnie must have thought the rain was too heavy for she wagged her tail when Radcliffe invited her to go along but returned to her spot in the stable.

Once in Tosten he entered some shops, keeping greetings and York reports to a minimum and making a couple of purchases. He was shocked to see Ormand crossing the square. The two exchanged greetings, and Radcliffe, anxious to be off, took his leave. It surprised him when the constable haled him as he mounted his horse. "Radcliffe, it just occurred to me that you might assist me if you would. I have to meet with a community group in Kirkston tomorrow night. We shall have to stay over, of course. I can give you the details as we ride."

Thinking of no way to avoid going, he promptly agreed. "Damn," he mused as he rode his horse toward Compton Heath.

Carinna and Flora entered an inhospitable house. Because the Gunnings were to be gone, Squire had given his housekeeper a few days to return to her own home. Other hired help was limited to two caretakers for animals, the stablemen having gone to York to assist Gunning with racing.

Unobtrusively Flora checked on her sister who was in her room. Silently she flung a cloak about her shoulders and left the house, skirting the stable so as not to be seen, avoiding the main gate and meeting the lane well below the house. When rain came down harder, she chose a tree for shelter. Radcliffe found her under her temporary cover. He pulled her onto his horse, covered her with his great cape so that for all appearances he was the only mount, and rode in the direction of his own stable. Dismounting, he kept her hidden and entered the house by the back entry. He could hear cook in the kitchen talking to Mrs. Esterham. "Good," he commented to himself. "If they had seen me Mrs. Esterham would have come out." Quickly he motioned Flora to follow. Silently they went up the back stairs, crept down the hall and entered his room. The bolt was shoved into place and secured.

Motioning for her to be silent, he removed her cloak and began toweling her, drying her face, then on his knees he removed her shoes and rubbed her feet and legs. Such attention aroused her emotions and she raised her skirts higher. He allowed his finger to become free of the towel to stroke her bare flesh. She loosened her bodice and leaned over so that her bosom was level with his face. "If not pregnant now I shall be," she encouraged herself.

He felt his own ardor rise at her movements. Deliberately she teased him until he dropped the towel and he pulled her to him, burying his face in her breasts. She loosened her skirt as he kissed and nibbled at her bare breasts. When her petticoats were dropped she grabbed his hair and pulled his head back, kissing him hard on the mouth. She pushed his face into her abdomen and gyrated her body, forcing him to cover her with kisses. She raised him to his feet and began to disrobe him. He acted as a puppet, completely dominated by her aggressiveness. She took liberties of his naked person that he had not dreamed of.

A Strangeness

Arroused beyond endurance, she pulled him to the floor, placing herself beneath him. Such ecstacy he had never known. He felt strength growing his arms and hands. They clamped around her waist and moved to her shoulders. She felt herself in a vice and struggled to free herself. Her strong movements only served to increased his desire. She tried to force his hands downward, recalling the marks on her neck he once made on her but she could not pry them loose. He looked at her with glassy, watery eyes and fear began to grow within her. She felt his hands leave her shoulders and she fought to bring them down. His strength was too great. He was gaining dominance, overcoming the control she thought she had. She felt fingers about her neck and a scream broke free. Instantly a towel was in her mouth and the clasp on her neck tightened. She struggled for breath. Pain increased. Fright consumed her as she felt herself drifting - drifting - drifting -----.

Radcliffe collapsed on her.

When he came to he was beside her. He glanced at the window and saw darkness. He turned to face Flora. There was a towel in her mouth and she was still. He sat up, alarmed at what he saw. He could not understand how the towel got there. Her face was blue. He pulled the towel from her mouth. She just lay there, still. He touched her. She felt cold. He put his ear to her mouth. No breathing could be detected. He shook her. She remained limp. He got himself up and lifted her shoulders. She made no response. His eyes stared at her neck. Bruises. He placed her back on the floor and looked at the marks.

A realization of his deed struck him. He continued to stare at the dead Flora. He recalled looking at another young face, the face of a child. The face of Emma was taking the place of Flora's face. His hands covered his own face to hide his agony. The plan he designed called for Flora to leave this world but the deed accomplished was revolting.

He dressed trying to decide what to do. He knew he had planned what to do with the body but he could not recall what it was. "Flora. In my room. Dead. What can I do with her? Where can I take her? I have to hide her. Where?" He sat at his desk debating with himself what he could do, his eyes moving unconsciously about the room trying to recall what he planned to do. They fell on the south wall. He remembered his father. "Yes. That is it. That is what I planned to do." He rose and walked to the side door, an entrance to his mother's room along the north wall. He was a boy again. He was a boy watching his father from the side door. His father was at the south wall. His father pressed the second panel. A lower panel opened. His father went through the opened panel. He dragged behind him a person, a girl in a white frock. The little boy ran from the door in fright.

Radcliffe went to the second panel and pressed, the picture of his father vivid in his mind. Instantly the lower panel opened. He knelt and looked inside. He found a narrow cubicle. Bones lay in one corner. He looked at Flora. He rose, went to her, lifted her body and carried it to the open panel. He pushed her through it. He returned to pick up every bit of her clothing and pushed all through the opening. He crawled into the small room. He spread out some of her clothing and placed her on the pieces. He covered her with her cloak then stood to look at her. He stooped to pick up a cloth and jabbed it into her open mouth. "Say no more you will be Mrs. Radcliffe Roche," he snapped.

Leaving the room, he pressed the second panel and watched the lower one slide into place.

He looked about to make sure that all was as it had been and walked to the window. Rain had stopped and skies were clearing. A moon cast intermittent light on the landscape. He stared at the abbey bewildered. "How does it happen?" He looked at his hands. A sigh was audible.

He returned to his desk and sank onto his chair, his head dropping to rest on his arms spread across he work area.

In the morning Radcliffe met the constable in Tosten en Dale.

Carinna knocked on her sister's door. "Come to supper, Flora." Carinna had put together a light repast from food she found in the buttery. She returned to the kitchen to complete the preparation. When Flora did not appear, Carinna climbed the stairs, knocked on the bedroom door then entered. The room was neat, all clothes from the travel trunk having been put away and the trunk left open. Carinna looked in the drawing room then called loudly, "Flora!" A check with the caretaker in the stable brought no help. He had not seen her. It was not like Flora to just up and leave without saying where she was going. "She would not go out in the rain and she was tired from the trip."

Carinna returned to the house and called in every room. "Perhaps she did go out for a walk, maybe to get a bit of exercise after the long ride." She poured herself some tea and ate a bit of cheese. She tried to think of York but fears for Flora would not leave her. Thoughts of Emma and Otley crowded her mind and her imagination quickened until every sound suggested an entry by a killer. She locked the back door, closed several shutters, then went to the drawing room, rekindled the fire and sat before it. She was in the same position when dawn broke.

Cook called out, "Why, here comes Carinna Gunning." Mrs. Esterham looked out the window to see Carinna ride into the stable. "Come here, child," she called from the door. "You look upset. What is the trouble?"

"Flora is not home. Is she here?"

"Why no. I have not seen her."

"She left the house after we arrived home from York, and she did not come home last night."

"Perhaps she went to other neighbors."

"Flora has never done that. I am afraid. I remember Emma."

"Now child. You just stay here. Sit down and join us for tea."

"I must see the constable."

"Dear, Constable Ormand is away. Radcliffe left this morning early to meet him. They wont be back until tomorrow. Stay with us. We expect Mrs. Roche and Kendall to arrive this afternoon."

Carinna did stay but it was a nervous wait. She sat, drank tea, walked outside, petted Bonnie, came inside, but by noon Mrs. Esterham had her resting. She was asleep when the travelers arrived from York.

After greetings and introductions, Radcliffe's absence was explained. Elizabeth and Diana were assigned rooms and maids assisted them in unpacking. Mrs. Esterham asked to meet with Mrs. Roche and Kendall. "Carinna is here. She arrived this morning greatly agitated. She reported that Flora left home before supper and did not return. She was gone all night. Carinna is afraid because of what happened to Emma."

"Poor child," Mrs. Roche sympathized. "Let her rest but when she awakens I want to see her. Since Radcliffe will not be here tonight, prepare his room for her. I want her next to me where she can reach me if necessary. She needs a great deal of reassurance."

At tea Elizabeth and Diana were informed of the situation. When Carinna entered the room, the two guests withdrew. "My dear," Mrs. Roche spoke soothingly, "Kendall has informed Constable Ormand's men and he is assisting in organizing searching parties. Word has been sent to your father. We want you to stay here tonight. You will be in

Radcliffe's room which is next to mine, anytime you feel distress you are to come to me."

"Thank you, Mrs. Roche. I do feel better. No more can be done."

Kendall returned home in time for supper and explained what had happened. "We have search groups organized and the entire community has been notified. We didn't do much searching because of darkness, but all is in readiness for tomorrow. We start early and will continue until Flora is found."

Mrs. Roche accompanied Carinna to her son's bedroom and remained with her until she was in bed. "Now, dear, call me or come to my room if you need me."

"I am so sorry, my dear," Kendall apologized to Elizabeth. "I have had no time with you and tomorrow will be the same. I am in charge of the search groups until Constable Ormand returns."

"I do understand. I am proud of the way you have taken hold. We shall have time together."

Diana, too, was understanding, although she would have preferred to have Radcliffe near her. "I can see that the Roche men are called on at any time for help. We don't have this kind of service need in London."

"We must always give as we are called on to give. That is the motto of the Roches." Mrs. Roche's comment was filled with pride.

Sleep came slowly to Carinna. Although the unexplained absence of her sister caused her anxiety it was being in Radcliffe's bed that bothered her more. "I could have had all this. I could have been his wife. Here I would have been Mrs. Roche, mistress of the manor. Here I could have received his loving, borne his children, continued the line, become leading lady of North Riding and have been a lady of distinction." She rolled over and spread her arms across what she thought would be his side of the bed. She pretended he was there, feeling his flesh. She thought of him responding, reaching for her, but it was Kendall whose face was above her. Kendall. The cave. Of course Kendall. He was superb that day. I know the pleasure of his loving."

Later when it came, Carinna slept soundly.

Sometime in the early morning hours she bolted up in bed fully alert, listening. Fearfully she looked about. All was silence. She looked out the window. The first light of dawn had already appeared. She stepped out of bed, rolled Mrs. Roche's wrap around her shoulders and strolled to the window. A soft mist hung a gauze atop the meadow. The abbey seemed to float on the silken mass without foundation. Light brightened as the sun's first rays broke over the hill beyond the Dale.

The scene was calming to Carinna. She felt enraptured and for the first time since arriving home from York she experienced a peacefulness. She felt inner strength developing and courage surfaced.

Rays of the sun were falling more fully on the meadow slowly dispelling the mist and presenting the abbey in total reality, the stark ruins of the arches, their feet imbedded in the earth. Her eyes went to the south transept. Emma. The face of the murdered girl appeared to her. Instantly she thought of Flora. The confidence she had just known vanished like the mist on the meadow. "Will I find Flora in the abbey?" Fear was with her again.

She closed the shutters except for a narrow opening and returned to bed keeping the wrap around her shoulders and drawing the covers to her waist. She sat resting against the pillows she had piled behind her and tried desperately to rebuild the lost confidence. "Surely they will find her. She probably is home now wondering where I am. She may even now be on the way to Rochedale Manor looking for me."

A moan. Carinna listened. Nothing. She glanced outside thinking a wind had come up to shove a tree branch against a pane. All was in full daylight. Trees she could see through the shutters were as statues. Intently she concentrated on the room, listening. All was silent until - scratching.

She tilted her head and waited. The sound appeared again, more like a rubbing than scratching. She tried to identify its source, darting her eyes around the room. A moan. This time longer, louder. Carinna sprang out of bed and ran to the south wall. She put her hands on the paneling. Scratching. She felt a vibration on her palm through the wood. She screamed in shock, a piercing scream that was an impulsive reaction. She screamed again, a loud prolonged scream that grew out of fear.

The bedroom door opened. Radcliffe stood within its frame. "Carinna! What are you doing here?"

"Oh, Radcliffe!" Not expecting his entry, she stared at him bewildered. Recovering, she ran to him and threw her arms about his waist. He held her more out of reflexive action than out of care. "I am so frightened. I heard noises beyond the paneling, a scratching, a moaning."

"There is nothing. It is your imagination. Tell me why you are here."

"I can explain, but first, what was the screaming I heard?" It was Mrs. Roche speaking. She had opened the door between the two rooms.

"It was Carinna, mother. Something she imagined frightened her."

"Carinna has had a very difficult time. Flora has not been home since she returned from York and the poor child is worried for her sister. Little noises will frighten her. I had her stay in your room last night so she could be next to me."

"I heard about Flora, mother. Word reached the constable and me early this morning. We returned immediately. We will take responsibility for the search parties."

"Good. Your brother went into town some time ago to manage them."

Mrs. Esterham entered the room.

"It is best we leave, Radcliffe," Mrs. Roche directed. "Mrs. Esterham can assist Carinna."

A low moan was heard. Carinna screamed and grabbed Radcliffe. "Did you hear that?"

Mrs. Roche questioned. "Did you recognize the sound?"

"It sounded like a moan, as if someone was in pain," Mrs. Esterham answered.

"Let me get my gun," Radcliffe volunteered, releasing Carinna and going to this desk. He took out a hand gun and made some adjustments. "It is loaded."

They stood as if transfixed, listening. No one said a word. Kendall stepped into the room.

"What is all this?" His question was like thunder in the silence.

"Ssssss," Mrs. Roche quieted him. We are listening for strange noises. Any news?"

"Search parties are out. The constable will be here as soon as possible to question Carinna." A scratching was heard and Kendall stopped speaking.

Ormand appeared in the doorway. "Come in," Mrs. Roche invited. "You want to talk to Carinna. Sit at Radcliffe's desk. Kendall, get a chair for Carinna."

Still frightened, Carinna began her story. A long moan interrupted her. The constable stood and listened. "What is that?"

"We don't know yet," Kendall whispered. "We have been listening to locate the location."

"I heard it early this morning with a scratching sound. I think it is on the south wall," Carrina volunteered.

"Who's room is this?" the constable inquired.

"It is mine," Radcliffe spoke up.

"Have you heard that sound before?"

"Never."

"The scratching could be rats," the constable suggested, "but rats don't moan." He walked to the south wall and motioned the group to be silent.

The scratching noise was heard followed by a long moan. "It's on the wall, I'm sure. Radcliffe, what is beyond this wall?"

"It was a priest's room during the Tudor period."

"If so there is a priest's hole. How is it opened?" The constable began moving his hands on the surface of the wall panels. Kendall stepped to the wall and began pressing, placing hands on areas not touched by Ormand. A panel began moving. It slid to the side until it created an opening. The constable quickly got on his knees and peered in. "There is a body in there!"

"Get up, Constable." The command came from Radcliffe. "That is Flora. There was an accident."

"If there was an accident then will you tell us what happened?"

"Now all of you stay still. Hear me. Flora and I had an affair. At York she told me she was pregnant and that I had to marry her. It was a trick. It was the same trick Emma used. Emma asked to meet me in the abbey. It was I you saw go to the abbey, mother. As I left the house by the stable entry I took Kendall's coat. That was not intentional. I didn't realize at the time I had taken his, not until I returned and saw my coat still in its place.

"Emma told me I had her pregnant and insisted I marry her. She wanted me again. I obliged. When I recovered I found her at my side, dead. I could see red marks on her neck."

As Radcliffe gave his testimony, Ormand recalled Flora's story about Emma. "The dead girl used pregnancy as a ploy to get Radcliffe. Flora thought she could make a similar story stick, but Radcliffe is no fool. He thought about the vulnerability of young men of means. "What about Otley?" he asked aloud.

"I don't know about Otley," constable. I saw Otley. He was sick, very sick. I lifted him onto my horse. I don't know if he was dead when I put him on my horse of if he died on the way to Tosten."

Radcliffe glanced quickly at his mother. Her face was pale. Kendall reached for her. She crumbled into his arms.

The constable, seeing Radcliffe's attention diverted, made a quick move for his gun, but the movement alerted Radcliffe who instantly pointed his gun at Ormand. A hand grabbed at his arm. It belonged to Mrs. Esterham. There was a scuffle. The gun discharged. Mrs. Esterham fell. Radcliffe staggered a moment then dropped to the floor. Both began bleeding, she from the neck, he from the head.

Ormand knelt beside Radcliffe. "It is better this way, sir," he mumbled slowly then closed his eyes. Mrs. Roche came to Radcliffe and peered down at her son. Kendall helped her to the floor so she could sit next to him. Carefully she lifted his head to cradle it in her lap. Tears rolled down her cheeks and dropped onto his face. His eyes opened to look at her. "Forgive me, mother." His voice was weak. "I have a terrible affliction. Headaches. Kendall knows. I love you."

He gazed at her for a moment, closed his eyes and she felt the tenseness in his body relax. Gently she placed his head on the floor then looked up at Kendall. The tears she saw on his face were for his brother. She motioned for his assistance to rise, saying, "I must see to Mrs. Esterham."

Kendall assisted her to the floor next to the housekeeper.

"Rest gently, Mrs. Esterham." Her voice was a murmur.

"Tried to stop him, Mrs. Roche. How is our boy?" The words were spoken in broken whispers.

"He is resting."

Mrs. Roche saw Mrs. Esterham's hand move. She took it gently, patted it lightly and then clasped it lovingly. "Must tell you something before I go," she heard Mrs. Esterham say. Leaning over she placed her ear next to the dying woman's face. In gasps the housekeeper mumbled almost inarticulately, "My daughter gave birth to a boy then died. It was the night Radcliffe was born. I gave the boy to you." No one else in the room heard the confession.

Mrs. Roche showed the shock she felt for just an instant. A smile replaced the stare of dismay. "They are our boys, my dear."

"Constable," Mrs. Esterham mumbled.

Mrs. Roche motioned for the constable to come. He placed an ear close to Mrs. Esterham's mouth and listened. "Otley told me it was Radcliffe. I gave the boy a potion. May God forgive me." Her head rolled to one side.

The silence in the room was interrupted by a groan. Carinna reacted with a scream and ran to the priest's hole, crawled through it and pulled the cover from Flora's body. She saw her sister looking at her and slumped to the floor.

Ormand and Kendall entered the cubicle immediately behind Carinna. Ormand removed the mouth gag and looked for vital signs. "She is alive. Let's get her out of here." Bones in the corner caught his eye.

Together they got her through the opening and placed her on Radcliffe's bed. Ormond began rubbing her legs and arms. Mrs. Roche threw open the shutters. The crisp fresh air that struck her face helped revive her and she hurried to the opening to see to Carinna. Kendall ran from the room.

Carinna responded to the slapping and rubbing administered by Mrs. Roche. Kendall returned shortly. "I've sent for Dr. Poole and gave orders to call off the search."

Flora came round. Bruises on her neck were much in evidence, "similar," thought Ormand "to Emma's bruises." When Flora had established rhythmic breathing, Ormand motioned Kendall to follow him. Both left the room. "What was this terrible affliction Radcliffe spoke about?"

Kendall hesitated. He considered a reply that would answer the question but yet protect his brother. When he did speak he sounded remorseful. "Constable, what I say is for no one else's information. I shall have to tell my mother if she asks. If more than three of us learn of this, I shall hold you responsible."

Ormand nodded.

"I do not understand how or why but Radcliffe had at times a strange reaction to women particularly when his sexual interests were aroused. He wanted his hands on their necks. The strange part about it was that he could not remember he committed such an act." He told of the episode with the girl in the London club. "This is what undoubtedly happened to Emma and Flora." He suddenly thought of Diana. He would no longer worry about that girl's life with Radcliffe.

"Thank you, Kendall. I shall respect your confidence."

Ormand returned to the bedroom and went immediately to the priest's hole, crawled through, and examined the bones.

When Dr. Poole arrived Squire Gunning was with him. Carinna instantly reassured her father and Flora gave him a comforting smile. Mrs. Roche motioned Squire and Carinna to leave the room with her.

Flora had more than sufficient time to think during her ordeal in the priest's hole. When consciousness returned she had no strength to move, and the darkness of the place frightened her almost to second death. She acknowledged that her plight was retribution for her lie. The scratching came from fingernails she managed to play along the base of a wall panel immediately next to her, and moans filtered through the loose fitting mouth gag. Comfortable now in bed she felt remorse for her deed that resulted in the death of Radcliffe and Mrs. Esterham whose bodies she could see stretched out on the floor. "Well," she thought, "I made it to his bed although I didn't need it. I had him twice with no bed beneath us. They can't blame me for his death. He would have had the gallows for Emma's death anyway."

Dr. Poole examined the bodies and gave approval for their removal. He could prepare death certificates with accuracy.

"Doctor, what do you think of these bones?" The constable led the way through the priest's hole and into the cubicle. Dr. Poole examined the bones. "They belong to two girls. They have been here for a long time."

"Would you say about ten years?"

"That is a reasonable estimate."

When he returned to his office, Ormand checked his files and reread the entries made on homicides that occurred ten years ago, one of the girls being the Roche child and two missing girls who were never found. He also read a file on Mr. Winsford Roche who was killed in a shooting accident in his own bedroom. "The girl found in the abbey had been sexually abused and strangled, heavy bruises testifying to the cause of murder," he read aloud. He sat thoughtfully considering the facts as he knew them. "Could it be Radcliffe Roche had the same malady as Winsford Roche. I wonder. An inherited disease of some kind handed down from father to son. Strange that. I wonder about Kendall having the same problem."

Alone at last in her own bedroom, Guy stretched out on his rug next to her, Mrs. Roche let go of her own emotions. Tears fell as she thought of her own losses. "Two of my three closest loved ones," she said softly between sobs. She considered her future without them and thought there was none. "How can I go on. Radcliffe, the whole future of Rochedale Manor was planned around you. I know you wanted to go to London, but you still would have managed the estate. Radcliffe. Why?"

"She raised you, Radcliffe. Mrs. Esterham was as much yours as mine. She was my great strength, always firm as a rock, always ready, always knowing. She was Rochedale more than I, protecting, doing, holding us together. I never could have survived those first years without her.

"Those first years, Radcliffe. They were hell. The man I married was no man. He preferred his mother. His father knew of her incestuous love for her son, but there had to be an heir. The line had to go on. After all these generations, there could not be a break in the Roche tradition. He came to me, Radcliffe. At first I refused, sickened by his proposal. But he kept after me. I would not give in. I would not share my bed with him. Even for one night. One day I fell ill. I was placed in bed. After I recovered I knew I was pregnant. She was a girl. No heir. Later I had the same sickness. I knew he managed to drug me. That was easy. Although I was on guard I could not prevent it. He was determined and I was watchful, but I had to have food and drink. You were born, a flowering from your grandfather."

A light knock was heard on the door. It opened slightly. She saw Kendall peering through the opening. "Come in, dear," she called in a muted voice.

The figure of her son prompted another thought of Mrs. Esterham. "What she told me I knew. I have know for years. I was aware her daughter was expecting yet nothing was said of her baby. I had supposed it had died with her.

"As I saw my boys grow I recognized great differences between them, more than one would expect in twins. One day as I watched them at play it occurred to me that I should do some checking. I did. Death records showed only Mrs. Esterham's daughter dying, not her child. Burial records listed only her daughter as well.

"It was Mrs. Esterham who gave me the clue. Shortly after I reviewed the records, we were observing the children at work in their classroom. 'My our boys are doing well,' I heard her say. It wasn't what she said so much as the way she said it, full of pride like a gloating grandmother. It was enough to tell me. She never favored Kendall. Always she shared her love for them evenly. Always they were our boys."

Kendall approached her. "Forgive me for leaving you for so long, mother. It has been a tragic day for us." He kissed her then knelt beside her. "I want to tell you our plans so you wont wonder. Funeral arrangements are cared for. Services will be day after tomorrow. Both will be buried in the family plot.

"Diana wants to return to London immediately after the burial and Elizabeth will accompany her. I will join her in London later when we will announce our engagement."

"But you will live here, dear?"

"Oh, yes, mother. Elizabeth thinks it is beautiful here. We shall go to London for socials, but Rochedale Manor is to be our home."

Mrs. Roche bent over and cupped Kendall's face in her hands. She kissed him gently and gazed on his countenance. "You are the next Roche generation."

Printed in the United States
72358LV00005B/1-111